Y

HARD TO FORGET

A warning ignored...a love denied

Four years ago, Major Jack Ballentyne followed Special Agent Lowry Fisk into a death trap. Fortunately, both of them lived to tell the tale, but when he had Lowry drummed out of the British Intelligence Service for her own safety—and his own peace of mind—he knew she'd never forgive him.

Lowry Fisk knew, she just knew, that the Service had a mole, and it was up to the Assassins, the secret black-ops unit of the Service she and Jack belonged to, to find him. And as the Assassins leader, Jack should have believed her, even though she had little evidence beyond a gut feeling. But when he hadn't, she'd taken it upon herself to find the traitor—and ended up assaulted, shot, and left for dead. Jack had come to her rescue, but it had been too little, too late. Now all she wants to do is forget the attack, the Service, and the sexy, steely-eyed Major with the power to make her feel weak.

But the mole is on the move, and he's coming for Lowry to finish what he started. Jack has to get the stubborn, dangerously gorgeous woman to let him back into her life and allow him to protect her—without allowing her to worm her way into his heart.

HARD TO FORGET

INCY BLACK

Entangled Publishing, LLC
2614 South Timberline Road
Suite 109
Fort Collins, CO 80525
Visit our website at www.entangledpublishing.com.

Ignite is an imprint of Entangled Publishing, LLC.

Edited by Tracy Montoya
Cover design by Heather Howland

ISBN 978-1507844786

Manufactured in the United States of America

First Edition October 2014

ignite

Hannah, Rupert, Josh, Dylan, Max: Live, love and laugh—
always.

Prologue

A slum warehouse in London. The air rank with cordite and death. Hardly the most auspicious place to die.

And she *was* dying… Frankly? Bring it on.

Men, wholly dressed in close-fitting black, their faces ugly with smears of olive camouflage paint, hovered in uneasy formation, ever alert as the wide arcs of their flashlight beams cut the dark.

Four, maybe five, crouched beside her. Fussing.

Not a one of them urged her to focus. Not a one of them pleaded for her to hang on. No one muttered her name. Not to encourage. Not to comfort. Not to calm.

She'd broken ranks.

Even close to death, she was *persona non grata*.

So, with her life slipping away, she reminded *herself* who she was. Lowry Fisk. Special Agent. Purportedly a conspiracy theorist—most definitely a pain in the ass to them all.

Them being the British Intelligence Service. *Them* being

the Assassins, a "plausibly deniable" unit loosely affiliated to both MI6 and MI5.

Them being *him*.

Jack Ballentyne. Her commanding officer. A man she loved and hated in equal measure. There, with nothing to lose, she could finally admit it. If just to herself.

"Water," she croaked.

Jack looked up.

Christ, had she not been all-too familiar with it, his grim expression would have stopped her heart.

His lips drawn thin in the barely there light, he shook his head. "Nil by mouth." Then he went back to ministering to her leg.

What, did he honestly think she would survive this injury? What difference could a few sips of water make? *Bastard.* But no way would she beg.

She shut her eyes. Why wasn't she cold? Surely the concrete floor, hard and unforgiving beneath her back, should have chilled her? What came after numb? Because she was obviously way past that.

Hardly surprising, when she was lying in a small lake of her own blood gushing freely. Warm. Wet. Slippery. Definitely slippery, given the number of sliding hands trying to fix tight around the flesh of her thigh to stop the flow.

Getting shot was messy.

Funny, she'd always imagined a bullet would bring agony. She didn't feel a thing. Did a body shut down that fast? She hoped so—for the sake of those poor girls they'd tried and failed to save.

Her heart fluttered weakly. Like a frantic but fatigued bird caught in a net. She eased her head to the side. Her gaze skirted humps of fallen men, tumbled barricades of wooden crates, two abandoned cars, doors wide open to provide cover that had failed. All obscenely small in the shadowy, wide expanse of the warehouse.

A row of steel cages, animal-sized, lined the far, far wall. She'd spent forty-eight hours cramped in one of those. Waiting for the Assassins to strike as scheduled. Confident she'd be rescued. Fully aware that once the warehouse was secure and the heads of the United Baltic Cartel had been dealt with, she'd be disciplined for daring to pre-empt Jack and his team's mission to finish the UBC once and for all.

Her defense that they'd left her no choice but to go maverick wouldn't save her from sanction. Not when she'd contravened Jack's direct orders to leave all things connected with the UBC the hell alone.

For months and months, she'd tried to warn them that the UBC—vicious orchestrators of the tidal crime wave, including the sex trafficking of underage girls, that had lashed Britain's shores for too many years—had protection from someone high up within the Intelligence Service.

Naturally, given her reputation as the Service's pet serial fantasist, eyes had lifted heavenwards and sighs had been heaved.

Before this mission, there'd been other instances of black ops going awry. Subtly, occasionally, so very cleverly avoiding suspicion. The wrong address, a mistaken time, missions delayed. Bad guys slipping the net—hey, shit happened.

But she'd noticed a pattern. Connected to the United Baltic Cartel.

With admittedly only her gut instinct as evidence, she'd

confided her suspicion that someone connected with the Service was dirty. Discreetly at first, only growing more adamant and vocal when her fears were ignored. Then, as the jokes at her expense had increased and her credibility had plummeted, she'd shared with anyone who might believe her.

No one had. They'd been too busy smirking and, eventually, too busy beating a hasty retreat whenever she approached. *Bastards.*

Not that she had let that stubborn wall of blind denial stop her.

No. She'd dug deeper for details. She'd watched each of her colleagues more closely. She'd publically held Jack to account, defying his orders when necessary, in her struggle for vindication.

And hadn't that just backfired spectacularly.

Desperate for concrete proof, and suspecting the cartel would have prior warning of the Assassins' planned attack against them, she'd gone in undercover to intercept a "shipment" of young women from Moldova with neither the safeguard of a handler nor permission. She'd hoped one of the traffickers might let something slip—a clue as to the identity of the Service agent or agents selling information and protection to whoever could pay the price.

Passing herself off as one of the stolen young women destined for the sex trade had been easier than she'd anticipated. With half the "fresh flesh" shipment dead from dehydration on arrival at the makeshift dock on a deserted stretch of the river Thames, she'd used the ensuing panic and chaos to blend in with the surviving girls and joined them in their trapped-animal confinement.

From her cage, she'd whispered promises to the remaining eight girls. Two not yet sixteen years of age. Promises that they'd be safe, that good men would come.

And come they had, just as planned. But too late to save. Either her or the terrified young women.

She dragged her eyes away from the row of corpses still trapped. Each in their own cage. Each shot in the head.

Straightening her own head, she stared at Jack. The tourniquet he'd lashed around her thigh pinched deep as he tightened it savagely. He could have prevented this. The senseless body count. *He* should have listened to her.

The cartel had known Jack and his team were coming. A man in a balaclava, full of authoritative swagger, had shown up at the warehouse to alert them while she'd been in the cages with the girls. He'd ordered the traffickers to weapon-up heavily and prepare for a fight. To the death.

And then he'd noticed her, the man who was likely tied to the Service and had betrayed them all time and again. Not cowering at the rear of her cage like the other girls, but crouching forward. Watching him. Listening.

He'd looked at his watch and had smiled a smile as cold as the mid-winter Siberian plains. Then he'd ordered her release. What had followed, what he'd done to her—

She battened down her eyelids tighter and swallowed. *Not going there. Not going there.*

She focused her mind on the way, just minutes before the Assassins had hit the warehouse a half hour earlier than scheduled, he'd casually walked the line of cages after finishing with her. Calmly killing first one girl, then another, then another. Turning to gauge her reaction following each execution, the smug smile contorting his lips a macabre promise that her turn would come.

The traffickers, who only moments before had been caterwauling filthy jeers of encouragement, scattered into position at the earlier-than-anticipated yelled warning for all weapons to be dropped. Not the man with the flat, dead eyes, though. No, he'd frozen momentarily, his gun mid-aim at the head of a cowering girl. Then, with gunfire, shouts, and death cries filling the warehouse, he'd moved fast, using the dark, the stacks of wood crates, and the confused chaos to cover his escape.

Still prostrate on her back, her arms thrown wide as if nailed to a crucifix, she could have lain prone. Should have lain prone.

But her broken promise to the girls that she'd keep them safe, and a fierce need to see justice done for those she had failed, had launched her to her feet. No way was that faceless, nameless, murdering rapist bastard getting away.

She'd given chase. A bullet had brought her down.

Unable to move, she'd watched the hidden steel door swing close as he disappeared, unchallenged, into the night.

She'd overheard her rescuers talking about all eight girls being dead. But only three girls had been killed by her attacker. She knew that for a fact. Bile, sour with revulsion and seasoned with fear, burned her throat. Five of the girls had still been alive when she'd chased after the man intent on escape. Who'd killed them? Who among the agents scattered in the dark was a traitor? Who was working with the man in the balaclava?

She forced her eyelids to lift.

Jack was staring at her. His face gaunt in silent fury. Oh, he had a temper, a temper he wasn't shy to show. But never before had she seen him actually shake with rage. "Survive the bullet I drilled into you, and I *will* see you discharged."

Her mind, sluggish and distant, centered abruptly and sharpened. Jack had shot her? *He* was responsible? For letting the sociopath who had violated her and murdered those girls in cold blood get away? "You always were an arrogant son of a bitch, Ballentyne." Her emotional scale swung all the way in hate's favor.

One last chance. She was fading fast. She'd share what she knew, make this her final statement. Then they'd get no more from her. Not the Service. Not Jack. They could have the facts, but nothing personal. *Not the rape. Not the rape.*

Their problem, should they choose not to believe her.

Her tone hollow, she began a slow account detailing the past forty-eight hours. *Not the rape. Not the rape.*

When finished, she raised a wall of silence and refused to engage. At all. With anyone. Her retreat, her control, against the pain of defeat and betrayal.

And no one dared protest when three months later, Special Agent Lowry Fisk — survivor against all odds, mute, and still a patient at the private hospital for those suffering from post-traumatic shock — was court marshaled in her absence. Not when it was Major Jack Ballentyne, Commanding Officer of the elite unit unofficially nicknamed "The Assassins," who leveled the charge of gross insubordination against her.

Chapter One

His back to the jostling guests, Jack Ballentyne studied the wild spread of vivid canvases lining the expanse of whitewashed brick wall. Lowry's work was good. Damn good. The colors strong and vibrant. The brush strokes bold and unhesitant, spirited even.

He hadn't broken her, not completely.

For the first time since the order had come through for him to get back in contact with her to deliver a warning, the knot in his gut eased. Turning his back on the paintings, he leaned against a faux-rusted iron girder—one of twelve such vertical supports lending an artisan chicness to the excruciatingly fashionable gallery.

He scoured the heaving throng of guests for his target—Lowry-*bloody*-Fisk. Finding her in this mob wouldn't be easy. But then, when had she ever done simple?

Certainly never in the two years she'd spent under his command. Not even for one goddamn day.

That she had compromised him as a professional, he could forgive—just. That she had compromised him as a man? Not. A. Chance.

He'd unashamedly shagged half of London to lay her ghost to rest. Yet still she haunted him. Four fucking years of her drifting into his mind uninvited. One thousand four hundred and sixty disturbed sleeps—those stormy gray-green eyes of hers dark with pain. Accusing him of betrayal, of letting her down. Small wonder he was an insomniac.

Irritated, suddenly impatient, he re-scanned the press of bodies. The rich, the titled, the celebrated. Standout colors of couture frocks hurt his eyes. The heavy mix of competing scents and colognes curled his nostrils. Before joining the Service, with his pedigree, he'd been destined for a lead role among the socially elite. *Thank fuck he'd rejected it.*

Now where the hell was she?

As if warned of his darkening mood, the throng magically parted.

And all breath slammed from his chest.

Lowry-bloody-Fisk. Standing surrounded, yet isolated. Her eyes, wide and watchful, darting over her guests in an exclamation of distrust and suspicion. Her body, long and lithe, delicately turned with tempting soft curves, taut and under strain, poised for imminent flight.

Fuck. A tethered goat, helpless bait in a lion's den, could not have looked more panicked. Was he to blame? Is that what he'd done to her? There was no denying he'd been tough on her. He'd had to be—she'd redefined pain in the ass. And, not content with taxing his patience and testing his temper, she'd had to go and tempt him. Tempt him into giving a damn, when he'd long ago vowed never again to allow anyone to get close enough to make him care. He'd only screw up. Best way to keep them safe? Get them to stay the hell away.

Lowry's head swung in his direction, a stray tendril of her hair catching in the crease of her lips.

His lungs kicked back into action. He spun on his heel fast. Oh, they'd duel tonight—but not yet. Not until he had a grip. Not until he *remembered* he was not supposed. To. Give. A. Fuck.

Teeth clenched, he rolled his back muscles against the knot bridging his shoulders. Christ, he needed a drink. Something strong to scorch on the way down, then slow-burn like a sonofabitch when it hit his gut.

Lowry-bloody-Fisk.

He'd first hyphenated her name on learning she'd been assigned to *his* team. Within a week, his curse had strengthened to the unprintable. Across the seven languages and innumerable dialects in which he was fluent.

Her first public challenge to his leadership, he'd laughed off. Her second, third, fourth, and fifth, he'd let pass with a sharp reprimand. He'd benched her for the sixth, insisting she be anchored to a desk. Even then she hadn't quit. If anything, she'd become even more of a pain in the ass. Imagining subterfuge and corruption where none existed. Quietly defying his orders as if they were nuns' farts, best politely ignored.

Her seventh challenge had finished her—he shot her. Fuck near killed her.

His gut twisted. The memory of her—prone, her blood leaking a lake between his fingers, the pearl-blond of her hair a halo against the filthy concrete floor—as crystal clear as the night it had happened four years ago.

Some man, all soft, sweaty, and city slick in tailored pinstripes, staggered against him carelessly, jolting him back to the present.

Without thought, Jack shouldered back hard. No apology. Not even when the man stumbled and would have fallen, had his indignant companions not caught him.

Deadpan, he stared the group down, not giving an inch until they shambled off. Idiotic, because his orders had been simple, but specific—stay the fuck off radar. But Lowry had him ready to split open his own skin. A minor contretemps eased the pressure.

A silver tray floated into sight. He snatched a flute of pale gold liquid, the bubbles still rising and breaking in a soft hiss. Bloody champagne. He'd have sacrificed his right bollock for something a lot stronger.

The pretty server—body like a goddess—paused, checked him out, and, judging by the blatant invitation in her eyes, she liked the view.

Jack saluted her with his drink and slow-grinned his own appreciation. His eyebrows slowly climbed of their own volition when she winked in an unspoken promise that she'd be back to collect…and he knew she wasn't referring to his glass.

His body tightened in anticipation. Maybe a few hours solace in the arms of a beautiful woman was just what he needed—because his job sure wasn't providing the distraction he craved like an addict. It hadn't for a while.

He scoured an open palm across the length of his face and grimaced when his fingers met the two- or maybe three-day-old stubble shadowing his chin. *Shit.* Casually—and, he had to concede, carelessly—dressed head to toe in black, from his grandfather's battered leather flying jacket to his scuffed, albeit hand-tooled leather boots, he had to look like an over-aged delinquent with a Goth complex. Not that he cared, but he couldn't afford to be memorable. His job might not be cutting it right now, but it was his life, and recognition would see him flying a desk faster than Alice from Data Retrieval shucked her panties.

Shit. Shit. *Shit.* When the order had come through to warn Lowry off, he should have delegated. Sent in someone with whom open combat wasn't a given. She'd only have to suspect *he* was close, and she'd bristle and spit, her tight little body quivering with fury. Not good, when his own body was already revving in hungry anticipation.

He looked down, saw his hand was less than steady, and clenched his jaw tight enough for the crack to be heard above the hubbub of the chattering masses.

Jesus, one glimpse of her, Lowry Fisk—the first in four years—and he was as twitchy as a raw recruit, first time under fire.

Sonofabitch and to hell with this. He'd confront her. Caution her, then get the fuck out of her orbit. Is wasn't like he hadn't done it before.

In a single belt, he downed his drink, making no effort to hide his grimace. Reaching forward, he placed the now-empty glass, with its impossibly delicate stem, on the waiting tray. The flirty server, as wickedly promised, had returned.

With a forced grin as close to civilized as he could muster, he shrugged a flattered-but-not-tonight-darling apology, which earned him a disappointed pout. Hell, the foul mood he was in, Miss L.W.A — luscious, willing, and able — should count herself lucky for the narrowest of escapes.

Lowry-*bloody*-Fisk, on the other hand, had just run out of time.

• • •

Lowry had taken refuge near the rear of the gallery. Butterflies with blades for wings swooped in her stomach. She wrapped her arms across her midriff, her hands rubbing her upper arms against a sudden chill. Someone was watching her, tracking her; she could *feel* it. Or it might just be another hated flashback, brought on by the pressure of her opening night.

Adrian, her agent, would kill her if he discovered she'd deliberately released the lock to the back exit. A wise precaution to her way of thinking, but he wouldn't agree. His priority was to protect property. Her only concern, escape — should the need arise.

She tried measuring each inhale and exhale of breath against a slow countdown from a hundred. Maybe if she just focused hard enough, she could pretend her skin didn't itch and her spine wasn't threatening to rip free and leave her to her own damned fate.

Suddenly conscious of the pathetic impression she must be giving, she straightened her shoulders and forced her arms to her sides. Not quite sure what to do with her hands, she fisted them tight. Better that than allow her fingers to clutch and twist the slate-gray silk of the dress skimming her thighs.

Her throat, already as dry as week-old toast, tightened. She snuck out the tip of her tongue to moisten her lips. God, she didn't want this. Not the tittering. Not the strangers. Not the fear.

Especially not the fear.

What the hell had she been thinking? Tonight — the solo show, the blaze of publicity — huge mistake. If her little foray into the public eye backfired, it could finish her. For good this time. Four years was a long time. Long enough for her attacker to forget her? The lighting in the warehouse had been poor, but what if he recognized her? What if he didn't trust her to keep her mouth shut? What if he came after her to make sure that she did?

Gritting her teeth, she damped down the gnawing anxiety fast. Losing control wasn't an option. Not when she'd only just seized it back.

Bloody past.

Her history didn't exactly qualify for a cheer or even a hesitant ripple of applause. But she hadn't let it beat her. Change her, yes. But not beat her. And *that* was what tonight was all about — vindication.

Only mildly emboldened by that reminder, she darted quick little glances at her milling guests, trusting not a one of them.

The tiny hairs at the nape of her neck pricked. The little pants escaping her mouth puffed at loose strands of her hair. To hell with the promise she'd made herself not to run. To stop hiding. She could *smell* the threat in the air.

She twisted her body, her hips going one way, her shoulders the other, and it was all she could do not to claw at those obstructing her path as she attempted to thread a fast exit through the crowd.

A heavy arm draped around her lower back and pulled her in tight for a quick squeeze.

"Seventeen red stickers, only six left to sell. Unbelievable!"

She stared blankly at her agent. Couldn't Adrian see she had more important things to worry about than the sale of a few pictures?

Survival for a start.

His brow puckering, Adrian dipped his knees to better capture her line of sight. Then, his eyes rolling heavenwards, he reached forward and positioned his forefingers at the corners of her mouth. The gentle pressure he applied was upward in direction. "I know this isn't easy for you, but could you at least pretend to smile?"

"Someone's watching me—I need to go," she blurted, thrusting him aside. He was blocking her view.

"Lowry, *sweetheart*, everybody's watching you. What did you expect? They're insanely curious about the hermit-girl responsible for the paintings. You've worked hard for this; we both have. Don't blow it, not after you've come so far. Please, cupcake, your adoring public awaits."

Sweetheart? Cupcake? She bit back a sharp reprimand. Adrian didn't know about the man who, while holding her down, had used those same sweet nothings and a whole lot more besides. No one did. Not even the staff at the PTSD hospital after her last mission with the Service, who— clueless about anything beyond her bullet wound and fracturing mind—had thought it comforting to shower her in obscenely affectionate endearments.

Adrian, clearly determined to draw her back into the

melee, seized her hand and tugged. She dug her heels deep, resisting. She also freed her fingers and scrubbed her palm against her thigh as if contaminated.

His look, ever patient but pitying, flooded her cheeks with color. She hadn't meant to be rude, but touching was a no-no. "Fifteen minutes more, then I leave," she warned him quietly, hoping to make amends.

"Make it an hour, and I'll not only call you a taxi, I'll even cover the fare," he pleaded.

Her nerve endings flashed worse than any lightning storm. Another sixty minutes? Could she last that long? One quick look at her best — her only — friend's excited face, and she knew she didn't have a choice. "Okay, lead on," she agreed weakly.

Smiling hurt. Her cheeks ached with the strain, as did her muscles from the effort of trying not to jerk and recoil at every stranger's touch. With no wall to protect her back, people hovered dangerously close, outside of her line of vision; the brush of their unknown bodies jolting bolts of anxiety the length of her spine. Where the hell was Adrian?

Not for the first time, or even the fourth or fifth, she smoothed a moist palm against the silk of her dress and ran through her particular fashion "must" list for reassurance. All pieces dark in color to blend with shadows, check. Skirts and dresses short and cut loose to allow uninhibited flight, check. Stiletto heels — normally avoided — a half-size too big, so she could kick them free and run, check —

From behind, a hand clasped her shoulder.

She squirmed free, staggered forward, quickly stifling the squeal on her lips in case the touch had been an innocent mistake. Deafened by the sound of blood gushing through her head, she spun around, her arms instinctively raised somewhere between attack and defense.

Her assailant swore and raised his palms to calm. "Easy…I didn't mean to startle you."

Battling the palpitations threatening to crack her chest, she pushed the humiliating weight of paranoia aside and forced herself to make eye contact, an apology for her skittishness ready on the tip of her tongue.

Her vision cleared, and she stopped herself just in time. "You!"

That past she'd buried? She should have staked it first. Dead center through the heart. It might have prevented its resurrection.

"Yes, me." Jack, visibly bracing his shoulders, closed in. Probably to halt a line of braying men from cutting between them. "I take it you have yet to forgive me?"

With the crowd tight behind her, she couldn't run. She couldn't even step back. "Damn right. So piss off." Language she hadn't used since being tossed out by the Service, but in this man's company, the coarseness flooded back. Some words, however ugly, said it all.

She stared fixedly at his long fingers, now curled around her wrist. "Let go, Ballentyne, or so help me, I'll scream, and a man like you doesn't need the attention."

His grin was lazy. Deliberately provocative.

Her heart dithered with indecision. Speed up, or stop beating altogether?

"A man like me? And what kind of man is that, Lowry?"

A rash of invisible pinpricks danced the surface of her skin. She leaned back into the crowd behind her. Distance from Jack Ballentyne, more imperative than any danger strangers might pose. "A stained man. A violent man. A heartless, brutal, scary bastard who—"

"Okay, okay. I get it," he interrupted, one palm back up. "You don't like me much."

"Wrong. I don't like you at all. You embody everything I abhor, what any decent, person would abhor." That should cut his misplaced amusement off at the knees.

She jerked her wrist.

His fingers squeezed, his grin slipping into a hard, straight line. "Point taken, Fisk. We'll keep this short. I'd appreciate a word. Somewhere less public."

Her lungs flattened. The gallery spun, colors swirling, the disconnected snippets of chatter from her guests, too loud for her ears. "Appreciate away. This is as private as I ever want to be with you. Now get the hell away from me."

"Not until you hear me out."

She opened her mouth to make good on her threat to scream. Closed it again when his fingers tightened further and he jerked her flush against him.

"Don't." Though the word was quietly spoken against the shell of her ear, the warmth of his breath whispering against her skin, it was not a request. It was a warning. A promise of swift retribution.

Her body began a slow shutdown, the numbness starting in her toes and slugging upward. Dear God, never above the dirtiest of tactics, Jack would kiss her into silence if he had to.

Ice frosted her skin. Jesus, the bastard had an erection, and his hot male scent—predatory, lawless, just as she remembered—had strengthened. The frost began to melt away. Stupid, traitorous body.

One hand flat to his chest, she ignored the fierce pounding of his heart beneath her palm. She pushed and wrenched her wrist free, not caring about the bruises she'd carry in the morning. As injuries went, he'd given her far worse. The memory of his bullet plowing into her was all the reminder she needed.

Locking her spine, one vertebra at a time, she looked up, way up, ready for some hostile eyeballing. The mighty Jack Ballentyne, as drop-dead-or-drop-your-panties gorgeous as he was, looked stunned.

She immediately pounced for the first strike. With this man, it paid to seize the advantage. "You look a touch strained, *Major*. Don't tell me you've come to apologize."

His tight scoff put her right. "Hardly."

Ordinarily, she avoided prolonged eye contact at all costs—four years ago she'd had her sanity stared right out of her—but not this time. She scoured the depths of violent blue, and found the shocking. "My God, you want absolution," she gasped in disbelief.

"I don't *need* absolution."

"You shot me, Ballentyne."

"To save your life! I shouted for you to stay back, but noooo, you had to run straight into the crossfire. If I hadn't taken you down fast, you'd be dead."

She crossed her arms. "You were letting him get away."

"There was no *him*."

"Yeah? Try telling that to the three agents who died."

"It was damned near four," he fired back. "The angle was tight. I nicked your femoral artery. And your recklessness that night not only put your own life at risk, it compromised months of undercover work. You shouldn't have been there,

Lowry. I'd banned you from anything more active than shuffling paperclips."

"That's right, you shut me down. Why? Because I refused to let you intimidate me? Because I dared to disagree with your ethics? Because I dared asked questions no one could hear, because they had their heads too far up their own behinds?"

"My ethics stand up to scrutiny. Your suitability for front-line duty never did. Face it, Lowry, just as I'd predicted, you panicked when the shit hit the fan. And it got you shot."

She ignored the personal slight. It wasn't like he hadn't leveled it before. Incessantly. "I didn't panic. I was trying to stop him from getting away."

His snort had her wishing she had a gun in her hand.

"Here we go again. The evil mastermind scenario. A figment of your imagination, in which we, apparently, let "Mr. Big" get away. Tell me something, *ex*-special agent Fisk, was it worth it? Preserving your pride at the expense of your reputation?"

Lowry lifted her chin a smidgen, only dimly aware of the crowd funneling around the pair of them. "By then, thanks to you, I didn't have much pride left. And as for the cost? What do you think? I lost my job. Hell, I lost my mind. You let him go, so you tell me."

"There. Was. No. Him."

By now, Jack was giving a damn good impression of a furious bull pawing at the ground, ready to charge. But she'd stood up to him before and survived.

Tilting her head, she leaned in close. As close as she dared and stared him straight in the eye. "Go to hell, Ballentyne. Trust me, I can show you the way."

"Lowry…"

"Don't *Lowry* me. Not in that tone. I don't need your pity, I've moved on. Sadly, it appears you haven't, and it's eating you alive. So, I absolve you, Ballentyne. Let it go. That's what my very expensive therapist would have advised."

In a gesture screaming frustration, Jack plowed an untidy furrow through his too-long-for-regulations, mucky blond hair. "And maybe *you* should have listened."

"I did, right up until I found out you were personally footing the expense. Now, I'm self-healing."

"Really? And how's that going?"

She threw her arms as wide as the pressing crowd would allow. "Take a look around you, Ballentyne. Read the press reviews. I'm making quite a name for myself."

He nodded, his hard stare cutting through to the bone. "I know. That's why I'm here. Concern has been expressed at all the media attention you're attracting. People are worried it might lead you to forget you remain bound by the Official Secrets Act."

The butterflies that had sliced earlier swooped high into her chest, along with the nausea that had been swilling low in her stomach. By people, he meant the Service and her father. The very bastards who probably wished she had died the night of the raid. Her insistence that they had a traitor in their ranks hadn't been much appreciated, thank you very much. "Well, that's the thing about guilty secrets, isn't it? They just refuse to lie down and die," she challenged, rashly.

"Lowry, this is a warning. Leave. It. Alone."

"Or what? You or someone like you, will silence me for good? Don't worry, Jack, I learned my lesson. Some battles can't be won. Those traitorous bastards you work for are safe. On condition my past stays where it belongs. Way, way behind me, so I can get on with *my life.*"

Oh, he did not like that.

His eyes spat ice chips like an icicle shattered by the flat side of an axe. "Is that a threat?"

She tightened her lips, needing her words to be Kevlar-vest hard. "I wouldn't know. Thanks to you, I'm longer in the business. But put it this way: I'll be ecstatically happy—and hold my silence—but only if I never see you again, nor any of your associates."

She didn't wait for his response. Turning on her heel, she plunged into the heaving mass behind her, for the first time in years grateful for the warm embrace a tight crowd provided.

Chapter Two

The number of guests had thinned, their muted conversations now barely audible in the small office at the rear of the gallery where Lowry had sequestered herself.

Damn Jack Ballentyne. Damn him for dragging her back into his world. And double damn him for reminding her that she'd never be free. Not of the past. Not of him. Not of what had undeniably sparked between the two of them all those years ago. It wasn't just bad temper that flared when they were around each other.

Oh, they'd denied and fought and refused it. Blamed and punished and hated each other for its cause. They'd both wanted. They'd both resisted. *She* remembered the physical hell well. In the end, he'd hated enough to shoot her, and she'd hated him right back for his betrayal.

Not only did Jack Ballentyne have the empathy of a rock, the heartless bastard was completely without conscience. It's how he'd risen to the top. It's why those who dared cross him feared him. His motto, as always: the ends justify the means, and fuck the collateral damage.

With a puff of pained resignation, she reached down for her small backpack, the one she took everywhere she went. It was fat with a change of clothing, £5000 in cash, and a small leather folder full of fake documents, including three passports supporting her different identities — her survival kit, should she need it.

Slinging the strap of her backpack across one shoulder, she made her way back to the main exhibition space of the gallery.

Heart stampeding, she pulled to an abrupt halt. Oh, God, who'd dimmed the lights?

Her eyes urgently mapped an escape. Then, just as quickly, she recognized what was going on. Laughing softly, without conviction, she shook her head, her braid penduluming against her back. Paranoia was a bitch.

Dimming the lights was just Adrian's way of sending a discreet message to the few remaining guests that it was time to go. That was Adrian all over. Determined but subtle, not a rude bone in his body, because who could tell the direction from which their next big sale would come? As her agent, he wasn't just good, he was the best. And he was the only man — the only *person* — she trusted enough to call a friend.

He was busy glad-handing the last of the guests. No point in interrupting; she'd call him tomorrow. He'd understand her need to keep to the shadows and quietly slip away.

Straightening the strap of her backpack, she cast a final look over her shoulder.

And the past drove an iron fist smack into her chest.

Lips, thin and brutal, pale, uniquely bloodless. When

she'd last seen them, they'd been framed in navy wool, the balaclava scratchy, the edges of the cut-a-way mouth sodden where he'd licked. Now, nothing hid his face.

Black eyes—hideously cruel. Onyx, reptilian eyes—indelibly imprinted in her memory. Eyes—horror-struck with recognition.

Him. Staring at her. Her. Staring at him.

Rapist to victim. Victim to rapist.

Killer to witness. Witness to killer.

She didn't hesitate. Kicking free her heels, she sprinted across the almost-empty gallery, ignoring Adrian and the last of her guests. Pain fired up her wrists as her palms slammed hard against the heavy, double-thick glass door.

The chilled night air, still raw this early in the spring, razored her cheeks. She barely noticed the sting. She ran flat out, blindly, her unshod feet slapping the hard paving stones. One hand fisted tight around her low-slung braid to keep it forward, terrified that, flapping free, it might give her pursuer a place to grab hold.

She hit something. Not a wall. Too warm, too leathery, but just as solid. She struggled, flailing with her fists, kicking uselessly. Hard arms clamped round her, lifting her from the ground. Oh, sweet Jesus, he was carrying her toward the narrow passage bisecting one hulking warehouse from another.

She used her head to butt his chin. Heard a grunt, but the arms didn't loosen.

"Lowry. Stop fighting. You're going to get hurt. It's me, Jack, Jack Ballentyne. I said stop, damn it."

"Not until…you…let me…go." She needed air, wouldn't cease struggling until she got it. "Please, Jack…I'm near…

phobic…about restraint."

His arms loosened immediately, he set her back on her feet. She stumbled backward, her spine protesting when it hit brick. "No closer," she begged as he advanced.

• • •

For the second time that night, Jack raised his hands to calm. What the hell was going on? Had her mind finally broken? Had the pressure of all those people at the exhibition tipped her over the edge? She'd certainly fought in a crazed frenzy, all discipline and training forgotten. "You're safe, Lowry. No one is going to hurt you. I won't let them, Lowry. Want to tell me what's going on, Lowry?"

"Stop patronizing me for a start. Repeating my name like that is what people do when they need to talk you down. When they want you to reconnect with reality. I should know."

Despite the temper behind her words, he could see she was having difficulty staying upright, that but for the wall behind her, she'd collapse in a heap. "Do you need to reconnect with reality, *Lowry*?" He didn't have a bloody clue what he was doing. His experience had never extended to managing a full-on psychotic meltdown. But he knew he had to calm her, or she'd take flight again. When what he needed was for her to share *what the fuck* was going on.

"Get lost, Ballentyne. I had a flashback, that's all. It's not unusual. I panicked for a moment. Now I'm fine."

Lie. Jesus, she sounded like she could barely breathe. "Really? So, why are you shaking worse than an addict in withdrawal?" Instinct told him not to crowd her. Slipping down the zipper, he shrugged free his leather jacket and held it toward her at arm's length. The wait for her to take it—to trust him—was interminable. Strangely, it also hurt. Like a sonofabitch saber cleaving his sternum.

"Thanks," she muttered, snatching it, her fingers bloodless white against the folds of black leather as she clutched it to her chest.

He nodded curtly, rubbing his bruised chin with one hand. "Put it on. You're going to need it. The sudden crash after an adrenaline hit can be as cold as a witch's tit." He watched a shudder grip her and figured he'd better show something akin to humanity by moderating his choice of language and tone. "Come on, I'll take you to your father's house. You shouldn't be alone."

"I'm used to it. Being alone. I prefer it. Besides, my father and I haven't spoken in years, not since…forget it. I'm going home."

Her relationship with the Commander of the Service, her father, had always been difficult. He wasn't an easy man to like, let alone love. Had the heartless bastard abandoned her when she'd needed his support most? The sonofabitch saber struck his chest again. "Okay, I'll have Special Agent Will Berwick pick us up. He's in the area. You do remember Will? Terrible flirt, but one of the good guys, and a friend of yours as I recall. God knows, you soaked enough of his shirts with your tears every time you received a bollocking from me."

"Yes, I remember, but I still prefer to make my own way home. I don't want anyone knowing where I live."

If her teeth chattered any more violently, she'd lose them. He knew shock when he saw it, and he didn't want to alarm her and set her off again. But what choice did he have? None. "You're good at flying below the radar, Lowry, better than anyone gave you credit for, and I'm not saying tracking down your home address was easy. But did you seriously believe I couldn't find you anytime I wanted? You live at 3 Danby Mews. Alone, even with Adrian Wainwright's name on the title deeds. Accept my offer of a ride, or I'll follow you on foot. Your call."

Waiting for her to see sense again seemed to take forever. The stink of stale refuse from obese garbage bags piled a few feet down on the left soured the frigid air. A destruction of cats growled, then rumbled deep in the darkness, the squalling violent enough to raise the hairs on his neck.

She flinched at the battle sounds. Then surprised the hell out of him. "I'll take the ride."

But her back still hugged the wall. Her eyes never once ceased skittering left, right, low, high, scouting the dark.

He watched her scoot sideways, stoop, and grab her battered leather backpack from where it had fallen during their struggle. Something, or someone, had spooked her to hell. Christ, she'd even ditched her shoes...

The inexplicable impulse hit him with the force and weight of a mountain dropping from the sky. He wanted to pick her up and cradle her. Hold her close and swear a blood oath to keep whatever terrorized her at bay. Bloody pathetic.

He delved for his phone and hit speed dial the second it cleared his pocket. "Will? You've got three minutes to get your ass to the corner of Pound Street—and we've got a passenger." He cut the call and put away the device. When Will pulled up exactly three minutes later, he opened the door to the Land Rover's backseat and jerked his head. "After you." He made no further offer to assist as she clambered in. Not after she'd visibly flinched when he'd reached out to help her.

It shouldn't have annoyed him, but it did. Lowry, all tight and huddled in the far corner of the Land Rover's backseat, maximizing every inch of space between them, the very epitome of "I'm a victim." His eyes shifted to her hand. He noted the way her fingers gripped the door release. Christ, he hoped Will had had enough sense to engage the child locks.

He inched closer just in case, halting his slide when she pressed deeper into the corner, her eyes wide in the darkness, flickering mistrust and accusation.

That pissed him off, but not as much as hearing himself snarl at Will in a way that implied he'd gone and bought into Lowry's overflowing bag of the crazies. "Make sure we haven't picked up a fucking tail. Someone might try to follow us."

When Will finally pulled to a halt in the narrow street in front of her house, Jack resisted the impulse to help her down from the high step of the vehicle. Again, she wouldn't thank him for the body contact. Not with the signals she was throwing.

Except, he had no choice when she stumbled on the cobbles, and he had to catch her elbow to save her from falling flat on her face. He felt the shudder of her recoil right down to the marrow of his bones and released her immediately.

Coloring the inside of his skull blue with a string of foul mental curses, he promised himself he'd risk her full wrath should she try to slam the door in his face. He was going nowhere until he had some answers.

• • •

Lowry bit down a scream of frustration. The protection of the fortress she'd built for herself, a single small footstep away, and she couldn't get in. A cold bead of sweat trickled down her spine. She slapped her front door for defying her. If the complicated locking system didn't cooperate soon, she'd borrow Jack's gun and shoot her way in.

Jack's fault. He was standing too damn close. If she were a head and a half taller, his breath would be warming the nape of her neck, rather than just ruffling the hair on the crown of her head. "For God's sake, Ballentyne, can you give me a little space? You're making me nervous." The admission didn't cost her anything. He knew full well the effect he had on people, and she'd never known him fail to use it to his advantage.

Once inside her private sanctuary, she'd be safe. And free to unleash the humiliating panic clawing beneath her skin. But not in front of him. She'd rather die. Which, given the events of the evening—that man with his reptilian, dead, flat eyes—was kind of hilarious, in a sick sort of way.

The bubble of hysteria lodged in her throat. All those precautions she'd taken to stay safe?—waste of time.

As sure as blood ran crimson, the man from the gallery would be coming for her. He couldn't risk leaving her be. Not after she'd seen his face. Not when she might chose to spill her guts about what she'd witnessed and suffered at his hands.

She went back to battling the lock.

Finally, it relented, and her fingers flew to stop the spring-loaded door from falling fully ajar. Jack wasn't crossing her threshold. She didn't trust him. Anymore than she trusted anyone employed by the Service. "Okay, safe, sound, and calm. You can go now. Leave."

His reached over her shoulder, pressed his hand against the door, and shoved.

She instinctively leaped inside and spun to face him, her hands tight fists. The slightest touch from him—from any man, right now—and she'd unravel.

He followed her in and kicked the door shut behind him, his "make me" smile unapologetic.

She'd once stood fearless against this man, but that was before. Before the fear. Before the rape. *He can't possibly know*, she reassured herself. *No one knew.* So much less humiliating to let them all believe she was sick in the head from the trauma of being shot.

"You going to stand there while our ears bleed from that infernal beeping, or are you going to key in the code to stop the alarm proper from going off and deafening us both?"

Her eyelids fluttered like the wings of a moth caught in a web, the spider fast approaching. Brushing him aside, she stabbed the panel of flashing lights.

It took her two attempts to silence the squawking, the abrupt hush when she finally succeeded so cruel it hurt.

Forgetting how sensitive the device was, she dipped her forehead to rest it against the cool glass of the deactivation unit. The tiny bulbs reignited in warning. She immediately panicked, her fingers, heavy and clumsy, jabbed at the keypad as if she were playing the piano wearing a baseball mitt.

Jack brushed her stabbing fingers aside and keyed in the correct code. Flawlessly. She'd forgotten how keenly observant he could be. Also, that he had eidetic memory. Damn it, now she'd have to reprogram a new number. And memorizing eighteen random digits and symbols had been hard enough the first time round.

Determined to salvage what little pride she had left, she struck fast in the hope that a dig at his background would draw some blood and encourage him to leave. "What do you want, *Viscount*?"

"I'll take a coffee and an explanation," he said acidly.

"You're not staying long enough for either. Get out."

"Fine, I'll pass on the coffee, but I'm not leaving until you tell me what caused you to—"

"Unravel? Freak out? Descend into insanity?" She deliberately added several octaves to her tone. Jack Ballentyne loathed hysteria, heightened emotions of any kind. If believing her to be a lunatic guaranteed his departure, she'd stage her own full-scale crazy opera if need be.

His response? To lean his back against her front door, fold his arms across his chest, and stare her down. "Everyone's crazy, Lowry, it's just a question of to what degree. Now, about that explanation... I'm still waiting, and you, of all people, know I'm not exactly renowned for patience."

The unexpected humor in his eyes was as surprising as it was dangerously persuasive. Not trusting this change, she laced her tone with frost. "I don't owe you an explanation. Leave. I don't allow people in here."

His eyes swept the wide-open, uninterrupted space she'd hollowed from the two-story, former coach house and stables. She watched his patent disbelief build at the stark-white plastered, windowless walls. The solitary black, low-backed sofa—more a bench—and the absence of little else, bar the collection of metal trunks she'd artfully sculpted to screen the bulletproof glass walls of the bathroom. Just enough to afford her some privacy, without obstructing her view of every single corner of her home.

His face grim, he didn't even try to hide his shock. "Considering you put the minimal into minimalist, I'm not surprised. This is a bunker, not a home. God, how do you live like this?"

"Securely."

"Why, Lowry? What do you have to be afraid of?"

"Men like you."

"Too easy, try again," he countered with a flick of his wrist, clearly still distracted.

A naughty thrill trickled her spine. Time to turn up the burn. His buttons had always been easy to push, and she'd missed needling him, needling anyone. Four years of avoiding social interaction was a long time.

She gestured dramatically toward the heavily barred skylight comprising half the high ceiling and injected more insanity into her voice. "Wickedness, evil, and assassins, out there..." she dropped her arm and jabbed her forefinger at the sea-green stained, polished cement floor, "...sanctuary in here."

She savored his marked incredulity, then let him off the hook, readjusting her tone back into the normal range. "Oh, for God's sake, I only moved in a month ago."

He ventured deeper into her home. With a shake of his head, he turned slowly to face her. All sign of his earlier amusement had vanished. She'd have settled for his bewilderment, but he'd retreated behind a blank mask. "Considering you've been running and hiding all these years, pretty brave of you to risk re-surfacing, braver still of you to finally decide to put down some roots."

Sarcastic bastard. He'd never know just how much courage it had taken. "Oddly enough, the nomadic life lost its charm. Now, if you don't mind," she stared pointedly at the door. He still didn't move, forcing her to blatant rudeness. "Well, what are you waiting for?"

"My jacket."

Heat hit her cheeks. "Oh."

She quickly slipped her shoulders free and cursed as her elbows caught in the heavy folds. Flustered by the tangle, she looked up. Jack's lips had slanted in a lazy half-grin. He made no move to help her.

Cursing him under her breath, she struggled loose. The sudden loss of heavy protective leather and the subtle scent of him—a hint of gun oil and cordite—compressed her lungs. No. Absolutely not. She refused to miss him. "Here, now go," she muttered, her eyes fixed on the vacant space behind him.

As if in slow motion, he took the jacket and nonchalantly tossed it in the direction of her sofa. Leather hit the polished floor in a dull huff of insult. "Still not going anywhere, not without an explanation."

She settled her hands on her hips, content to let the empty silence hang.

"No? So, where do I sleep?" His gaze drifted.

Given the scant choice of furnishings, she didn't have to hold her breath for long.

His gawk came to a halt on her flush-with-the-ground, super-king-sized bed. The one at which her contractor had nearly balked when she insisted it be sunk level with the floor.

Why? Because, four years ago, she'd met a monster. And monsters could hide in the void between a mattress base and a floor.

Jack, calm as you like, crossed to get a closer look at where he no doubt thought he'd be spending the night.

Goose bumps prickled her skin. Mimicking madness wasn't working. She needed a change of strategy fast. She'd tell him just enough to satisfy and then figure out a way to repair the damage when he was gone.

Turning abruptly, she stalked to the surgically precise kitchen area—spotless, clutter-free stainless steel—a glass plate of lemons, sculpted into a high pyramid, the only color.

She flicked the switch on the kettle and unhooked a single mug. She swiped at the stray tendrils of hair that had escaped her braid and expelled a deep sigh. "Black, three sugars?"

For an instant, her blood ceased to flow. There was careless, and then there was just plain dumb. Now he'd know she remembered how he took his coffee.

She waited for the hot-pink scorching her cheeks to subside before throwing a look over her shoulder. He confirmed with a nod, an unmistakable gleam of triumph in his eyes.

Teeth snapped tight together, she glared, daring him to utter one word. The neat row of knives, all varying lengths and hanging to her left, was temptation itself.

She filled his mug, edged it in his direction, and retreated a safe distance—a good two yards—before turning to prop her hip against the counter. Staring at her feet, bruised and sooty with London grime, she took a deep breath. "Tonight at the gallery, I think I recognized someone. Worse, I think he recognized me…from the night of the raid."

Looking up, she watched his eyes narrow, his lips tighten. Black cotton stretched as the muscles in his chest expanded. She curled her fingers around the edge of the counter. Would he believe her?

"Forget "think"; I trained you better than that. You either recognized someone, or you didn't. Which is it?"

As unhesitant as a master surgeon's scalpel, and just as unsympathetic, this was the Jack she remembered. She curled her fingers tighter, the edge of the counter cutting into her palm. "The former. And you can stop looking at me like that. You asked for an explanation, that's it. Now drink up and leave."

"This person, I presume it was a man, describe him."

"I can't, not precisely. Noting details wasn't exactly my priority at the time." That seemed almost reasonable. Rational. Calm. Pity she sounded as if someone was strangling her.

He was staring into the depths of his mug. She relaxed her fingers a smidgen to ease the cut of the counter. She was handling him just fine.

"So, describe him from the night at the warehouse."

She blinked wildly and retightened her grip on the counter. One of her fingernails, already moderately short, split.

Chapter Three

"You know full well I can't describe him. As I told you at the time, the man who got away…he wore a mask, a balaclava… tonight…I…I recognized his eyes." *Hideous eyes. Empty eyes. Windows to the soul, only he didn't have one.*

She looked up in time to catch Jack's eye-roll. She didn't blame his lack of belief. Her words sounded fanciful even to her ears.

"Why do you do this to yourself, Lowry?"

She hated when his voice took on that soft, placating tone. It didn't suit the hard, ruthless man she knew him to be. He epitomized loyalty and integrity to the extreme when it came to just causes, a.k.a. the Service and defending the realm. But when it came to people and their messy emotions, he faked like a shiny Rolex watch for sale on the streets of Hong Kong for five dollars.

He pinched the bridge of his nose, then shifted his stare to the high skylight, as if the very sight of her—strung out and disheveled, emotionally and physically—offended him.

"Sooner or later, Lowry, you are going to have to come to terms with the fact that there was no other man. The violence you witnessed, the trauma of being shot, the doctors said—"

She held up a hand, palm facing Jack. "I know what they said. That to deal with the trauma of that night, I created a new reality, someone to blame because I couldn't handle the guilt of failing those girls. They were wrong; so are you." She accepted her share of the blame for those poor women dying. Someone stronger might have saved them. But she didn't deserve the undying fear. And she hadn't deserved that animal ripping her hymen.

Jack's silence was more condemning than any words he could have found to denigrate her. Not helped by the fact that he had to be the only man alive able to control the blink reflex.

The mean-as-all-hell butterflies colonizing her stomach took flight once again. "There *was* someone else there that night," she insisted. "Someone whose sole purpose was to ensure no member of the cartel survived to finger those selling them information, and providing protection for their operation. The whole thing was a setup. Pre-arranged and supremely well-orchestrated pest control, with you and your team the unwitting exterminators. You allowed yourself to be played, Jack."

From his expression, he looked like he wanted to hurl his mug against a wall. "So how come you didn't warn us? Good agents died that night. A single shot would have been enough to put us on alert."

"I. Wasn't. Armed." The short red and silver beaded

cocktail dress she'd worn that night to fit in as one of the stolen glory girls hadn't allowed for the secreting of a weapon.

"You've got a voice haven't you? You could have yelled. A single scream would have sufficed. Trust me, I'd have recognized your voice."

Except she'd exhausted all capability of making sound a half hour before the team arrived, having screamed her larynx raw during the rape.

The inner lining of her throat corrugated at the memory, just as it had done that night. She raised a hand to cover her mouth and choked discreetly to ease the dry constriction. "Ever felt helpless, Ballentyne, so raw and frightened, you disconnect from your own body?" She hadn't meant to whisper, but that's what emerged.

"Shooting you wasn't much fun. Before that, only when my brother, Richard lay smashed up and..." he stopped abruptly, took a gulp of coffee, then subjected her to another punishing glare. The fierce cobalt of his eyes looked sharp enough to slice veins. "Aside from the fact that you had no right to be there in the first place, hand-to-hand combat was your forte. What went wrong?"

"I froze, just as you always said I would." Not true. She'd fought for her life, initially. But guns had been pointing, and the laughter had been raucous. The filthy comments of what should be done to her had been the foulest she'd ever heard. And, dear God, no matter what, she'd wanted to live. But she wasn't sharing that with Jack. Some things were too horrendously shaming to share. Better to let him think she'd messed up. He wouldn't find that too hard to believe.

"Uh-uh. No way. I'd trained you myself. Tell me,

Lowry…" his voice softened to the texture of warm honey, putting her on immediate alert. "Tell me what *really* happened that night."

Thanks to her confinement in that cage and her fear that the bastard who had raped her might one day reappear out of the shadows, she favored space and unobstructed views, but she now regretted insisting all the internal walls and ceilings of her home be removed. She had nowhere to run. "You've seen my statement; you took the bloody thing. If you need a reminder, contact Data Retrieval. They'll forward a copy."

"When I want fiction, I'd buy a book. So, let's try cold, hard facts for a change. Every member of the cartel died that night. No one survived. No one."

"Because they weren't supposed to!" Yelling would only reinforce her reputation as a hysteric, but years of resentment at not being believed lent extra power to her straining vocal cords. "What about the men behind the cartel? Those in control? The bastards who covered and provided protection for the drug- and flesh-trafficking operation? Did you get them, too? Or did their undoubted connection with the Service put you off?"

"What the hell is that supposed to mean?"

She swiped the back of her wrist across her eyes, not to dry tears—of which she'd long stopped being capable—but to clear the dancing dots disrupting her vision. "It means the Service was, and most likely still is, dirty. I tried to warn you, Ballentyne, but you wouldn't listen. No one would. You were too busy laughing at me. But *I* knew something was wrong, and I would have proven it, too, except not content with half killing me, you got me kicked out of the Service before I could do so."

The sudden silence was suffocating, the temperature in her home crawling slowly into the red. Her attack on his precious Service had stirred the cobra in him. She winced as she felt the sacrifice of another nail as she retightened her fingers around the edge of the kitchen counter in her fight not to retreat out of strike range.

"*You* got yourself kicked out, Lowry. How the hell you kept passing the mandatory psych tests, I don't know. I've never come across anyone less suited to tackling violence and danger head on. I can only assume your father used his influence."

This time, she did step back. She'd fought harder than anyone to prove her worth. She'd rejected the offer of a place at the prestigious Slade School of Art for the rigors of the special, fast-track program designed more to break Service recruits than to progress them. Eighteen candidates started; only she and one other had successfully completed the brutal training. "If my father did, which I doubt, he soon regretted it. I was the Service's embarrassment, remember?"

"Pain in the butt, not embarrassment," Jack corrected.

She wanted to swipe his sudden smirk right off his face. "Either way, I was hung out to dry…along with the truth."

"So, the exhibition? All the publicity? That your way of thumbing your nose at the Service?"

She cocked her chin an inch higher. "Maybe. Though I prefer to think of it as proof of survival." And boy, had that little vanity just come back to kick her butt.

"Stupid though," he said, never shy about stating the obvious. "If you genuinely believed someone would deem you a threat and come after you. Why not just keep your head down?"

"Hope, the one thing neither *he* nor you could take from me. Hope, that because you and your team hushed up my involvement in the raid, he wouldn't remember and recognize me. Hope, because he'd never known my name and wouldn't associate me with the woman he..." She swallowed thickly and turned away to fiddle with the kettle. She'd come too close to telling him the truth.

Jack's voice dropped to a growl. "What exactly did he do to you, Lowry?"

Struck dumb by the sudden wave of simmering aggression he was throwing, she shrugged helplessly.

"What the hell are you hiding, Lowry?

She swung back around to face him. Hiding the truth was probably the only reason she was still alive. Now, she'd have to disappear and start all over again—if she wanted to live, that is. "Get out. Or I'll call the police. No, I can do better than that, I'll call the press."

Public exposure. The one thing Jack Ballentyne couldn't afford. With his cover blown, he'd never work in the field again. He'd be tied to a desk, and the slow rot of redundancy while he watched others risk their lives would set in. She ought to know; it's what Jack had done to her.

Without warning, he was there, right beside her. He leaned in close, his stubble rough as his chin brushed her cheek on route to her ear. "Don't. Ever. Threaten. Me. Little girl."

Instantly, it struck her. What it must feel like to have this lethal man as a foe. The promise of violence straining at the leash should have terrified her. Instead, a painful longing unfurled. He'd keep her safe. If she begged.

The hell she would. Palms flat against his chest, she

pushed and stumbled back, her lungs clawing for oxygen. She daren't trust him. He worked for the Service. He *was* the enemy.

With controlled deliberation, he set his coffee mug on the counter, turned, and crossed to retrieve his jacket. His aura of suppressed violence was gone, replaced by a brutally emphatic sense of *I'm done here.* She wasn't sure which was more chilling.

But when her front door clicked shut leaving her on her all alone, she knew.

She sprinted after him—even used her sofa as a springboard to add to her speed—and slapped the locks home. She threaded the titanium security chain in place.

She wasn't locking him out. She was locking herself in. To stop herself from following him.

Dear God, and she'd thought herself immune to bone-numbing loneliness, the complete absence of friends, save for Adrian. Damn it, now she'd have to add deluded to her list of little ailments. It would slot in quite nicely between acute anxiety and paranoia. Oh, and let's not forget deep self-loathing.

Burying her fingers into her hair, she slid slowly to the floor, the steel of the front door hard and cold against her back. She tucked her knees to her chest and, arms wrapped around them, hung on tight.

What the bloody hell had gotten into her?

Jack, the professional, so hard he made granite seem like putty, she'd always been able to handle. But Jack the man? Not a chance. She ought to know; he'd sucker punched her enough times in the past. She'd do something wrong. He'd rant and threaten, all the while, his eyes promising he'd protect her back. Always.

Liar!

One day, out of the blue, he'd abruptly stopped yelling and, instead, had made it his mission to get her to quit the Service. Which had only made her more determined to stay. Their battle of wills had become the stuff of legends. To Jack, her refusal to concede had been an insult too far. He'd had her court marshaled for gross insubordination.

The day she'd found out he'd actually made good on his threat to secure her discharge, something inside her had died. Torn and battered as she had been by the rape, what Jack and his team had stolen from her—her faith in them— was far worse. She hated them for that.

And, right now, she hated *him* enough to pull herself upright and cross to her sculpture of dented, paint-worn, metal trunks. He deserved to suffer. To feel what it was like to torment yourself with questions of "what if" and "if only." Most likely, the bastard had never tasted guilt. It was time someone introduced him to the possibility.

Now, where the hell was her old voice recorder?

• • •

When sleep had finally come, she'd fallen off a cliff into its nothingness clutch. Now, damn it, the incessant trill of the intercom buzzer was interrupting one of her few moments of peace.

Through weighted eyelids, she tried to make sense of the image pixilated on the screen of the television that doubled as a front-door security monitor, easily viewable from her sunken bed. Jack-*bloody*-Ballentyne, blowing vigorously into his cupped hands, and stamping his boots on her doorstep.

She'd suspected he'd be back. With her luck, it had been inevitable. But so soon? No matter, she'd made her decision. He wasn't running her off. Nor was the psycho bastard she'd recognized at the gallery. She'd prove her silence to both and hope that would be enough for them to leave her the hell alone.

A shiver racked her to the bone. She put it down to the morning chill. It was easier than admitting she dreaded another run in with the man on her doorstep. She shot a glance at the pyramid of lemons standing proud against the steel of her kitchen counter. Christ, she'd been embarrassingly intoxicated on hostility and the need for him to hurt last night. Once she got rid of Jack, best she destroy the recording she'd made.

The electronic demand for attention started up again.

She hauled herself upright with a groan and stumbled to her front door. She propped her forehead against the cool concrete just to the side of the intercom. "What do you want, Ballentyne?"

"More hot coffee. It's been a nippy night. Balls and brass monkeys spring to mind."

Her blood started to fizz in a most disconcerting way. Balls, right! Why, could she never catch a break? Even distorted through the intercom, his voice sounded dangerously tempting. Its rasp, deep, warm, and undeniably…something. Sexy?

A mortifying heat flushed every inch of her skin. She didn't want to know what the hell the muscles of her womb thought they were doing. She flapped her hands frantically in front of her face to cool down. Ohmygod, ohmygod, *ohmygod*. She didn't have thoughts like that. Not anymore. She really *was* losing her mind. No way was she opening the door to Jack now. No way.

With her heart beating triple time, she stepped back from the intercom.

The hideous buzzing started over.

She damn near exited her skin. Bugger, Jack Ballentyne wouldn't recognize "no" if it bit him on the ass. If she didn't let him in, he'd likely shoot the door down.

She slammed her hand against the intercom. "For Christ's sake, is a moment too much to ask for?"

Closing her eyes, she pictured a ripening field of wheat awash with swathes of scarlet poppies. Her happy place. Maybe, if she played this just right, convinced Jack that she wouldn't share her suspicions about the Service with anyone, he'd leave her alone.

She unhooked the security chain and spun the multitude of metal grips to release the deadlocks, gritting her teeth at the too-loud sound of steel grinding on steel.

She hoped she wouldn't live to regret this.

Leaving the door very slightly ajar, she retreated fast. Back to her bed, the safest place she could think of. She ducked under the covers and pulled a pillow over her face. Suicide by self-smothering struck her as remarkably appealing.

His boots thudded against the concrete floor. Getting closer. "I taught you better than that. Anyone could be standing here, and you'd now have a gun to your head."

God, did his every comment have to be a reprimand? "No one half as annoying as you, Ballentyne. What's the time?"

"Five-thirty."

She groaned. "If you've a gun handy, shoot me. This time, it would be a kindness."

"I guess you're not a morning person. I need coffee."

It wasn't the morning. For her, it was the middle of the bloody night. Pillow still to her face, she waved an arm in the rough direction of her kitchen area. "Help yourself, and when you've finished…" Wait a minute, had he stood sentry all night? And why, if he hadn't believed her wild claims? She wanted to ask, but refused to give him the satisfaction of doing so. By refusing to engage with him and pretending full command of her senses, she trusted he'd get the message and leave.

Which was just wistful thinking. He'd switched her wide screen from security mode to entertainment. Insufferably chirpy voices trilled with enthusiasm, discussing the *simply marvelous* day ahead.

She groaned again. What in a previous life had she done so terrible, it merited a punishment as horrendous as Jack Ballentyne?

She threw the pillow aside, sat up, and scrunched her fingers into the tangle of her hair. Jack had tossed his jacket. The muscles of his back flexed as he reached for a mug. Black cotton hugged and defined his shoulders. Lower down, black denim hugged too. Hot damn, but did he have a butt to tempt a nun—which was a *wholly unimaginable* observation for her to make.

Prickly heat seared her skin. She'd no doubt pay in spades for the creeping dereliction of her mind. In fact, she was as already paying. He'd started whistling. Bloody terrific.

She drilled her frustration into the back of the man making himself at home in *her* space, then flicked a glimpse at the TV screen, her attention caught by the news program's change in tone from insufferably light and breezy to measured seriousness.

An interview. A calm, emphatic denial of possible corruption in the corridors of power. A rebuke that such a suggestion was not only unsustainable, but also unconscionable.

Her skin no longer burned; it iced, as if touched by death itself. "Jack, who's that?" The strain of trying to sound halfway casual nearly severed her vocal cords.

He turned his head to the side and threw a glance at the screen. "Patient Peter Forsythe. So called for his tact and diplomacy in easing conflict and settling quarrels between state departments. He's the acknowledged doyen of the Civil Service. Powerful, very influential. Respected for his integrity. Governments will come and go, but he'll be a permanent fixture in Whitehall—thank God. I've met him a few times. I like him. So, incidentally, does your father. He's one of the good guys. Why?"

She was out of bed and force-feeding random clothing into her rucksack. Arms crisscrossed in front, she clasped the hem of her faded pajama top. Pausing, she glared at him. "A bit of privacy Ballentyne—turn your back."

Not waiting to see if he'd comply, she turned her own instead. Discarding the top—wildly thrown, who cared where it landed?—she pulled on a long sleeved, black T-shirt. She tugged her hair impatiently when it caught in the collar, then shimmied free of her tiny boy shorts, replacing them swiftly with hip-slung, dark jeans. She had to spring upward on her toes to release her heels from the hems before plunging her bare feet into sneakers.

"What in hell's triggered you this time?"

She was at the door and spinning tumblers before he could stop her. Her final words, muffled by the slammed door were, "Check the lemons."

. . .

By the time Jack had wrestled past the trap of locks and followed her into the narrow, empty street, she'd disappeared.

Hurling the door shut, he glared at the barred skylight that rattled under his violence. Last night, Lowry'd base-jumped the edge of reason, and, damn it all to hell, he'd followed her. Without a parachute.

Because she'd looked so damned vulnerable. And, fool that he was, he'd felt the heavy knock of responsibility. Not regret. Not guilt. Responsibility.

He'd once been her commanding officer, for God's sake. And, because of that, he'd borrowed trouble. First, by escorting her home. Then, by standing guard over her through the night. Now this. She'd flipped and gone.

A soft growl, low and deep, rumbled at his feet. He looked down. Right into the amber eyes of the ugliest looking cat he'd ever seen—part ginger, part black, huge, one ear missing.

He dropped to his haunches. Trust Lowry to have befriended an outcast. Two damaged warriors, both abandoned, together against a world they couldn't understand and didn't trust.

He extended his arm, then snatched it back, hissing in

concert with the beast. Rubbing the lacerations on his wrist, he cursed extinction on all things remotely feline, especially Lowry-*bloody*-Fisk.

Pushing upright, he surveyed the concrete prison she had tellingly called her sanctuary, and shuddered. Vast and pin-neat it might be, but it was coffin-like nevertheless. How the hell did she live like this? *Why* the hell did she live like this?

His eyes flicked to the TV screen.

Icy fingers danced along his spine. If Lowry went public with her insane theories—that the Service was corrupt, that agents were selling secrets and offering protection to criminal elements—given her reputation and medical history, this god-awful space would seem like utopia in comparison to where they'd lock her up. And no one, not even he, would be able to save her this time.

Turning the empty space indigo with his curses, he reached into his pocket for his phone and hit speed dial. "Will, I need a pick-up. Same drop-off address as last night. Fifteen minutes."

He wandered over to the recessed platform she called a bed. The sheets were crumpled. She'd had a bad night.

Stepping to the side, he stooped and picked up her discarded pajama top. Then dropped it as if it had burst into flames. Jesus, had he really been intent on raising it to his nose to inhale her scent?

He'd run out of things to call himself by the time he reached the kitchen area. Retrieving the remote, he killed the television. Resting his hip against the counter, and arms folded across his chest, he glared belligerently at the lemons. He suspected they were mocking him. Gritting his teeth, he reached for the one on top, examined it, and then tossed it aside, uncaring that it rolled free of the counter and thudded dully on the floor. He did the same with a further five.

The seventh, he paused over. It didn't feel right. He squeezed. Juice trickled from an inch-long slit, and the scent of lemon cut the air.

He inserted his forefinger and damn near made *himself* blush with his language when he hit something solid. Curling his finger, he hooked free a mini-cassette wrapped securely in cellophane. Who used these anymore? Damn thing belonged in an antique shop. He peeled free the protective covering, scrunched it into a tight ball, and slipped the cassette into his pocket. Where the hell was his ride?

He'd almost escaped when unfamiliar concern pricked.

He eyed the cat, which eyed him right back. Who knew when its mistress would return? He grabbed his jacket, dropped it over the brute, and moved fast to grapple with the wildly undulating leather. Earned himself a sharp nip for his trouble. Will Berwick had better like cats, he decided, because he was about to acquire one.

• • •

Back at his Notting Hill home, which few knew about, Jack riffled through a deep kitchen drawer. The one where he dumped everything useless, but with which he was reluctant to part—wrenches, their grip too worn for further use, wall plugs, plastic lighters, keys without a home, and…an old mini-cassette recorder.

He flicked the switch. Lifeless. Back to the drawer. He must have some spare batteries somewhere.

He slammed the drawer shut, scanned his various kitchen devices for likely bounty, and, savaging the air with a curse, strode through to his den. He wrestled free two batteries from the television remote. He looked up. The ugliest cat in the world seemed to be grinning at him. The scratches on his wrist burned.

Even when Jack had pulled rank, Will had refused point blank to take the beast. "Sorry, boss, I'm allergic." The man would pay for wimping out. Finally set, Jack reclined back on his sofa with his feet braced on the antique coffee table in front of him. He took a belt of whisky—straight from the bottle, high-five to the bachelor life—and depressed the play button.

Lowry's lilt broke across his den.

Ballentyne, if you're listening to this then I've gone. For good this time. To anyone else, I'd be obliged if you would forwarded this tape to him...

She reeled off his home address. He frowned. That was classified information. In the wrong hands... Christ, she wouldn't sit down for a week once he got a hold of her again!

...You want to know why I was so damn certain the man I saw at the gallery was the same one from the warehouse the night of the raid? You want to know why all that rigorous training you subjected me to, failed?

He raped me, Jack. Caught me unaware, took me down, and raped me. Admittedly, it was my own fault. You were right. I shouldn't have been there. You were also right with your prediction that I'd freeze in the face of raw violence. That I would panic, lose my head, and put the team at risk. I should have saved those girls. Someone better would have.

But you failed too, Jack. I wouldn't have had to go it alone if you'd just had a little faith in me. If you'd just kept an open mind, done your job, and had the decency to assign someone to check out my theories.

You let me down, Jack, but you let yourself down more.

Who knew your team would strike the warehouse at midnight? Who warned the cartel to expect you? Didn't you find the high level of resistance you met odd? And who authorized your use of extreme force? In London, for Christ's sakes. Why was your team even sent in? There was no threat to national security. Those men were criminals, not a terrorist threat.

Find him, Jack. The man inside the Service. The one providing protection for the cartel. Start with the list of guests who attended my exhibition. Adrian will have a copy.

One more thing. A personal request. Keep the matter of my rape to yourself. There's nothing to gain by sharing it, and I've earned the right for that little humiliation to remain private.

Bye, Jack. Don't take this the wrong way, but I hope we don't meet again. Watch your back and, as always, mind who you trust.

The torturous hiss of discordant white noise reached through his numbness. Jack depressed the stop button. Rewound the tape a few revolutions, and hit play.

...He raped me...

He hit stop, then rewind. Pressed play again.

...He raped me...

He couldn't stop himself repeating the stop-rewind-play action, any more than he could silence his mind screaming over and over—find Lowry. Save her. Fucking apologize.

Chapter Four

Peter Forsythe dismissed his secretary without thanks or a smile. No need for politeness, or niceties of any kind. There was no one watching, no one listening, and she wouldn't gossip. Not with him holding those decidedly distasteful photos of her doing the nasty with three men—none of them her husband—in his safe.

His pocket vibrated. He didn't need to check caller ID. Only one man had the number to his "special" cell phone. "Speak."

"I've tracked down the girl's address. I'm on my way now. She rarely goes out, so she'll be there."

"You sound certain of that."

"Not as certain as the person in the trunk of my car. According to him, she connects with no one. Has her art supplies and groceries delivered by courier. If she communicates at all, it's by email. She refuses to carry a phone. She doesn't trust them. She's out in the cold, has been for years. If you want her to disappear, no one will miss her."

"No. Not yet. Not with Jack Ballentyne sniffing around. He was at the gallery."

"Hah, that bastard I'll do for free."

Patient Peter clicked his tongue in a staccato of fussy *tut-tut*s. "No one 'does' Jack Ballentyne. You, of all people, should know that. Turn around. Don't go anywhere near her. I need time to think. Keep your phone on, and take care of your passenger. We might need him for leverage."

Patient Peter cut the call and took advantage of the backward tilt of his cushioned leather desk chair. He smiled. "Patient Peter"—the nickname pleased him. It was so very, very apt.

But never less so than at this moment. In an eruption of violence, he thrust to his feet and swept the files from his desk, papers scattering like leaves in the wind.

There was no doubting the girl had recognized him. And she was Lowry Fisk? The Commander's daughter? Stupid. Stupid. Stupid. He never made mistakes. And he wouldn't tolerate this slip up.

Breathing heavily, he sank back into his seat and clasped his hands as if in serene prayer. Now, how best to neutralize her without arousing suspicion?

• • •

His Sig in hand, Jack left the lights off as he made his way, silent as an unshared secret, through the kitchen to his back door. He wasn't expecting a visitor, not at three in the morning. Bold of them to ring his bell. Foolish too, the mood he was in.

He slipped outside and checked the shadows of the rear courtyard behind his home and then hefted himself up onto the nine-foot wall. He dropped down the other side, landing soundlessly, and edged his way to the front corner of his house.

His back flush against the wall, he ducked his head forward to see around the brickwork. Christ. He'd know that silhouette anywhere. Lowry.

Holstering his gun inside the waistband of his jeans, snug against his spine, and with one hand for leverage on the black metal railings marking his front boundary, he vaulted and then triple-jumped the front length of his house. He barreled into the slight figure, pushing her tight into the shadow of the small alcove protecting his front door, his fingers simultaneously punching the code to release the lock.

He surged forward into the house, the unwelcome visitor caged in his arms, then kicked the door shut with the back of his heel. He hustled his prisoner down the dark corridor to his kitchen. "Where the bloody hell have you been?"

No answer. Something was wrong. He released her, stepped back, crossed to the wall, and hit the lights. "Fuck, Lowry, what the hell have you done?"

Blood stains, richer and darker than the brown of her T-shirt—not the same one he'd seen her pull on that morning, before she'd fled her home—soaked her front. Crimson whirls coated her hands and naked arms. Dried blood, dead claret in color, smudged one high cheekbone. Jesus, it was even in her hair.

Her eyes, tortured green and dull, stared back at him, unfocused.

With an oath, he grabbed her wrist and dragged her to

the sink. He spun the faucet and plunged her arms into the gush of water, rubbing briskly to dislodge the horrific stains.

The sink turned pink.

He all but begged her to resist, to protest, yell at him, anything.

Not a sound.

Her puppet-like countenance as he adjusted her body to better take advantage of the flow spooked the hell out of him. Fuck. She'd disengaged. "Oh no you don't, Fisk, not this time, not again," he muttered furiously.

Scooping her into his arms, he ran back into the hall and charged the stairs to the upper floor. He imprinted the tread mark of his boot on the bathroom door, and one arm tight around Lowry, set the shower to hot with his free hand.

That she didn't slap at him, or even protest, when he stripped her down to her underwear, scared two decades off his life.

He shoved her into the cubicle and positioned her dead center beneath the full force of the spray. Her feet slipped, and she tilted precariously. Bollocks. Bollocks. Bollocks. Left alone, she'd hurt herself.

Shuffling out of his boots, he joined her in the shower.

He scrubbed and rinsed her head to toe, calling himself every kind of deviant for registering how delicious she smelled with his soap clinging to her skin. Damn stuff, it wasn't supposed to have a scent.

When she did respond, it was to lean in close. Wrapping her arms tight around his waist, she lowered her forehead to his chest. Somewhere in the vicinity of his heart.

Awkward.

Scrubbing at her skin was one thing. Placing his hands

on her naked skin—all slick with water and promising heaven—for pleasure, quite another.

His teeth ached. He strained against the need to hold, his arms two pillars of lead by his side.

Bloody hell, he didn't need this. Had he lost his sodding mind? That had to be half a crime scene swirling down the drain. Anyone else showing up on his doorstep, injury-free but coated in blood—someone else's blood—and he'd have had them at gunpoint.

Hands firm around her shoulders, he eased her away and, stretching behind her, abruptly cut the downpour. He bundled her into a towel, rubbing vigorously, as he maneuvered her to his bedroom.

"Ditch the bra and panties, then get into bed," he said quietly. "I'll be back in a minute." He snagged a fresh pair of jeans and a top for himself before quitting the room fast. Christ, he only hoped she'd registered his instructions. No way in hell was he removing her underwear—no-nonsense white cotton, modest in cut, but which had turned tantalizingly transparent, thanks to the shower.

· · ·

Her fingers fumbling with the fussy clasp on her bra, Lowry did as he'd ordered and climbed between the sheets. Turning her head into his pillow, in need of an anchor against the nightmare crashing around her, she inhaled his essence deep. Then she remembered. Remembered his first reaction when he'd flicked on the kitchen lights. Accusatory.

Jack returned, glass in hand, his face unreadable.

Not good.

Sitting upright, she skidded her back tight against the headrest of the bed and pulled the sheet high and tight beneath her chin. "I need to leave," she blurted. "The first thing you asked me was what I'd done—not if I was okay, but what I'd done. You didn't even give me the benefit of the doubt."

"You're in my bed aren't you? That should tell you something."

His snarl cut the fading remnants of her earlier dulled state. "What? That your reputation for being a fast operator is true?"

"Charming. Now who's not giving the benefit of the doubt?"

She glared distrust. He glared offense…and something else. Oh, Christ. The tape. She'd been falling off an emotional cliff when she'd recorded it. Full of vinegar and spite and self-pity. Yes, she'd wanted to punish him. And, yes, she'd hoped he'd go after the truth. But she'd made the recording believing she'd never see him again.

Cracking open her eyelids, unsure of quite when they'd fallen shut, she caught him frowning, staring pointedly at her hand, as she gnawed at a cuticle of her forefinger. "I'm not a victim. I won't be labeled one," she whispered fiercely, more for her own sake than for his.

"Then stop behaving like one. Here, drink this."

Didn't matter that she knew Jack to be abrupt by nature, that eschewing all emotion himself, he never spared the feelings of others. His bluntness still made her gasp. The man was heartless. No, worse. He had no soul.

She took the glass from him, her hand trembling so badly, the rich amber fluid threatened to spill. She set it aside on the small cabinet beside her, un-sipped. "I didn't do it."

Reaching forward, he lifted the glass, took her hand, and fixed her fingers around its base. "Knock it back. All of it. Then start from the beginning."

Fire scorched the back of her throat. Mid-splutter, she nearly heaved when the whiskey-burn hit her stomach. Eyes watering, she waited for her breath to return. Would he believe her? Or, given the damning evidence stacked against her, would he judge her guilty and turn her in? Hard to tell with Jack. He wasn't an easy man to predict.

Though it had failed to protect her before, she fell back on the truth. It was all she had. "I went home. I was worried about Claude."

Jack's eyebrows took flight, his eyes drilled.

"Claude, my cat," she hurried on. "He needed feeding. Adrian, my agent, was there… He was…he'd been brutalized. I barely recognized him…so much blood…I tried to help… but…but…"

Whiskey, now sour, returned to her throat. She immediately shut down the vision of her friend, pulped and dying. Then, needing to gauge Jack's reaction, she forced her eyes upward. Uncompromising blue stared her down. "I didn't do it, Jack, but everyone will think I did."

"Why come to me?"

She flinched. Hard not to when faced with a man who could flay skin with his tone alone. "I…I don't know." She rubbed at her forehead. The furrow creasing her brow refused to smooth. "One minute, I was running along the alley behind my house, the next I was here. I don't know why, I don't even know how I got here. "

"Anyone see you?"

She shrugged helplessly. She had no idea, but guessed instinct would have kept her to the shadows. "It's him, Jack. He set me up. My home...that scene of depravity... Adrian..."

Her fingers tortured the sheet at her throat, bunching, kneading, creasing the impossibly soft cotton into desperate folds. "God, what if they think I finally snapped. They'll lock me up. He'll be able to get to me. Please, you have to —" She realized Jack had disengaged. Gone all granite-hard, black ops agent on her, all interest beyond the facts locked down.

"Have to what, Lowry?"

"Nothing...just...I didn't do it, not that anyone will believe me, not even the members of your team."

"And why the hell should they? You didn't give them a chance."

"I'd been labeled crazy, even before the PTSD," she defended weakly, tightening her grip on the sheet.

"Hardly surprising. You were unpredictable, deliberately combative, and that was before you started weaving conspiracy theories...and keeping secrets. Like the fact you were raped. You withheld that crucial piece of information, Lowry, and in doing so you called into question the integrity of every man under my leadership. Men ready to die for you. I made a call. As of ten minutes ago, your 'sanctuary' officially became a crime scene. You did yourself no favors by running."

Sheet tucked tight with her elbows, she raised her hands and covered her ears. His disgust was too much. His team had been right in their assessment of her. She was crazy — coming here, subconsciously believing Jack would help, proved it. Time to go.

She wrestled with the swathe of sheets and tried to get to her feet. Hands, hard and heavy, gripped her shoulders. Pressing her down. Not letting her go.

And her world crashed.

Limbs crazily uncoordinated, she thrashed, trying to fight. She tried to breathe, but her chest locked tight. Black dots danced before her eyes. From far in the distance, she heard herself whimper, then cry out.

The hands holding her down lifted immediately. She twisted and scooted to the other side of the bed. She swiped at the tangle of hair blocking her vision and glared, her chest in agony from the too-vigorous workout.

On his hands and knees, he stalked her across the bed, pulling up short when she raised her hands to ward him off. "Jesus, Lowry, we have got to get you some help."

She let her arms fall to her sides. "No. Just…just don't touch me like that again. And there is no 'we,' Jack. There never was, and there never will be."

He pulled back. She heard his feet hit the floor. Then he drew himself up to full height. Never in a million years would she have credited the highly delectable Jack Ballentyne as capable of looking ugly. But, just for a moment, he did. "When I get my hands on that bastard, I'll kill him."

She held his death-promise glare for as long as she could, before twisting onto her side and giving him her back. "Thanks, but why bother? Killing him won't help Adrian… and it won't fix me."

She felt the mattress dip.

He was beside her in less time than it took her to expel a sharp breath. His forefinger and thumb to her chin, he forced her to look at him. "You're not broken, Lowry, but you do have some serious trust issues. The call I placed was anonymous and to the police. This is a civil issue. The Service shouldn't be involved. I'm going out for a bit. Be here when I get back, or I will hunt you down and prove to you the true meaning of insanity. Got it?"

She nodded. She didn't doubt he'd have refused to relinquish his hold on her chin, if she hadn't acquiesced.

He might have closed the bedroom door softly when he quit the bedroom, but to her, it still sounded like a slam. A loud slam of disappointment. She'd thought her rape would revile him, and maybe it had, but her failure to trust had repulsed him more.

Her father's favorite platitude about the futility of weeping over spilled milk swept into her mind. He'd callously used it when her mother died, and he'd muttered it every time *she'd* done something wrong thereafter. Only in this instance, the milk hadn't just spilled; it had soured. And it was too damned late to cry about it.

Years too late.

The tears wouldn't come. They never did.

• • •

His body flush against the roof tiles, Jack angled his head so he could see through the skylight into the depths of Lowry's studio without detection. The front door was open, the flash of emergency blue from the vehicles parked out front casting deep, unholy shadows into her home.

From what he could see of the scene inside, it was as gore-splattered as she'd described. Adrian—what was left of the poor bastard—lay *in situ*, grotesquely twisted in a pool of deep magenta. Anonymous white figures were clearing the studio, bagging and tagging Lowry's personal belongings. Two fussed with small, lurid yellow flags plotting the blood spray and spill. They were particularly busy.

Official-looking characters in ill-fitting suits stood to one side. Civilian detectives from the local police precinct, he suspected.

But it was the two men in dark conservative suits — immaculately tailored this time — who snatched his attention. Ramrod straight, in control, hands neatly tucked behind their backs, they exuded silent authority. Intelligence Service. He'd have known that even if he hadn't recognized them.

Their rank was the highest, and he wasn't surprised by their presence. He focused on the most senior of the men. Lowry's father.

Stoic to the last, the man wore an emotionless mask.

The tight fist that had settled in his chest from the moment he'd seen Lowry drenched in blood flexed its grip and twisted. The Commander couldn't possibly believe his daughter capable of such violence. She might have been a proverbial pain in the ass to her father since birth, but he had to know her better than that.

Yet nothing in the man's expression suggested he'd given her even the smallest benefit of the doubt.

Jack inched away from the skylight, turned on his back, and stared into the darkness.

If the Commander believed his daughter capable of such carnage, was Jack in any position to refute it? He'd taken orders from that man and trusted his judgment implicitly. Whereas Lowry? He'd never fully trusted her. Too defiant. Too suspicious of authority...and too damned bloody tempting!

Grit scratched his skin as he scoured his face with a mucky palm. Fuck. What was he waiting for? All he had to do was contact HQ and request that they take her off his hands. What the hell did he care? Lowry wasn't his problem.

He inched his way over to the street-side edge of the roof and furtively copped one last look. Lowry's father and his ever-present lap dog aide, Smith, had moved outside to the narrow cobbled street. Another man had joined them. Patient Peter Forsythe. No doubt, here to commiserate and limit any damage to the Service's reputation and, thereby, the government.

Patient Peter's soft, conciliatory voice caught and drifted on the light breeze. "I know she's your daughter, Harry, but the risk is just too great. We can't have a mentally unstable, ex-agent running amok through London. You've just witnessed for yourself the level of violence of which she is capable. I give you my word every effort will be made to bring her in safely, but you need to know extreme force has been sanctioned, should she resist."

Needle-sharp beads of icy sweat pierced the surface of his skin. Extreme force? Shoot her dead? What son of a bitch had authorized that? No way would Lowry allow herself to be taken into custody without a fight. He'd seen the familiar spark of her old defiance the night he'd confronted her in the gallery. It might have dimmed a bit since he'd shot her, but it had still been unmistakable.

Fuck. For her own protection, he'd have to take her in himself.

• • •

Jack stared down at the woman slumbering in his bed, the ice white of his sheets hugging curves that dared to be stroked.

Christ, she was beautifully dangerous, even when asleep. That his body should alight with lust, he could deal with. What red-blooded male wouldn't harden as the sight of something so bewitching? But the sudden and inexplicable whip of longing to slay dragons and lay them proudly at her feet, damn near had him clawing at his own chest to rip his heart out and stomp it beneath his boot.

Why couldn't she have just disappeared into the night? She'd never bloody obeyed him before. If she'd lost her mind completely and decided to put her trust in him, he'd find it hard not to wring her neck. But she did look surprisingly right in his bed—safe, like she was where she finally belonged—a scary thought that brought his own damned sanity into question.

Blanking his mind to the pale bruises underscoring the crescent of her closed eyes, he leaned forward and shook her awake. Roughly. To remind himself he didn't care a smidgen.

She awoke with a snarl. Her ugly cat spat and hissed. He ignored them both.

Stomping to his dresser, he riffled through the drawers. He pulled free an ancient pair of jeans and a ratty, once forest-green T-shirt. Neither would fit her. Both would have to do.

"Get dressed. Kitchen. Five minutes. Dress fast."

He tried not to slam the door on his way out. And failed.

· · ·

Lowry made it to the kitchen in four minutes flat. "What's

going on, Ballentyne?"

"There's a black fleece by the front door. Put it on. Use the hood to hide your hair."

She'd had bad feelings before, but as far as bad went, this one was the worst. Folding her arms tight across her chest, she lifted her chin and hoped Jack couldn't hear the voices in her head screaming at her to run. "Not until you tell me what's going on."

"I can't afford for them to find you here."

Ice crawled through her veins. "I presume you're referring to the Service. Why should they find me here? Everyone knows you're the last person I'd turn to for help. Oh, for God's sake, you didn't tell them, did you?"

"No. But…"

Her heart skipped a few beats. "But what, Ballentyne?"

Damn. His eyes had gone all permafrost on her. She preferred him yelling and livid. Temper kept him human. His ability to detach completely scared the bejesus out of her.

"But I'm taking you in."

"Sorry. I didn't quite catch that."

"I said I'm taking you in."

She shook her head. "You can't. Don't you get it? He'll kill me."

"You'll be dead if I don't. You're the Commander's daughter. As a professional courtesy, the civvies called in the Service. You're wanted for murder, Lowry. You're considered dangerous, and the order's gone out to shoot should you resist arrest. And I mean shoot-to-kill. Wounding wasn't offered as an option."

She actually felt the blood leach from her face. "Why Jack? Why the need for extreme force? Or didn't you ask?"

Pure Jack, he ignored her challenge, his face implacable. "Just move. Door. Sweatshirt. Put it on."

She could have argued. Once would have done so. But it would only have wasted time. He'd made his decision.

Her spine rigid to hide the pain of betrayal, she turned and stomped the length of the darkened corridor toward the front door, her bare feet slapping against the intricate tessellation of antique parquet flooring.

She finished tucking her hair deep out of sight beneath the hood of the fleece she'd found hanging on a hook and paused to consider her options. The streets would be crawling with agents trying to find her. All cleared to kill; no questions would be asked. She'd be lucky to make it out of London alive. How convenient.

She looked down at her bare toes peeping out from beneath the overly long jeans. Jack's. His T-shirt and fleece, too. She wanted to rip them from her body and hurl them in his face. But with her life on the line, pride was cheap.

She reached for the door latch.

A deadly *click* broke the hush of the hall.

"Touch that door and, so help me, I'll shoot you again."

Chapter Five

She stared down the ugly eye of the barrel of the gun he pointed, his arm straight, fully extended. He would, too. Shoot her, that is. Jack Ballentyne did not make idle threats. "God, I'm stupid. I hoped you'd just let me slip away. This is wrong, Jack. You know it is."

"You're not stupid, Lowry," he said so softly, she almost missed it.

"Jack, I—"

"Get back in the kitchen," he cut in. "I don't have time for this. We leave by the back door."

Shoulders in a slump, head down, she braced her back against the hallway wall. "Not without Claude."

"You weren't too bothered about him the other morning."

Her head jerked up. "I went back for him, didn't I?" She couldn't believe they were about to argue about her cat's domestic arrangements.

His detached-mode mask came down. "I've only got your word for that. It's not as if we can question Adrian Wainwright for his version of events."

She pushed her spine tighter against the wall to steady the treacherous sway that threatened to knock her horizontal. Jack thought her capable of the depravity Adrian had suffered? Seriously?

She sucked in a breath. If being an ass is what it took for him to feel better about what he was doing, shame on him. "Claude comes with me, or, by God, I'll fight you every inch of the way. I was dumb enough to trust you with my life. I'm not trusting you with his."

"Fine. Call the animal. Any resistance on his part, and he stays put."

He turned his back and disappeared down the corridor. Her jaw dropped. He actually trusted her not to make a bid for freedom? Then, she remembered. Barefooted as she was, he could easily outrun her. And he was the one with the gun. Though not for much longer, if she got her way.

Jack showed a level of forbearance of which she'd never have credited him capable. Claude was far from cooperative at being stuffed into a large sports bag. She and Jack would carry scars. Jack looked fit to kill. He also stuck rather too close as they crossed the enclosed courtyard, the size of a tennis court, behind his home. But he didn't touch her. Not even to steady her when she stumbled on a loose paving stone and damn near pitched head first into a potted fern.

"Jesus, Lowry, wake the whole damn neighborhood, why don't you?"

"It's dark, and I can't see," she hissed.

"For fuck's sake." His hiss definitely out-hissed hers.

Long, strong fingers curled around her own. Heat shot up her arm. Instinctively, she tried to tug her hand free. Which just made Jack all the more determined to hold fast. Slowly, very slowly, her muscles relaxed, and her lungs stopped trying to escape her chest.

She'd never held hands with a man. Boy-men, yes, years and years ago. But never a *man*-man. She shouldn't have, but she quite liked the feel of Jack's hand. Rough, calloused, sure with intent. A big hand. Capable. Very Jack.

Jesus, had she just licked her lips? What in the hell was wrong with her? No one indulged a private fantasy while stumbling around in the dark with a man who repeatedly broke faith. Except, it would seem, her. Crazy. Completely insane.

Distracted, she almost careened into Jack when he came to an abrupt halt. She followed his gaze upward. No way was she getting over the wall that encircled the rear of his property. Not without help.

And she damn near separated from her skin when Jack stepped behind her and fixed his hands, yes, those very large and capable hands, around her waist. She didn't as much twitch as jerk like a puppet with its strings yanked.

"Easy," he growled, clearly misinterpreting why her body should flex violently and then lock tight. "You need a boost. Once up, straddle the wall. I'll pass you the damn cat."

The cat which she nearly tripped over in her hurry to escape further physical contact when he lifted her. Stupid fleece. Stupid T-shirt. Both had ridden high beneath his sliding hands, laying bare her naked skin from breastbone to navel. But at least she hadn't screamed. Hadn't even yelped. Not even inside her head.

Once astride the top of the wall, she hastily tucked the wayward T-shirt into the bagging waistband of her jeans as if it were life-saving Kevlar. She definitely wasn't right in the head. Her skin should not be tingling—not with pleasure. Her blood should not be hot—not with thrill. And she sure as hell shouldn't want his lips hard against hers. Not now. Not ever.

She chose to jump down from the wall, her ankles unimpressed by the impact, rather than wait and let Jack assist her.

"Jesus," he whispered furiously, staring down at her, his hands full with the sports bag and cat. "What're you trying to do, kill yourself?"

She reached up to take Claude. Jack swiveled onto his front and lowered himself from the wall. She spotted the outline of his gun, resting snug against his spine. She'd have that off him the first opportunity that came her way, she promised silently. God alone knew what had driven her to run to him for help, but whatever insane instinct was responsible, it had been way off base. He'd betrayed her. When he had to have known that with her medical history, not to mention her reputation for being delusionary, she wouldn't stand a cat's chance in hell with the authorities.

Factor in the way her body hummed, the way her mind wandered a dangerous path—wanting, longing, tempted by him—and that instinct had to be...well, fucked. No better word for it. To save herself, she had to get away.

The opportunity to snatch his gun came sooner than expected. He turned his back on her to open the passenger door of a black Land Rover waiting for them on the street, ominous with tinted windows. Which was unusually careless of him.

Placing the bag containing Claude on the pavement first, she lunged forward, one hand pushing hard between his shoulder blades, the other reaching for his gun.

Just as swiftly, he linked a leg around one of hers, at the same time shouldering her off balance.

She hit the pavement hard. Her head gave an audible crack. For a moment, she actually saw stars, but didn't have time to ponder the phenomenon. She heard "stupid," may have heard "crazy," and "brainless" was in there, too. A savage tug on her wrist, and she was upright, the stars now a galaxy of wildly flashing pinpricks.

"Fuck, can't you even remember how to break a fall right?" He bundled her, none too gently, into the SUV. There was a yawl and soft thud as Claude hit the rear seat. Next thing, Jack was crawling over her without ceremony, the shortest route to the driver seat. She'd get no second chance at trying to seize the advantage from him again.

He stabbed a key into the ignition. Turned toward her, swore again, then leaned across her once more. His tug on her seat belt was furious, the way he jammed it home, savage. There was nothing civilized about the way he raised her chin and forced her to look him in the eye. Who knew blue could burn black with fury? Dark blue, yes. She'd witnessed that herself on too many occasions. But blue to black? Never.

She held back the need to blink, her eyelids burning at the strain. She'd surrender, but she wouldn't beg.

"Don't ever try that again. I've killed men for less."

She was still trying to get her breathing under control when, half an hour later, he pulled the Land Rover to a halt, unclipped his seat belt and angled his body to face her.

"There are two ways of doing this, Lowry. The hard way, or the even harder way. Your choice. You either walk in there with some semblance of dignity or I cuff you, hands and legs, and shoulder you like a sack of potatoes. What's it going to be?"

She'd opted for dignity. Pride alone kept her back ramrod straight as they crossed the stark concourse fronting the building she'd learned to loathe.

The Cube—headquarters for the "plausibly deniable" units of the secret service—had none of the elegant symmetry its name suggested, and none of the legitimacy enjoyed by MI5's elegant Thames House, or MI6's Babylon-on-Thames monstrosity. A mash of concrete and sickly green glass, it rose three squat stories high. Those floors accommodated IT, research, and administration. But the real business took place in the sprawl of sub-terrain levels, buried below.

Few knew of the Cube's existence, and fewer still the true nature of the various task forces for which it served as HQ. It didn't matter a jot that lines were regularly crossed and laws broken, so long as the public interest was protected.

Four years since she'd last set foot in this building. Right now, she wished it could have been four hundred more. Her pride and humiliations, her protests and indignations, her messy past—all were entwined in the fabric of the Cube. A monument to the seriously murky side of the Intelligence Service.

She shot a sideways glance at the rigid profile of the man who, while not actually touching her, marked her every move. He was ready to take her down, hard and fast, should she try anything.

Surreptitiously, she raised her hand and tested the

throbbing, raised knot at the back of her head. What the hell part of her Frankenstein mind—a crazy stitching of fear and obstinacy, conviction and doubt, traces of humor and futile tragedy—had induced her to trust him? Jack-bloody-Ballentyne. The man who wore his complete absence of conscience as if it were a badge of honor.

He pushed through the bulletproof glass doors without sparing her a look. She curled her fingers round the tail of her fleeing courage and followed him. Not easy when her skin wanted to slough free and desert her.

At the request of security, he reached sideways and tugged down her hood.

Great, now she'd be fully exposed. Bring on the curious stares.

From the way the anonymous pressed against the walls as they passed, she knew Jack must be glaring, but even he couldn't stop the looks of quiet condemnation. Her identity was clearly no secret.

She realized she was tiptoeing and forced extra weight into her heels. She'd be damned if she'd admit to one fraction of the fear polluting her veins like a river choked dead with factory waste.

He held a frigid silence as he escorted her down into the bowels of the earth.

The artificial lighting burned bright. She narrowed her eyes to defuse the glare. Three levels down, she lost the battle to hold her head high and settled her attention on the battleship gray linoleum instead. Uncaring of why, she edged closer to her betrayer. When her step faltered, he didn't reach to steady her, but he did curb the length of his stride, which was kind—for Jack.

"In here."

She raised her chin, seared him with what she hoped was a look of disgust, but suspected revealed nothing but her dread. Spine snapping straight, head balanced high, she stepped across the threshold of the cell-like room.

Without a word, he clicked the door, shutting her in.

She blinked wildly to ease the insistent sting in her eyes. She'd shoot herself before she gave way to tears. Designated agents, experts in interpreting body language, were sure to be watching her. She couldn't afford to show weakness of any kind.

She glanced nervously at the darkened mirror taking up the length of one wall, and seeing no reason why she should make the job of whoever was on surveillance easy, she tugged her hood back up.

A metal table and four facing chairs, all screwed to the floor, stood in the center of the cell. Ignoring them, she moved forward, turned and settled her back against the mirror, and inched her way down to the floor.

She drew her knees to her chest, wrapped her arms around them, and hugged tight, her stare fixed on the door. She'd fight when they came — she'd lose, but she'd take a few of them down with her.

Because "they" could be on either side, good or corrupt. There was no way of knowing, and she daren't take the risk of getting it wrong. Secrecy was endemic at the Cube. The various task forces neither questioned nor shared. That was the unwritten rule. A stupid rule, because it made identifying traitors and holding them to account impossible.

Where the hell was Jack? She doubted the rogue agents would try anything too obvious in his presence. He might be an utter bastard but...but what? The damned man had shot her. If ordered to dispose of her, would he question, would he even hesitate?

She glanced at her wrist. Where the hell was her watch? How long would it be before someone came? She started counting down time in her head.

• • •

The meeting ended.

Not bothering to hide his offense at the political step dance that had just taken place, Jack glared down the barrage of hostile looks he received from those filing out of the conference room, including Smith, the Commander's right hand man. Smith hadn't appreciated being dismissed when Jack was ordered to wait behind because the Commander wanted a word.

He had done his best for her. Defended her corner. But what if he hadn't done enough? He closed his eyes and took a moment while he waited for the burning in his stomach to ease.

"Thank you," the Commander said when they were alone. "It would not have been appropriate for me to argue my daughter's case. I'm grateful that you were here, and even more grateful that you troubled to bring her in safely."

Jack didn't acknowledge the man's quiet appreciation with the customary "Sir." What kind of father put his own position before that of his daughter? They'd been ready to disappear Lowry off to the nearest military containment facility. No investigation. No trial. Everything under the radar.

All of it happening too damned fast for his liking.

Christ, without his protests, she'd already be on her way to GKW—God Knows Where. To face what? A little something in her food? A little something in her vein? Lowry had been pretty adamant about someone wanting her dead, and after he'd witnessed what had happened to Adrian Wainwright, maybe a touch of her paranoia had rubbed off on him. Or maybe he just needed a decent night's bloody sleep.

He cleared his throat to catch the Commander's attention. "Will that be all?"

Lowry's father nodded, shuffled papers, and used the surface of the boardroom table to tap them into uniform order.

Jack's hand was already reaching for the door handle when the Commander spoke. "Do you think she did it?"

Jack turned. "Excuse me?" His hearing wasn't impaired; he just couldn't believe her father would ask that question.

"You know her better than I do. Do you think she did it?"

"No." He swallowed *don't be stupid* with difficulty. "Lowry couldn't kill to save her own life. Why do you think I never sent her out into the field? She had a hard enough job getting her head around the fact that to be effective in the war against crime and terrorism, an agent has to be ready to cheat, trick, collude, and deceive, without conscience. For her, joining the Service was the wrong career choice. But her opting to work out of the Cube? To sign on with the Assassins? Pure suicide. It's what broke her."

The Commander poured himself a glass of water. Jack noticed his hand shook. "Bruised, not broke. That's why she remains such a threat. She might not cope well under fire, but offend her sense of what's just, and nothing will stop her. And, God knows, we — the Service — offend her. The danger that she'd come back at us and fight has always been real. It was just a question of when and how. Anyone who worked with her will have known that deep down here." The man thumped his fist against his abdomen.

He conceded her father the point. That niggling pain in his head? The mysterious twist in his gut that kept him awake at night? Her fault. Lowry-*bloody*-Fisk — refusing to be set aside and forgotten. He should have known.

"Think she'll ever forgive us?" the Commander asked quietly.

"Not if we screw up the investigation into Wainwright's murder. Not if we ignore the possibility of someone trying to frame her and fail to ask ourselves why."

"We may not like what we find. Politically, things could get…complicated."

Jack fixed his concentration on the oil portrait of Queen Elizabeth II hanging its somber over the boardroom. He'd heard and made the toast "to Queen and country" more times than he could count. He wondered if the poor woman had a clue about the shit that went down in her name. Just as he wondered how the Commander couldn't see that his first priority should be Lowry. "She's your daughter."

His boss's head snapped up, uncustomary sparks of anger flaring in his eyes. "Are you sure you want to debate the issue of family, Jack? The ties you have with your own are tenuous, to say the least. Some advice: Put that right in the near future, or you'll just end like me — wondering if this *god-awful* job's worth it."

He managed to keep his arms stiff at his sides, but there was little Jack could do to stop his hands balling into fists. *His* family was strictly out of bounds. "She's in holding room 12B; maybe you should speak to her," he pressed stubbornly.

"No. The greater the distance between us, the better. I won't risk whispers that the investigative process has been in any way compromised by my interference."

Jack's throat narrowed. His mouth filled with dust. "So, she's on her own."

"If she's innocent, she'll be cleared by the internal investigation *you* insisted upon. I'll put my best men on it."

But would those best men be good enough? Jack doubted it. Lowry had few supporters. Her conspiracy theories, which she had not been shy about sharing, had ostracized some, worried others, and brought ridicule from too many. Christ, she didn't stand a chance.

Not his problem. She wasn't *his* responsibility. Thank God. And he didn't want her forgiveness. What the hell would he do with it? No, what he needed was distance from her. She tied him in knots. Example: Earlier, when helping her down from that fucking wall. Her smooth, feather-soft skin naked beneath his fingers, as his hands slid from her hips to the narrowness of her waist. Her hot little gasp. The fact that she'd clung to him for just a moment too long, her curves pressed tight against him. He'd wanted. Any other woman, he would have accepted her invitation, taken her fast, and bugger the consequences. But Lowry had found and tugged on the single thread of decency left in him. A thread of decency, which, if allowed to unravel, would compromise his ability to do his job. *Goddamnit.*

"You're not going to like this, Jack, but when I said I'd

put only the best on my daughter's case, that included you."

No. Not him. Aside from the fact that she'd already messed up his sleep pattern and screwed with his head, he didn't want her shining a too-bright light on the integrity of the Service. Not when he'd made it his life. He'd already had one lesson on the catastrophic consequences of exercising poor judgment—just ask his brother, Richard—he didn't need his ass kicked with a metal-toed, size-whatever, but definitely huge boot, again.

"Use someone else. Nick Marshall."

"Marshall will lead the investigation. *You* will be in charge of her protective custody. And Jack, if she's even halfway right about one of our own wanting her dead, she's going to need it. Besides, who else is she going to trust?"

Fuck. Good point. "Has the shoot-to-kill order has been rescinded?"

The Commander surprised him by chuckling. A rare sound, if not unique. "Distrusting the Service already? It didn't take her long to get to you, did it?

If her father knew just how much she'd gotten to him, he might not be as keen to hand over his daughter into Jack's charge.

· · ·

She pointedly ignored Jack when he re-entered the cell. His impersonation of the grim reaper hadn't slipped. If anything, it was more convincing.

"Get up, Lowry. I'm taking you into protective custody."

She ignored his instruction to rise. "Protective custody? What's that a euphemism for, exactly?"

Four fast strides, he dropped to his haunches, his glare easily capable of flaying the armor-plate from a tank. No hesitation, he got smack up in her face. "Don't. Piss. Me. Off. I'm not in the mood."

She bit back a furious protest. He was right. This was not the time to be obstructive. Jack didn't do turmoil. He didn't do inner conflict. Yet, behind the anger, that's what swirled in his eyes.

The hairs at the base of her neck pricked. Was Jack compromised? Had he been ordered to do something he didn't want to do? What? And where the hell did that leave her?

Not once did he relax his fierce grip on her arm as he frog marched her back along the corridors of the Cube, through Reception, and back out to his vehicle — into which he didn't so much hand her as bundle her inside.

This time, she snapped home her own damn seat belt.

Before activating the ignition, he paused and gave her a long, hard look as if searching for an answer.

Goose bumps the size of mountains stretched her skin. How was she supposed to respond if she didn't know the question? She held his stare for as long as she could, then, conceding defeat, turned her head away to look through the passenger-side window.

Yup, the Cube was just as ugly as it had always been.

"So who was dumb enough to step on your toes, Ballentyne... And who's got my cat?"

She gasped and gripped the edge of her seat as, with eye-watering speed, Jack pulled out into the heavy flow of rush hour traffic.

"Your father. On both counts. Now, shush and let me

concentrate. I need to think."

Shush? Not an expression she'd ever expected him to use. A soft word, so totally at odds with the hard, brutal-when-required man she knew him to be. On top of which, he was mega-smart with a mind that could solve problems at warp speed. So just how complex had things become for him to demand silence "to think?"

Chapter Six

Since when had protective custody necessitated the need to switch cars—twice? Cars Jack had broken into and hotwired, because they weren't a part of the Service's fleet of vehicles.

Odd behavior, for a man tasked with taking her to a Service-maintained safe house. At least she presumed that's where they were heading. Jack hadn't exactly been forthcoming with any explanation.

But she was done with his silence. He could think his deep thoughts some other time. "So, what's the safe house like?" she ventured conversationally to disguise her anxiety.

"Not exactly taking you to an official safe house," he muttered, his eyes on the traffic. "I don't appreciate playing a game I don't understand, so I've reset the rules. You'll be safe; just don't get your hopes up about the standard of the accommodation."

Her heart stopped. That explained the stolen cars. He'd been covering their tracks, making sure their whereabouts

remained uncertain—even to the Service. "You've always been unorthodox, but they're not going to like this, Jack."
Christ, was he mental?

"Tough. My play. My way."

Lowry rolled his words around the inside of her head. Jack bent the rules, but he'd never before gone rogue. The Service was too important to him. And he was destined for the top. One day he'd have her father's job, a position for which he'd been in contention for from the moment he joined the Service.

And she had a nasty suspicion he was putting all that on the line. For her. "Pull over, Jack. Let me out. Break all the rules you like, but not because of me. I *won't* be responsible for ruining your career. You can tell them I overpowered you."

"Yeah, like they'd believe I'd let that happen," he scoffed, his eyes raking her slight frame to drive his point home.

"Fine. Lend me your gun, and I'll shoot you. It'll hurt, but at least your reputation and your macho pride will still be intact."

"Sweetheart, your views on violence? You couldn't shoot a corpse."

He was probably right. Didn't stop her throat thickened though, her vision fading from color to black and white. "Jack, you ever call me *sweetheart* or anything similar again, and I swear I'll prove to you just how wrong you are."

He threw her a sharp glance. She ducked it, angled her body to put as much distance between them as the narrow seats would allow, and pulled her knees high.

Mostly, she'd come to terms with what had happened to her. She was just damn glad to have survived. But certain triggers tipped her over the edge, back into the nightmare of those early days after the rape. "Sweetheart" was one such trigger.

"At some point, you are going to have to explain to me exactly what just happened, Lowry. Why—" He broke off, shifting gears to overtake a bus. If asked, she'd swear blind she saw the white of the driver's eyes. His hand gesture, certainly, left no room for misinterpretation.

"Why explosive hostility, then a sudden and somewhat scary, complete zone out?" Jack continued. "If we are going to be spending time together, a lot of it, I need to know everything. Everything you're thinking, everything you're feeling. Consider it a necessary check and balance on that psyche of yours, for however long this takes."

Bastard. He still considered her flaky at best, unstable at worst. "However long what takes?" she asked dully.

"For Nick Marshall to clear your name, and for me to extract that bastard rapist's name from you."

Such confidence that she would fold and share—but she wouldn't. Never. The first place she'd headed, after bolting from her home when she saw Patient Peter on television, was a public library. She'd Googled him. The number of pages denoting his accomplishments, his pristine reputation for being the best of the best, had run into the thousands. She'd quit reading around about reference two hundred and eighty-six, nauseated to her soul.

Once an international diplomat of renown, Patient Peter was a "close personal friend" to just about everyone—the Prime Minister, the German Chancellor, the presidents of France, China, Russia, and the United States—the list ran long. More popular than the color green on St. Patrick's

Day, it would appear the man sat right up there with Jesus, Buddha, and the Prophet Mohammad.

Smart fucker. No doubt wary of a capricious electorate, he hadn't sought political appointment, preferring to build his field of influence as a civil servant. And as chief liaison between the Treasury and all state departments, he wielded his power on the balance sheet. Supporting, or cutting to the bone, annual government budget allocations. The Service had enjoyed his special consideration for years. She knew that for a fact, having spent three hours cross-referencing the sanitized public accounts of income and expenditure across different government departments.

Her pointing the finger and screaming "rapist, murderer"—never going to happen. No one would believe her. Not with *her* reputation for imagining conspiracies. She'd be locked up. Stuck in some psychiatric facility for the rest of her life—no doubt, a very short life, if Patient Peter got his way.

She wasn't sure why Jack's opinion of her should matter, but it did. So she asked, "Do you believe I'm being set up?"

"I'm not sure what to believe. All I know for certain is that I want the bastard who raped you. You'll give up his name. Eventually."

"Well, just for the record, torture won't work."

He laughed loudly. He didn't seem able to stop. She liked the sound. Very much. Deep. Throaty. Strangely liberated. Her own lips twitched.

The too-taut internal wires holding her together slackened a few millimeters.

Then he had to go and ruin the moment.

"Torture? Jesus, Lowry, you would try the patience of a

saint. Next to your father, you are probably the most insulting person I know. I didn't ask for this assignment. In fact, I find it hard to imagine a worse one. Refusing it, however, would have meant inflicting you on some other poor bastard. But you so much as hesitate when I give you an order, you cry, scream, or complain just once, and I'll make you someone else's headache so fast your head will pull an *Exorcist* spin. Got it?"

She nodded. Now she knew where she stood. He would ditch her for the smallest irritation. That helped clear her mind. They'd be parting company just as soon as she devised a plan.

"Too easy. What's going through your head?"

Well, he did ask. "That I don't trust you. That doing so would be to make the biggest mistake of my life. That I hate you as much as I hate everyone involved with the Service." She watched his lips narrow. "Would you prefer that I *lied* about that, too?"

"No. But I do need you to trust me."

"You first. Promise me you don't believe I killed Adrian."

Another sharp look from him.

Another cringe from her.

"For God's sake, I'm thirty-four years old, long past crossing my heart and hoping to die. But no, I don't believe you killed him."

Eu-bloody-reka! She had little experience of anyone trusting her word. She needed a repeat of the rare little zing that had sparked deep inside her. "You sound very certain. What if I flipped out?" she pushed.

He screeched the car to an abrupt halt. But for the seat belt, she'd have catapulted through the windscreen.

He turned to face her, seemingly oblivious to the furious blast of horns behind them. "Lowry, that threat I made about dumping you? Add pretending to be crazy to the list of triggers... Okay?"

She jerked a few little nods, then lowered her head and blushed from the inside out, less than proud of herself for insulting his acute intelligence. Then her heart sprouted wings and fluttered inside her chest. Endorsement felt bloody marvelous.

"And one other thing, Lowry, in case you didn't get it the first time around. The name of the bastard who raped you? I want it, and you *are* going to give it to me."

Her heart de-winged and plummeted like a rock in free fall. No, she wouldn't. Not in a million years. He'd probably go straight to Patient Peter Forsythe with her accusations and together, they'd toast and drink to their shared mirth. Then have the men in white coats, and armed with a strait-jacket, collect her."

"You do have a name don't you, Lowry?"

She didn't hesitate. "No."

The silence that engulfed the car sizzled with resentment. And frustration. It only took a scrape-down-a-blackboard moment to ramp the tension even higher.

Jack provided the nail. "I don't believe you. Having seen the state of Wainwright's body for myself, you've got one hell of a manic fucker on your tail. My worry is how many other poor bastards are going to have to die before you wise-up and give me everything you know."

"Thanks, Jack. I'll sleep so much easier knowing that." In truth, she never wanted to shut her eyes again, because when she did, all she saw was Adrian's pulped body, Patient

Peter's soulless eyes, and Jack's face rigid with contempt.

"Kiss good-bye to any thought of sleep, Lowry. It's a luxury you can ill afford until this mess is sorted out. You want to sleep? Give me the name of your attacker. Then I'll tuck you up, nice and snug. Hell, I might even flip you on your back and give us both a good time."

Her lungs flattened. He was joking, but that didn't stop her inner temperature soaring at the stupefying vision of him lying across her, naked and strong, promising more than just to keep her safe. Love, connection, passion hot enough to put the flames of hell to shame, everything other women got to enjoy without flinching.

"Sorry. Rotten choice of words. I give you my word, it will never happen."

And that was the trouble. No man would ever "flip" her on her back. She'd probably kill them if they tried.

Even Jack? She rubbed at her too-hot cheeks and pushed that unwanted challenge aside unanswered.

She didn't want Jack, didn't need him. She didn't need anyone. She was better off on her own...and the people she cared about would be safer. Suppressing a shudder, she dared the acid burning her throat to climb higher. Had Adrian's last thought been to wish he'd stayed the hell away from her?

The car bounced wildly across rutted terrain. She gripped the edge of her seat with one hand, the dashboard with the other, bracing against the bone-jarring jolts.

The immediate landscape was open and flat. Bleak. Ripe with decay. A long-dead factory, windows broken and with ravenous weeds populating its cracked walls, loomed ahead. The affluent jut of Canary Wharf broke the distant skyline, mocking the utter desolation of the abandoned industrial site.

Jack had warned her not to have any expectations about the accommodation. But, seriously?

He drove straight into the belly of deserted building, pulled to a halt, and left the vehicle without so much as a word.

Her door opened, and she looked up at him warily, trying to think of something clever to say. Her mind blanked.

She eased free from the car and curled her arms around her midriff. God, it was cold. Not the razor-chill of winter, but damp and mean with the first kiss of spring. She tugged tight the fleece Jack had lent her to stop the draft shooting the length of her spine.

"It's not as bad as it looks. And it's safe."

Her face must have shown her dismay. She glanced down at the fractured concrete floor pockmarked with industrial stains, and curled her toes. Plotting an injury-free path through the broken glass gleaming with sinister intent would be a challenge.

She squealed when arms banded her, one across her back, the other behind her knees, and she was tipped off balance and swung high.

She went rigid. Concrete replacing the blood in her veins.

Jack heaved a deep sigh.

Feeling the sigh, long and deep, vibrate his chest, her lungs stopped mid-action. She tried to ease some space between them.

He tightened his grip, hugging her close. "It's this or lacerated feet. Your choice."

She glanced down at the carpet of glass shards and splinters. Game over. She'd let him carry her—just one more little humiliation to add to her collection.

Too aware of his strength, of every muscle sculpting his chest, of the body warmth he couldn't help but share with her, she made the mistake of looking into his eyes. And found what looked suspiciously like silent laughter. "Damn you, Ballentyne, you're enjoying this."

"Yeah, a part of me is. Better hang on tight. The accommodation's two levels up, and the staircase is less than stable."

He wasn't kidding. The steel construction swayed alarmingly under their combined weight, the rasp of metal against concrete a warning of fatigue.

When he dipped to avoid trailing electrical wires, she availed herself of his invitation, and clung to him for dear life. In this instance, pride could take a hike; she didn't want to fall.

He shouldered his way through a pair of swing doors, sidestepped the scattering of fallen ceiling tiles, and stopped in the center of what must once have been the employees' recreation area.

A heavy pool table slumped at an angle, two of its legs missing. Ugly padded benches and tragic armchairs spewed foam filling. The rotting orange and gray carpet tiles emitted a rank stink.

To avoid gagging, she stopped breathing through her nose.

He set her down…or tried to. The instant her feet hit the ground, her knees caved. Large hands to her hips, he had little choice but to hold her against the length of his body to prevent her from collapsing into a heap on the floor. *Goddamnit.*

"You okay?"

Her skin on fire, she nodded mutely. No way was she admitting that, held tight to his broad chest, she'd felt safer than she had in eons. Not when she was having a hard enough job admitting it to herself.

She chanced a look at his face expecting, and ready, for his wry amusement.

Her heart skidded to a halt.

Jaw locked so tight it was a wonder it didn't shatter, he had his eyes closed. Strain stretched his skin from stubborn chin to high cheekbone. Without doubt, the man was in pain.

Poised high on tiptoes, with her arms still anchored around his neck, she realized she was all but welded to him. Her breasts crushing against his chest, her hips pressed so tight, they cradled one hell of a hard and swollen erection.

Hot needles stabbing the surface of her skin, she jerked away from him and stumbled backward several steps. Good Christ. Physically, at least, Jack desired her. *Her.*

Her face must still have been full flush, because when she did look up, he slow-grinned at her. "Control is sometimes overrated. No need to feel embarrassed. I'm not."

He strode past her and dropped to a crouch beside an empty bookcase, only upright because it was screwed to the wall. "I know it's hardly a palace, but make yourself at home. You'll find a bathroom with a bank of showers through there, though I warn you, the water is only tepid."

Reluctant to even contemplate the state of the bathroom, she stayed put. And watched.

Using the blade of a vicious-looking knife, he worked

free a length of baseboard, then shoulder tight against the wall, he reached deep into the hollow behind. He pulled free a cell phone and what looked like a small cellophane bag stuffed full with SIM cards—the tiny data circuit boards found in all mobile phones identifying the carrier. Available over the counter, interchangeable and disposable, they'd become a must-have for those needing to communicate without risk of their activities or location being traced.

He thumbed a series of buttons and then spoke into the mobile. "You know where I am. Bring supplies. Include clothing. Size six for her and sneakers, size…" He cast an enquiring look in her direction.

"Five," she muttered, still disconcerted that he could have guessed her dress size so accurately.

He passed that along and cut the call. Then, reaching into his back pocket, he withdrew a pair of old-fashioned metal cuffs and walked toward her.

Her eyes widened in disbelief. "You cannot be serious."

"As the Ebola virus," he retorted, snapping one bracelet around her wrist, while using his body to shuffle her toward the injured pool table. "On second thought, you'll only pull the damn thing down on yourself. Over here."

He overrode her stunned resistance and tugged her toward a wall lined with fat metal pipes.

"This isn't necessary. I'm hardly going to run." She stared pointedly at her feet.

"Yes you will, given half a chance. It's what you do best, and a little glass won't stop you. You're in custody, Lowry. My custody, and I don't trust you. How's that feel by the way? This is absolutely necessary while I take a look around."

She didn't want to be left on her own. Not in this rotting

space. Vulnerable. Defenseless. "I'll come with you."

His eyes narrowed. "I got the impression you didn't much like being carried, but if you insist — "

Had he not been watching her so keenly, she'd have pressed a hand to her chest to keep her heart in place. "No... no it's fine. Hook me up. I'll wait here."

He nodded. "Figured you'd say that." He fastened the other bracelet around a pipe and rattled it to test it was secure. "Try and stay out of trouble."

• • •

Jack circumnavigated the perimeter of the vast decaying site, then worked his way inward, back to the abandoned factory in ever-decreasing circles. The terrain had been cleared. The few outcrops of vegetation were too sparse to provide effective cover, but the mounds of abandoned bricks and discarded twists of machinery were a threat. He made a mental note of each potential hazard, his senses alert to any untoward disturbance of the barren wasteland

Scouting mission finally completed, he leaned his shoulder against the wall of the dead factory and, for the first time in years, felt the nagging itch for nicotine. He'd quit his pack-a-day habit the day he'd secured Lowry's discharge from the Service, figuring the torment of withdrawal would offset the gnaw of guilt he refused to carry. Up until now, it had worked.

Witch. He could still feel her imprint against his body. Hard, callous bastard that he was, he'd hoped to unsettle her using the hot press of physical contact, the one thing he suspected she couldn't handle. He'd intended to tease, the start of his campaign to get her to talk. Fuck, had that backfired. He'd only let her step back when the pain of his too-hard cock became unbearable. Otherwise, he'd have happily kept her tucked tight. Like the nicotine, it was a craving he'd thought he had long conquered.

Exhaling deeply, he made a vow. No touching, no more clutching for her scent. No more allowing his eyes to skim and dwell on her curves. No more games. A three-foot buffer zone at all times. Maybe five. And a quick resolution to this mess. Historic in speed.

He'd make damn sure he was all over Marshall like a rash until her name was cleared. Then he'd be gone. Overseas. If the Middle East wasn't far enough away, he'd try New Zealand. He'd put in a request. Shouldn't be too hard to disengage from her. Christ, he'd managed to gain, and hold, the widest possible distance from his own family. Doing the same with Lowry should be a walk in the park.

But with him gone, who'd look out for her? Clearing her name as a suspect in Adrian Wainwright's murder offered no guarantee that her rapist would be pursued. Who'd put that right, if not him?

He buried the nagging concern. Once cleared as prime suspect, her father could fathom out the what-next. Hell, she could do it on her own. God knows, she was a survivor. She didn't need him.

He rubbed his sternum with his fist and cursed the dull ache that had become his new best friend.

A bright yellow Jeep caught his attention. He heard the grind of protesting gears as it struggled over the potholed terrain. The Jeep stopped and flashed its lights twice, then repeated the signal before moving forward.

Will Berwick. What the hell was the man up to? He knew better than to use such an attention-grabbing monstrosity.

Making his way around the side of the building, Jack went to greet their visitor, hungry to tear stripes off someone. Will would do.

"Boss." The man grinned, obviously pleased with himself.

Jack eyed the Jeep in disgust. "What the hell is that?"

"Borrowed it. And this." Will stuck a red hardhat on his head. "I let it be known in a couple of the local pubs that I'm a surveyor working for a developer with an interest in this site. A cover story, should anyone grow suspicious about visitors to this dump of a facility. God, Jack, of all the places to bring Lowry."

He didn't appreciate the other man's criticism. "She's in the rec area. Follow me, and watch your step," he growled.

"You left her on her own? In the dark?

"She's cuffed to a pipe. And it wasn't dark when I left her there." Fuck, how long had he been standing there, lost in his musings? Jesus. Lowry—he didn't know if the dark scared her. He quickly turned on his heel, only surprised that he was able to stop himself from running to her.

Will followed him. Bitching.

"Oh, very smooth move…not. She's been through hell, Jack."

He didn't need Will's icy reminder. The bullwhip lashing at his insides was chastising him just fine. "She's under suspicion for murder."

"Bollocks! She didn't do it, and you know it. You're just pissed off because she got under your skin a long time ago, and you can't scratch the itch. Well, she got under all our skins. Learn to live with it. There's no antidote. That's

Lowry."

There wasn't a lot he could say to that, he realized. A hot denial would insult his friend's intelligence and, knowing Will, he'd extract his revenge with a relentless barrage of jibes and bad-taste insinuations—something Jack could do the fuck without.

Mouth in a tight line, Will held out his hand.

Jack slapped the key to Lowry's restraints into the man's palm.

He didn't duck the hard fist Will planted against his shoulder to move him aside so he could go rescue Lowry.

Will didn't hesitate when he saw her. He shrugged the two rucksacks from his shoulders and moving across to her, swiftly set her free.

Teeth clamped tight, Jack bit back an acid snarl as Will helped Lowry to her feet. He noticed she didn't flinch when Will engulfed her in his arms—which he did with enthusiasm. Guess she had been scared all alone in the dark. Scared enough to overcome her aversion to a man's touch and welcome a reassuring embrace. Which *he* should have been giving her, he realized too late.

"Clothes, shampoo, girly stuff, et cetera in this rucksack, basic food and provisions in the other. Did the savage tell you there's a bathroom through there? Probably not. For a viscount, his manners shame the nation."

On a filthy oath, Jack booted a fallen chair from his path and left the two of them to it.

Chapter Seven

Lowry listened to the clipped retreat of Jack's footsteps and waited for them to fade. "That was brave of you, Will. He'll make you pay for that little dig."

He grinned. "The savage or the viscount? Don't worry, he'll get over it. The man hasn't slept properly in an age, and it makes him cranky. Give him a bit of breathing room, and he usually returns in a better mood. Although maybe not on this occasion. HQ is apoplectic because he's ducked below their radar. He's sure pushing the boundaries of his luck this time."

She moved across the grubby space to take a seat on the least damaged of the chairs. "So he's in trouble."

"You could say that, but he's used to it. And he knows the team has got his back. Marshall's pulling out all the stops for you—just so you know. Coffee?"

"No, thanks. Why would Jack do that, Will? Put his career in jeopardy."

He tapped the spoon he was holding on the edge of a mug, his face suddenly grim. "It would take a braver man than me to ask him. You know what he's like."

Yes, she did, but that didn't explain why Will was dithering over the making of coffee. Instant coffee!

"Will, what's going on?"

He abandoned the mug and walked toward her, his reluctance showing in his leaden feet. "Sorry, Lowry, but I've got to do this."

Her heart slowed to a heavy thump. She curled and flexed her fingers to encourage some blood flow.

His eyes sympathetic but wary, Will reached into his jacket pocket and pulled free a small device, to which he attached a somewhat tangled coil aerial. He also pulled out a couple of tear-shaped earphones, implanting one in his own lobe and gesturing that she should do the same with the other. "Marshall's waiting at the other end."

She swallowed with difficulty as she complied. "Uh... umm..." her voice faltered. Four years had passed since she'd last chanced a conversation with Nick Marshall, and he still intimidated the bejesus out of her.

"Hey, Lowry," Marshall started gently. "It's been a long time. Wish we could have met up under different circumstances. You okay?"

"Fine." Too abrupt, but the tension straining her body had ratcheted sky high. Will and Marshall worked for the Service. Once she'd trusted them. Could she now? Patient Peter had minions. She didn't know who. Where the hell was Jack? He might be an unpredictable SOB, but he was...he was...actually she didn't care what he was, she just wanted him here.

She glanced over at the closed swing doors, willing him to return. Fate must have heard her. The doors screeched on their hinges as Jack pushed through.

Uncaring that ardent relief was probably written large across her face, she attempted a half smile. And failed.

He crossed to her, dropped to his haunches behind her, and leaned in close to share her earphone. His breath puffed warmly against her cheek. For a moment, she was tempted to rest her head against his shoulder.

Not happening. She leaned forward to increase the distance between them so the tease of his breath wouldn't... well, tease. What in the hell was wrong with her? Will hadn't made her feel edgy.

She sensed, rather than saw Jack stiffen behind her. And what the hell was wrong with him? If the tension emanating from him tightened any further, they'd likely all be sling-shot across the skies above London when it broke.

Jack being Jack, assumed control. "Marshall. It's me. Let's get this over and done with."

Marshall's voice took on a regretful edge. "Things don't look good, Lowry. Forensics, naturally, put you at the scene. Your motive's a bit of a puzzle, but frankly with your history—"

"It's a slam dunk that I did it. Right?"

Marshall ignored her challenge. The poor man was probably embarrassed by the resentful bitterness she hadn't been able to hide. "The hard drive from your security system's missing. Any idea where it might be?"

Her mouth dried. Licking her lips with an arid tongue wasn't worth a damn. "Well, obviously *he's* got it," she rasped out."

"Who's *he*, Lowry? And why would he want to frame you?"

The questions she'd been dreading. In these men's eyes, the truth would put her in La-la-land. Without hard evidence, they'd never believe her. And as for admitting to being raped? No way. Absolutely, no way. Jack alone knew, and that was one person too many. She'd left him that stupid recording in a moment of madness, something she now deeply regretted.

Jack cut across her silence. "Adrian Wainwright will have had the guest list. Cross-reference the names with anyone connected with the Service. From four years ago. She recognized someone."

"The gallery was fire-bombed last night, so any list is gone. And I need her to answer. Back off, Jack."

All her precious artwork destroyed? Every single one of those pictures had been a notch signifying the slow climb of her returning self-respect. Proof that she hadn't let her past crush her completely. Her chest tightened, too-rapid palpitations threatened to tear her chest in two. She rubbed damp palms, to and fro, from her thighs to her knees and back again. Repeatedly. Patient Peter was taking precautions, covering his tracks. She stilled when Jack put his hand on her shoulder and squeezed gently.

"Put out a call for witnesses; work up a list of guests that way," he ordered.

She swung her head round and stared at Jack in disbelief. He was trying to spare her. Running interference for her. There went his too-tough-to-care reputation. Shot down in flames by his own hand.

"Don't tell me how to do my job, Jack. Right now,

Lowry's the only suspect I've got. She hasn't got an alibi, and all the evidence is against her. Unless she gives me a name or, at the very least, another direction in which to look, she's going down for murder. And I need to hear it from her, Jack... Maybe you should step outside?"

Nick Marshall was well past pissed off, she realized.

Jack, apparently, didn't give a damn. He was quite emphatic about what he thought Marshall could do with his suggestion. She winced at his language. The agonizing silence that followed his tirade had her heart back to beating double time.

She felt the pressure from Jack's fingers, still fixed around her shoulder, change from offering comfort to active restraint, and held her breath.

"Okay...there's a tape—" he started, his voice soft, his tone painful with regret.

A tremor ripped though her. "No, Jack, he can't. Please. What's on that tape is private. It's not essential to the investigation, not if you all just follow up on what I've told you already." For the second time in her life, she was ready to plead.

"In the floor safe under the dresser in my kitchen," Jack continued, his tone now strained. "Listen to it. Call me back." He reeled off the combination.

She shook her head wildly, her hair lashing at her cheeks. "No. You can't do this," she whispered.

"The truth about what happened that night helps your credibility, Lowry," he insisted quietly. "It provides a solid reason as to why someone is trying to frame you for a murder you did not commit."

It was her turn to swear. To rant about why the Service

wouldn't recognize any truth *she* spoke if it bit them all on the ass.

Another, much longer this time, awkward silence followed when she ran out of breath.

Marshall's voice eventually crackled to break the excruciating hush. "Lowry, I'm sorry, but I already found the tape, and I've listened to it. Jack's going to need a new safe, and a new floor, too. Now I *really need* that son of a bitch's name and all the details. I'll have Jack and Will step outside, if that would make you more comfortable."

Her stomach lurched. Jack and Will both had their heads down. God, Marshall had listened to the tape. He knew about the rape. Who else? "Does my father know?" she forced out with a whisper.

More silence.

"Marshall?"

"Yes, he knows, I was the one who told him. And, trust me, hearing about what had happened to you, damn near broke him."

The pain ripped through her. She yanked free the earpiece and staggered to her feet. Stumbling over debris that got in her way, she sped to the bathroom where she retched up the contents of her stomach. Then tried to do the same with its lining.

Jack went ballistic. She could hear his bellowing through the walls. "She won't discuss what happened. Certainly not with anyone connected with the bloody Service. By pushing her, Marshall, you've just cost me any opportunity I might have had of gaining her confidence and learning *who the fuck* was responsible for the murder of those women and for raping her. She was as close to opening up as I've ever known her to be, and now, she'll have shut herself back down."

Her stomach felt like a dejected, collapsed sack. She pushed from all fours and slumped her back to the wall. And she'd put his support, the glimpse of concern he'd shown, down to the fact that he must care? Stupid mistake. He didn't care about her. Only the information she held had currency and, if she shared, even that would lose its value, faster than tin counterfeit coin. Because they wouldn't bloody believe her.

. . .

Jack gestured for Will to go check on Lowry. He didn't trust himself to do so. He wanted to bundle her up and escape with her. Take her home. Stand in front of the ornate wrought-iron gates to his family estate, Sig in hand, and shoot dead the very next person stupid enough to try and violate her in any way.

Where the hell had that come from? He hadn't been home in years. A self-imposed penance for the trust he'd broken. For what he'd let happen to his brother.

The image of his brother in a smashed heap, destined never to move under his own momentum again, was all the reminder he needed of what he did not want—involvement, love. To give a damn. If that meant jack-booting all over Lowry's privacy, then so be it.

"Marshall, I'll tell you what little I know, then leave it with me. I'll get the identity of the rapist from her one way or another." He cut the connection, thrust upright, and paced to the window. Turning, he hurled the earpiece away and cursed a vicious blue-tartan streak.

Hands on his hips, he tilted his head back and stared at what was left of the ceiling. Hearing Lowry's wild suspicions about the Service being rotten trip from his own lips had only made her accusations sound even more far-fetched. He'd sensed Marshall had felt the same.

"She wants five minutes," Will interrupted, bending to retrieve the earpiece. "I heard what you told Marshall, and yes, it sounds crazy, but give her the benefit of the doubt. It's the least she deserves. If what she claims *is* true, the Service owes her a hell of a lot more than that."

He was saved from responding to his friend's marked disgust by Lowry's return. She looked broken or, at least, bruised. That was the expression her father had used. Dark smudges beneath her eyes stood in stark contrast to her pallor. She was hugging herself again, a trait he'd grown to loathe. It smacked of isolation and a distrust of everything, everyone. His own arms itched to wrap around her.

He rolled his shoulders. He'd be lucky if she allowed him to share the same air she breathed, let alone get within an arm's length of her. From the expression on her face when he'd offered up the whereabouts of that damned tape to Marshall, he'd been dead to her. Jesus, he'd been stabbed, shot, suffered broken ribs, endured three weeks of torture at the hands of rebels in the Congo—and none of it had hurt like this. Not even close.

He froze when she approached Will and slumped against him, his friend's arms folding around her to hold her tight. *Sonofabitch.* Four years ago—just how close had those two got? And how could he not have noticed? A white-hot burn seared through him. Jealous? Him? He'd cut his own head off first.

"Will, go and check the perimeter."

"I'm staying with Lowry. She's shaking."

"That was a goddamn order, not a fucking request. Now move." Jack ignored his friend's undisguised look of contempt. He'd begun to wonder just how well-suited Will was to the Service…and realized how very well-suited his friend was to Lowry. To heal, she needed gentle. Will could do gentle. She needed warmth and security. Will could provide both. He, on the other hand, wouldn't know where the hell to start. "So what's keeping you?" he barked.

He knew his reaction was way over the top. What he couldn't fathom was why he hadn't been able to reign in his temper. Yes, it escaped when he allowed it to, but never before had it had done so without his permission.

"That was completely unnecessary, Ballentyne, and you know it. Will's the only thing about this hideous situation that makes it half tolerable."

"Lowry, sit over there and be quiet." It would appear that his temper wasn't yet ready for containment.

"Or what, Jack?"

He couldn't believe the fragile woman he'd thought broken half a moment ago was standing up to him, hands on hips, her eyes flashing storms. "I'll cuff you and lock you in the car down below," he threatened gruffly. This was more like the Lowry he remembered. As irritating as all hell. Pissed off. Full of fire. Ready to fight her corner or die trying. Christ, she was magnificent. No wonder half his men had lost their heads over her.

The heavy weight he hadn't even realized he'd been carrying all these years eased a little. He hadn't destroyed her, not completely. She might look fragile, feel and act it most of the time, but the brat was still in there somewhere. He'd just seen it.

She held her defiant stance for a full minute before she huffed and followed his order.

It would only be a short reprieve, he knew. She'd hit back somehow; she always did. Eventually. And though she'd never handled violence well, there was no denying she was a master when it came to ambush. He ought to know. He'd lost count of the number of nights he'd lain awake trying to anticipate her next move.

A few minutes later, she broke the quiet. "I'm hungry. I'll make lunch."

He took one look at her pinched, pale face. "No. I'll do it."

"Worried I'll poison you, Ballentyne? Don't think I'm not tempted." He moved toward the rucksacks and checked the contents. "I hope you like Spam and beans...for lunch, supper, and breakfast."

"Will did his best. It's not as if you gave him time for a full gourmet shop, *my Lord*. He'll bring other provisions when he gets a chance."

He ignored the ridiculous curtsey she dropped and gritted his teeth to stop himself jeering at her for defending a man who, only a short time earlier, he'd been happy to consider a friend.

As he decanted the cold baked beans onto two disposable plates, he watched Lowry sift through the clothing Will had brought her. And very nearly choked on his tongue when she twirled a red silk thong around her forefinger. "Damn, that man must have had fun," she laughed shakily. "Great taste, too. No wonder he had little time to buy food." She added a few more skimpy insignificants to the one hanging from her forefinger.

He swallowed, not finding it easy. She was deliberately winding him up, and it was working. If there was the one thing he'd always been able to guarantee, it was that her revenge would be sweet…and it would hurt! Just as he was certain that beneath all that flirtatious bravado, Lowry was in agony. Distrusting, frightened, and appalled at having had her privacy invaded.

What worried him was what the hell else she would do to retaliate.

What worried him more was how he'd react when she did.

. . .

Patient Peter steepled his fingers as if in prayer, and surveyed the scene spread before him like a lavish architectural picnic. He'd chosen this penthouse for its bird's eye view across Whitehall toward the Houses of Parliament. His kingdom. A kingdom where information and dark secrets were the undisputed currency, and he reigned supreme.

Now his sovereignty was under threat. Because of her, Lowry Fisk.

Framing her had been a perfect solution. As predicted, the Service had moved super fast to track her down. He'd preordained her death in their custody. A supposed tragic suicide, understandable when dealing with a fractured mind. Of course, the Service would have hushed it up out of respect for the Commander. The investigation would have been quick. A few token slaps on the wrist would have been merited to convince any skeptics questioning the veracity of the enquiry, of course, and then his position would once again have been secure.

And his plan would have worked but for Jack Ballentyne who, in direct contravention of orders, now had the girl secreted God knows where. Something for which he would pay. Time that man learned he was a mere puppet. A small player on a much bigger stage.

Patient Peter smiled and reached into his pocket. Withdrawing his phone, he placed a call, caressing his lower lip with his forefinger while he waited.

"Peter?"

"Jack Ballentyne. Find him, and you'll find the girl. The Service has got the best technical equipment in the world. I know because I authorized the expenditure. Start using it. Track each member of his team. Trace their calls. Put a shadow on every damned last one of them. He'll be getting help from someone. Double the financial incentive for information on their whereabouts. Triple it if necessary, but find me that girl."

He cut the connection, cast his mind back. Leaving Lowry Fisk alive at the warehouse had been a colossal mistake, one of his few. Not that he'd known her identity when he "took" her, or even subsequently. He'd thought she was part of the shipment, delicious fresh flesh ripe for tearing—and he'd had time to kill. Or he'd thought he had. That bastard Ballentyne had brought forward the timing of the raid, and when the bullets had started flying, he'd panicked, and gotten the hell out of there. Forgetting all about her. Understandable when she'd just been another young thing, one of so very many.

Recognizing her at the gallery—young, new artists

often offered sound investment opportunities—had been a surprise. Realizing that she had *recognized him*, a shock. No matter, he had things in hand, and God help anyone who got in his way.

He felt a twitch. Looked down at his crotch. Something was hungry. He smiled. It had been a while. He would make an arrangement. Something slight and blond, like her. A final good riddance to Ms. Fisk, for she wouldn't escape him again.

He reached for his phone again. A second call would rattle Walter. He smiled at the speed with which his brother answered, and then Peter placed the order for his special brand of takeout. A girl. No side order, and no need to confirm clean-up services would definitely be required afterwards. Walter would know.

. . .

To and fro, to and fro, Lowry prowled the ruined rec area in the vain hope the perpetual motion would loosen the tautness straining her muscles.

An itch spread over her skin. The back of her neck prickled. Turning her head sideways, she saw Jack. Watching her. "What?"

His mouth tipped into a breath-snatching smile.

She tripped over her own foot.

Face aflame, she stuck her chin in the air and continued pacing—only a little less confidently.

Generations of selective breeding over hundreds of years, from warriors and statesmen, athletes and scholars, had gifted Jack something special when it came to looks.

Something compelling, a mix of danger, rebellion, and character — very inviting. Strong brow, firm chin, nose definite and straight. Fierce blue eyes, deep as a lake, and a mouth… God, that mouth.

Great looks, powerful personality, apparently charming when he wanted. She had a nasty feeling she was about to find out what would happen when he combined those weapons of female destruction into a single force.

She stopped pacing to glare at him. "Pack it in, Ballentyne. If you're bored, go find some insect to rip the wings off. I'm not in the mood."

His smile changed to a lazy grin. His eyes flickered a dangerous gleam. Reaching skyward, he flexed his arms high above his head. Muscles bunched, cotton pulled upward to reveal a two-inch-wide strip of taut, naked male skin, the color of light warm honey, stretched across the promise of a remarkably well-defined victory V.

Tiny flames ignited the surface of her skin. *Holy hell!*

She dragged her eyes away and swallowed hard. No need to stare. That was one image of raw sexiness that would be forever imprinted in her mind. *Holy frigging hell!*

She heard the hiss and crinkle of creasing foil. He must be adjusting position.

She bit her lip, and kept her eyes fixed on the damaged wall ahead of her.

"You and Will," he said. "You seem…close."

Chapter Eight

She halted mid-stride. Where was he going with this? Jack didn't make innocent observations, no matter how *apparently* laid back his manner.

A bead of sweat traced a furrow down her spine. This was definitely the start of a stalking game. One at which he excelled, and she, in comparison, was a rank amateur. "Will and I are friends, nothing more. Not that it's any of your business."

Impressed by the evenness of her own tone, she recommended pacing.

"He bought you sexy, almost nonexistent panties. Kind of an intimate thing for a *friend* to do." He deliberately and pointedly shifted his gaze to her chest. "No bras, though. So he either doesn't know your cup size or prefers you... unrestrained."

She bit the inside of her cheek hard. She would not react. No way. Then, hating herself, she caved and folded her arms to hide her breasts. Which had no doubt been bouncing energetically beneath the thin cotton of her long sleeve T-shirt as she paced. On that lovely thought, she confessed. "He was paying me back," she said acidly. "When I first joined the Service, Will made the mistake of sending me out to buy his great aunt a birthday present. I brought very naughty lingerie so he'd think twice, in future, about using me as a go-fer. It became a standing joke between us. He was just reminding me he hadn't forgotten."

Jack shrugged his broad shoulders and smiled. One of his slow, slow smiles.

Her blood flow didn't seem able to make up its mind of whether to race or freeze.

"If you say so. But I've seen the way he looks at you, sweetheart. And, I assure you, the last thing on his mind is his great aunt."

The *sweetheart* nearly stripped her of all control. But to lose it now would gift him the advantage he so obviously sought. Ignoring the palpitations threatening to crack her chest, the wave of revulsion rolling in her stomach, she shifted her hands to her hips. Then squaring her shoulders, she thrust her chest forward, fully aware that because her blood had opted for lightly chilled, her nipples were standing proud.

And she couldn't hold back the smile.

The satisfaction of seeing his eyes widen, his lips part very slightly to expel a sharp breath, was so worth the acute discomfort that brazen display cost her.

Jack dragged his stare from her chest to her face. A wild light backlit the blue-blue of his eyes. Not ridicule. Not anger. Raw hunger.

The blush started in her toes and worked its way slowly upward until her face glowed like a blood sun. She tried braving it out. Holding the come-and-get-it pose for a few precious seconds more. Then, conceding defeat, her arms fell leaden and limp to her sides, and she tucked her chin low.

She'd always been hopeless when it came to flexing feminine wiles. She'd failed abysmally every one of the "honey-trap" simulations Jack had put her through during training. It had become a standing joke within the team.

He laughed, albeit, in that strained way she recognized from years ago.

"Don't try that on Will, Lowry. The poor man's close to losing his dignity as it is."

"That man's your friend, Jack," she reminded him quietly, her head still down. "Don't forget he's putting his career on the line for you. Not for the first time, either. Every time you break the rules, you compromise your men. You issue an order; they follow it. You ask a favor; they grant it. Doing both without question, and regardless of any risk to themselves. Have you ever thought about that, or don't you care?"

She lifted her head and made eye contact to drive her point home.

His stare didn't waver, just drilled right through her. "You talk to Will."

She frowned. Jack made it sound like she'd committed a crime. "Yes, he's easy to talk to. He listens without making me feel a complete incompetent."

"Unlike me?"

She shifted her weight from one leg to the other and plucked at the sleeve of her top. "You don't talk, Jack. You issue orders, then dismiss. You listen only to what you want to hear and, even then, you do so under sufferance."

"Not true. Gathering intelligence is vital to the job, remember? I listen. I observe. And I'm pretty damn good at it. How else would I have pegged you and Will?"

"And got it wrong! Newsflash, Ballentyne. A man can connect with and show empathy for a woman without it meaning they must have had mad monkey sex, or even that they intend to."

His bark of laughter sounded strained, as if he was being strangled. "I wouldn't discount Will's intentions quite so easily if I were you." His expression hardened. "Have you spoken to him about the rape?"

The rape. Jack was able to drop those two little words so easily. Casually, as if it had been just some by the way incident, over and done with, ready for filing away.

Insensitive bastard. If only he knew.

Knew just how close she'd come to doing just that. Filing it away, burying the nightmare, putting it behind her. Right up until the night he'd accosted her in the gallery. Bringing with him the taint of the Service, and the taint of Patient Peter Forsythe.

She pressed her palm hard against her stomach. "What is there to tell, Jack? I'm not the first woman to be raped, and I sure as hell won't be the last, more's the pity. I'm over it."

"If you say so."

She narrowed her eyes. "What's that supposed to mean?"

"Just that for a person who thinks she's over what happened, you're a mess. As much as you accept that no woman is ever complicit when it comes to rape, you can't stop yourself wondering if you weren't in some way to blame. That maybe, just by being you, that was enough to provoke the attack. Manifested by the fact you find it incomprehensible for a man to like you, let alone desire you. You recoil as if burned when touched, though you fight to hide it. First you go rigid, then you get these little creases in your brow as you weigh up the motivation behind the touch. Even if you judge it to be innocent, you still have to force your muscles to relax. All, barely noticeable, except to someone watching for it. I pity the poor bastard who last tried to kiss you. Bet you lost your bloody mind."

She had.

Four years ago—Patient Peter was the last man to have gotten anywhere near her lips.

Jack wasn't wrong about her thought patterns either. Somehow, he'd slid inside her head and read her mental journal of fears. A violation in itself.

"When it comes to the blame game, *Viscount*, I hardly think you're qualified to offer advice. How many years has it been since you turned your back on who you are? Your title, your obligations, your family. When you get past what happened to your brother and finally accept that you were not responsible, try lecturing me. But until then—fuck off!"

Not a flicker of emotion crossed his face. He didn't even flinch. Had she expected him to? No, but she'd hoped. Wished that, just once, he'd prove he could be hurt. Show shock, even. At the fact she knew about the past that had shaped him into the soulless man he'd become—it would have made him less the invincible action-hero and more human.

"Interesting. Care to tell me how you found out?" He

might have arched his brow in a pretense of nonchalance, but the little pulse throbbing at his temple called him a liar.

She'd had it with his obnoxiousness. "Six years ago, I hacked your personnel file. Your fault; you should never have left me twiddling my thumbs back at HQ while you, and the rest of the team, played superheroes. Benching someone labeled as having a worryingly high degree of curiosity really wasn't the smartest of ideas."

The temperature, already chilled, dropped off the scale. "Accessing my file can't have been easy. I'm flattered you made the effort."

No he wasn't. He was bloody furious, she could tell— the narrow outline and pale hue of his lips a dead giveaway. Not that his file had revealed much. But, playing it calm obviously suited his strategy, for wherever the hell he was taking their little tête-à-tête.

Well, she didn't much like being maneuvered down a path she hadn't chosen for herself. Time to ruffle his calm. "Don't be. It was only your psych report I was interested in."

She inhaled sharply and took a step backward as Jack thrust to his feet, all cool control gone, his body humming with anger.

"For God's sake, Lowry, even I don't get to read those reports. That was an obscene invasion of privacy."

"Exactly. Still want to know about the rape, Jack? Or have I finally made my point clear enough for you?"

She'd bested him. She waited for his head to explode.

"Tell me what you know about Peter Forsythe, Lowry."

Christ, not that name.

The floor tilted beneath her feet. She reached for the wall and planted her palm flat against its damp cold surface, not trusting her knees to keep her upright. He'd bushwhacked her. Jack had set a trap, and she'd walked right into it. He'd used his nasty insinuations about Will and narrowed in on the rape to distract and fluster her.

She would not moisten her lips. Didn't matter that her mouth had dried to sandpaper. "Who?"

"That stricken look tells me you know exactly who I'm talking about. My guess is you know the man rather... *intimately.*"

A vicious choice of words. It implied complicity on her part. Her throat tightened. Jack Ballentyne redefined cruel.

Fingers trembling, she raked her hair clear of her face. The sharp pain as they snagged in the tangle helped ease the feeling that she was a captured moth into which he'd just stuck a pin. "Keep guessing, Ballentyne; you're getting nothing from me. I gave all I had to give four years ago."

He moved fast.

So did she. Backing up until her spine hit the wall.

He was too close. Too intense.

Her vision blurred.

"All signs indicate that you believe one of the most respected men in Whitehall capable of rape and murder, so you do not get to casually step back and walk away—or in your case, run away."

"I haven't accused your damned Patient Peter of anything," she shouted, her palms high on his chest, as she tried to push him away.

Jack didn't budge. Not a millimeter. "No. Your actions did it for you. You saw the man on television. I confirmed his name and status. You took off. My guess, confirmed by your reaction when I just said his name again, is you think he's the bastard who raped you."

"I don't think. I *know*."

"How can you be so certain? You said the man who raped you and shot those girls wore a mask, a balaclava."

"His eyes, Jack. Staring at me. Eyes, I can't forget. Eyes I hoped to God I'd never see again. But I did. Peter Forsythe *is* a rapist, and he is also a stone-cold killer. Though it was only three girls he shot. Someone else murdered the remaining five."

Jack shook his head, then pinched the bridge of his nose between his thumb and forefinger. "Lowry," he said with a sigh that sounded as if he'd dragged it up from the very depths of hell. "A statement based on evidence that nebulous wouldn't even get you into court."

"Don't you think I know that, Jack? Just as I know that if it ever came down to my word against his, I'd lose hands down."

"Yes, you would. Look, I know Patient Peter. He's just not that kind of man. He's all brain and no brawn. It was late at night. You'd spent two days trapped in a cage, barely big enough to contain a Labrador, not knowing if help would arrive on time. Extreme stress does funny things to the mind, distorts your perception of what's real and what isn't. Mistakes—"

The panic of being doubted, of not being believed, hit her with the force of a tsunami. She lashed out wildly with her fists. "No...No...No." Not her voice, not that desperate sound.

Strong hands pinned her. Strong arms banded around her tight. "Enough. Lowry. Enough."

Jack. Jack holding her, her back to his front, his arms a

large X across her body from her shoulders to her hips. Her arms pinned. Jack. Firm. Calm. In control. Her breathing steadied. Her vision cleared. She was safe. Very safe.

Will materialized in the doorway, his face a twist of wary concern. "Boss?"

"She's okay, now. Just give us a moment, would you?"

Will hesitated and threw her a questioning frown.

From somewhere deep inside, she dredged up a reassuring smile.

"Will. Out." She felt Jack's head jerk. She also felt his impatience. It was hard not to, given how tightly he was still holding her.

Will growled and then retreated, leaving the swing doors flip thudding violently.

The absurdity of the situation struck, she started laughing. "Do you have to intimidate everyone, Ballentyne?"

"If it gets the job done."

Her laughter stopped at the word "job."

"And to hell with the consequences?" She flexed and wriggled against him. He released her. She stepped away to give them both some distance before turning to face him, appalled by the sob stuck in her throat. She wouldn't cry. She never cried. She might never stop. "You should have asked your stupid questions and listened to my answers four years ago, Jack, because that was your *job*," she said quietly.

His hands cupped the curves of her shoulders. "I'm asking, and listening, now."

"I think you might have left it too bloody late. Patient Peter's invincible, and he knows it. You and—"

The kiss he brushed across her lips was as unexpected as it was shockingly inappropriate for its timing. But not as shocking as his second pass, his mouth now more certain. Firm and more insistent. Transforming from casual to demanding as if her surrender was not just inevitable but worth the risk and what the hell.

And nowhere near as shocking and inexplicable as her response. Feral and urgent. Like a wild animal caged for too long and suddenly released.

It was she who closed the distance. She who raised her arms to clasp him closer. She who hung on tight. She who opened to allow him a deeper taste. And she who all but climbed his body in need.

He was the one who pulled back. Unwinding her legs from around his waist, he set her firmly aside.

"I kissed you to shut you up about Patient Peter, Lowry, not to start anything," he said softly. "Think twice before you beckon me down that road, because I won't apologize later for taking what's freely offered." A calm warning. A slap in the face.

She returned the favor.

Her palm made contact with the flat of his cheek with enough force to knock his face from front to profile.

A spurt of bullets riddled an uneven line in the plaster above her head.

Reflexes kicking in, she ducked as more panes of glass shattered.

A heavy weight barreled into her, carrying her to the ground. The spitting retorts continued, plaster splintered, dust clouded the air. She couldn't breathe. She couldn't see, she couldn't hear over the cacophonous rush of blood through her head. The nightmare memory of a firefight four years ago clawed at her brain. Someone was screaming;

couldn't be her.

A hand clamped across her mouth. Next thing she was rolling, not of her own accord, and someone was fixed against her, toe to toe, hip to hip, chest to chest. Her back and shoulders screeched in protest with each dizzying turn. The weight, too heavy upon her, shifted. "Move Lowry. The corridor now!"

She scrambled and crawled, lost coordination, and slumped on her stomach. Bullets rained so close, they heated the surface of her skin. She curled her arms tight around her head, accepting escape as futile.

A hand fixed round her wrist, dragged her through the swing doors, and hauled her to her feet before forcing her into a sprint.

With a waist-high kick, Jack smashed down the release bar on the emergency exit and yanked her onto an external flight of metal stairs. Gun in hand, he ushered her at speed, his body adjusting to shield her with each twist of the fire escape that clanked and groaned its censure beneath their clattering weight.

Her feet hit the ground. He pulled her clear, spun her so her spine was flush against brick. He gestured for her to stay close as they edged along the wall of the building. His arm, a steel rod across her midriff, held her back as he ducked his head swiftly around the corner. It must have been clear because he urged her on.

He stopped abruptly, she collided with his back. "Stay down and wait here."

"But—"

"Do you really want to argue with me at this precise moment, Lowry?"

Not with that soulless look in his eye. Not with his face so granite stern, life appeared to have abandoned him. She shook her head and hunkered down, her eyes fixed between his shoulder blades as he disappeared from view.

Her lungs locked on expel, she gulped furiously, desperate for them to fill. How many men were there? Where were they? To hell with Jack's orders, she was going after him. He was the one with the bloody gun.

Before she could rise from her crouch, Jack was back. His face grim, those laser blue eyes of his glittering with single-minded intent. Instant calm washed through her. Violence was Jack's arena; he'd keep her safe.

"Will's down. Alive, but hurting. I've got to get you out of here. Head for that outcrop of brush over there. I'll cover you."

"Not without Will. You can't just abandon him."

"Damn it, I'm not abandoning him. I've called in our position, requested reinforcements. They'll take care of him. He was just an inconvenient obstacle in the way, not the target. You are. Now, get moving."

She moved.

She'd sprinted a bare seventy yards when she chanced a glance to the side. She spotted Will, bent double, struggling to get to his feet. He straightened, then stumbled. He was in trouble.

She changed direction. She'd almost reached him when the dirt kicked up in spurts at her heels. The shooter had her in his sights. Air locked in and scorching her lungs, she flung herself at Will, carrying him down. She screwed her eyes tight shut in petrified anticipation of the familiar sting of hot metal ripping into her flesh.

She cracked her eyelids, saw Will's gun on the ground. Some long-buried instinct from the past kicked in. She reached for it, twisted onto her back, and started firing blindly. Shot after shot after shot, until the trigger pulled freely without resistance and the chamber echoed hollowly. She rolled onto her front and collapsed over Will. She'd done what she could.

A hand clasped the waistband of her jeans and tossed her on her back. Winded, she stared at the pink evening sky hanging high above her, the edge of her consciousness registering the distant thump, thump, thump of helicopter blades and the eerie wail of sirens.

She glimpsed the inert body of a man hung halfway out the second floor window, head limp, his arms reaching downwards as if in a last desperate need to embrace soil.

Oh God, had she done that? Killed a man? Her mind darkened, threatened to close down.

Strong firm hands sped over her limbs, her ribs, her chest. Protest bounced against the walls of her mind, she tried to raise her arms to stop the trespass, but her brain and body refused to function in concert.

Someone flipped her onto her stomach, subjected her back to the same rough treatment. "Will?" Not her voice, it didn't sound right.

"No, it's me, Jack."

The mist smothering her mind began to lift. She tried again. "No, I mean, Will. Is he okay?"

Jack nodded and muttered colorful obscenities as he eased her into a sitting position. On his haunches, he scanned their surroundings before he lowered his weapon, tucking it into place against his lower spine.

Shuffling over to Will he placed two fingers against the man's throat checking for a pulse. Will's eyelids lifted, he attempted a weak smile. "How bad is it looking?"

"Flesh wound. Must hurt like a sonofabitch, but you'll live. Can't say the same about the bastard who put that piece of lead in you, though."

Will nodded and closed his eyes. "Think I'll just catch a bit of shut-eye. I need to rest if I'm going to have to keep pulling your ugly backside out of the fire."

Jack patted Will's shoulder and crab-walked back to her.

He expelled a deep breath, then let his ass hit the ground. Dropping his head to his knees while he sucked in oxygen. He looked up, and shook his head at her. "Christ, I thought you'd been shot. What is it with you and orders?"

He looked shaken. Gray veiled his normally disgustingly healthy skin tone, a fine white line tinged the outer edges of his lips. She wanted to reach out and smooth the specter of fear and disbelief from his face. But she knew he'd never forgive her for acknowledging what he felt.

Instead, a part of her crumbling, she confided a horror of her own. "Jack, I think I killed a man."

Chapter Nine

Jack, his brow knitted, followed the direction of her stare. "Lowry, the way you were firing…" He shuffled closer and dragged her into a fierce embrace, an embrace that he knew from anyone else, would have been too rough, too aggressive, but from him, a man who'd decided years ago he just didn't care, was entirely natural. He'd never finesse this woman. She'd see through the bullshit immediately.

Holding her. Too tight because his arms wouldn't relax enough to release her, he shut his eyes and hung on. "You didn't kill him. I did. You just distracted him." He adjusted his hold on her, dropped his cheek to rest momentarily on the crown of her head, and expelled another deep breath. His mind bucked at how close he'd come to losing her, how close he'd come to getting her killed.

Reckless. Stupid. Arrogant.

Fuck, you'd have thought he'd learned his lesson by now. First, his brother. Now, damn nearly her. He'd screwed up again.

Feeling ill, he abruptly thrust her away. "Next time I give you a goddamn order, you bloody well follow it. You ever do anything that monumentally stupid again, I'll shoot you myself." He surged to his feet, dragged a hand through his hair. Eyes huge, a stunned look on her face, she just stared at him. He loathed what she must see. Him shaken. Vulnerable. His emotions hanging right out there, out of his control and switching fast enough to give whiplash. He shook his head, slapped her with a glare, and strode away.

His chest hurt, a mild understatement given it felt more like a steamroller was using it as a parking bay. What the hell was that all about? When he took a woman in his arms, he did so because getting up close was necessary, in as much as it was damn near impossible to gratify his body's cravings without doing so. He did not hug; he did not cuddle; he sure as fuck had never clung to a woman as if his life depended on it. Jesus, he dare not trust himself around her. She had a way of making him feel things, things a man like him could not afford to contemplate, let alone indulge.

Like terror. Pure and unadulterated. And guilt. Heavy as a rock. Discounting when he'd damned near killed her, he'd only felt like this once before. When his brother, egged on by him, had made the climb. They'd both been too drunk to anticipate something going wrong. Yet it had. Horrendously.

He cupped the back of his neck and squeezed. He ought to get back to Lowry. Double-check she was all right before he handed her over into someone else's charge. Someone who knew how to play by the rules and who would keep her safe. She was right—he could be as reckless as he liked with his own life and career, but he had no right to demand that others endanger theirs. It was his fault Will was injured. He should have had his entire team guarding her. Two of them hadn't been enough. Foolhardy. Arrogant.

Just like that kiss he'd let get out of hand.

A spontaneous act of incredible stupidity that had all but blown his mind. It had also been all the warning he'd needed that his judgment was fucked. For that alone he'd deserved the almighty slap she'd landed. Some people just weren't meant to co-exist within a hundred miles of one another. Him and Lowry, for a start.

He stood aside as a black saloon screeched to a halt beside him. Marshall catapulted from the car. "Will?" Anxiety pinched the man's face, and so did censure. *Yup, he'd fucked up big time.*

"Over there. Lowry's with him." He didn't need to check over his shoulder. He knew she'd have crawled over to take care of his friend. That she'd be soothing and stroking, cooing words of reassurance while she beat back her own fear. That was Lowry.

"Ambulance is right behind me. She okay?"

He extended a flat hand, dipped it side to side to indicate he wasn't convinced. "She's unhurt though. You any closer to solving Wainwright's murder, or do I need to hand the investigation over to the civilians?"

His comment was a low blow, one Nick Marshall didn't deserve. He stamped down the impulse to apologize. Now wasn't the time. It was something he'd add to the list of apologies he owed, a list that was fast running out of control.

Lowry's fault?

Without question! Damn, but she ate at the very last crumb of his sanity. Twisted him in knots, skewered his judgment, frustrated him to the point of savage nastiness. Sonofabitch, he wasn't supposed to feel. He'd deadened himself against ever feeling again.

"For God's sake, Jack, give me a break. Someone just tried to kill my only suspect who, in case you'd forgotten, refuses to cooperate."

Jack scoured a hand through his hair and expelled a resigned sigh. Christ, he was tired. Worn out, sucked dry to the point he could taste his own ashes. "With the wild accusations she's likely to toss about, don't expect your job to get any easier."

"So she's talked?"

Jack shifted his weight to his other leg and fixed his eyes on the empty distance beyond Marshall's shoulder. He wasn't about to throw Peter Forsythe to the wolves just because he had unfortunate eyes. Not on Lowry's say-so alone. Marshall, and the rest of his team, would piss themselves laughing at his gullibility. "Not coherently. But had it not been for the shooter"—and that damned kiss—"I might have been able to calm her down enough for her to do so."

"Do I even want to know what you did to wind her up in the first place?"

Jack, his face implacable, stared the investigator's obvious disgust down.

"Okay, so what *did* she say?" Marshall demanded.

"Nothing I can hold her to, not yet, I pushed her too hard."

"I just bet you did. You might want to give her a break, too. If she didn't kill Wainwright then someone else did, and now they're after her. The Service abandoned her once. I won't be part of doing so again. Try and imagine how utterly

alone and terrified she must feel without anyone to trust."
With that, Marshall stepped forward, deliberately jarring
him with his shoulder, as he pushed past.

Jack held his ground. Tipping back his head, he stared
at the darkening sky and acknowledged he was behaving
like an ass. What the hell was it about that damned woman
that brought out the worst in him? Scared him? And what
the bloody hell had Marshall meant "without anyone to
trust?" She could trust him. Why the hell did she think he'd
contravened orders to protect her? On the other hand,
wasn't that the very mistake his parents had made? Trusting
him?

He stepped to the side of the rough track to allow the
approaching ambulance through and waved it toward the
anxious cluster hovering around Will.

Marshall had his arm around Lowry.

Jack's impatience busted through the top of his internal
thermometer.

And what in the hell was it with that woman and his
hardened men? First Will, now Marshall. Did he have to
erect a fence around her and pin notices on it not to touch?
Damn it, it was his job to keep her safe. Hell, the fear of
losing her had seen him empty an entire clip of bullets into
the bastard firing at her. More crass stupidity. He'd needed
the man alive, if only to make him talk.

His mouth arid with self-disgust, he forced himself to get
a grip. The night ahead promised to be long and punishing.
The thought of delivering his report of events to a board
of indignant suits—whose feathers were already ruffled
because he'd breached protocol—held little appeal. Not that
he cared a rat's ass about their ire, but he did care about the

fact that Lowry's protective custody had been compromised. How to explain that? He could hardly point wildly to leaks within the department or to Peter Forsythe. Not without evidence. They'd lock him up and throw away the key.

Much as he'd allowed them to do with her. Much as they would do to her again, given half a chance. How the hell was he supposed to prevent that?

Ten minutes later, he hoped he wasn't making the biggest mistake of his career, his life even. For her sake, not his.

He'd managed to subtly maneuver her to the fringe of the group anxiously watching as Will received emergency treatment. If there was one bonus to belonging to the Service, it was the guarantee that if you were injured, they'd call in the best.

Not that they had done that for Lowry. He'd hadn't let them, assuming instead full financial responsibility to ensure she received the best private care available. He made no complaint about the cost; hell, he'd been able to afford it. He'd met the bills of her treatment without a second thought. What nagged at him is why he'd felt compelled to do so.

Under the distraction of Will being loaded into the belly of the ambulance, he pulled Lowry aside, using his body to shield her from everyone's view.

"Take this." He yanked her dirt-smudged shirt free from the waistband of her jeans, reached behind her, and tucked his gun against her spine. He ignored the absolute stillness with which she held herself while he did so. At least she hadn't flinched or lost her mind. He also ignored how warm and soft her skin felt as his knuckles brushed, how his breathing had slipped from easy to almost labored.

He stuck a fat roll of high-denomination banknotes

into her hand and squeezed it in warning. He needed her to swallow the protest forming on her lips. "Go. Get out of here. Now." He thrust a mobile into the pocket of her jeans. "Disappear, head for...oh, I don't know, head for Wales. Bangor. In a university town, you can lose yourself among the students. Contact no one. I'll call in a couple of days."

He put his hand on her shoulder, turned her so her spine lay flush with his chest, and bowed his head to whisper in her ear. "I'm the only hope you've got. I know it's a lot to ask, but just this once, trust me."

He gave her a shove and glared at her when she threw a worried and bewildered look over her shoulder.

God, he hoped she'd be okay. He hated the idea of her being out there on her own. Damn near defenseless, with Christ knows who coming after her with the force of an armored tank in full throttle.

• • •

Patient Peter rose fluidly from his winged chair beside the open fire and made a show of straightening his bronze-and black-striped tie in the gilt mirror that hung above the fireplace. His fingers lingered and fussed with the silk knot until he was satisfied it lay dead center, plump and perfect.

He didn't invite Walter to take a seat. He wanted his brother edgy and uncertain. He turned around, retrieved his brandy from the top of the grand piano he couldn't play, and paced across to his favorite view. His kingdom twinkled in the dark at his feet. Still vulnerable. Especially with the girl back on the run.

Not a problem if she was sensible. Kept her mouth shut.

But could he count on that? She kept secrets. She'd already proven it. Her survival instinct was keen.

But his was keener.

It was a full five minutes before he turned his attention to the waiting man.

"This afternoon was an unmitigated disaster. What went wrong?"

"Yves forgot himself. His instructions were to call in their position should he locate them, that I would take it from there. Instead he chose to play hero. He paid for that stupidity. No one goes up against Ballentyne unprepared."

"Which leaves us with a problem. Jack Ballentyne never forgives an attack. He'll dig now, won't rest until he has answers. That's a complication I had hoped to avoid."

"Executing him is still an option."

"And how exactly will that help? That idiot Yves's clumsy attempt on the girl's life has already raised questions, cast doubt on her involvement in Wainwright's murder. No. You leave Ballentyne to me. I will find a way to neutralize him without arousing further suspicion. He needs isolating."

"And the girl?"

"Let's see how she responds to real pressure. I believe it's time I turned up the heat. She won't get far. Not on her own. And not with what I have planned. In the meantime, stay away from Ballentyne. The last thing I need is for your personal vendetta against him to compromise my efforts further."

• • •

Eyes down, Lowry studiously resisted the urge to glance at

her reflection in the windows of the many penny arcades cheerily fronting the promenade. She'd hacked her hair short, dyed it black, and added streaks of neon pink to distract the curious from focusing too closely on the details of her face. Which forty-eight hours ago had been splashed across the media with a warning that she was dangerous and, if sighted, the police should be alerted. Immediately.

A quick forage in the local youth market, a temple to all things garish, shocking, and student, had provided her with the uniform of a confused punk-Goth. Black jeans, tears manufactured, long safety pins holding the frayed edges of the fabric together. Black Doc Martins she'd pounded with a rock and scuffed on the damp saltwater beach so they wouldn't scream "new." Black faux-leather jacket, two sizes too big. Black T-shirt, too, though the motif, a faded crimson mouth caught full-scream, added a touch of color. Her necklace, the *pièce de résistance*, comprised three fat twists of silver rubber, shaped to look like vicious razor wire. Now, her appearance warned *troubled*, warned *disturbed*, and most importantly warned *stay away*.

Not her first choice of persona, but for some reason she had yet to fathom, Bangor's student population favored the visually anarchic, and her new look helped her blend in unnoticed.

Jack had promised to call. Ten days passed, and she was still waiting.

She resisted the compulsion to check the screen of her phone for a missed call. At the rate she'd been delving into her pocket for the device these last few days, she'd be lucky to escape a repetitive strain injury.

She'd grant him one more day, then she was gone. Forcing

herself to trust him, when she'd learned the hard way not to trust a soul, had been equivalent of sticking matches under her purple-enameled nails and igniting them one by one.

Jack readily broke the laws of the land when they got in his way, but he believed in the Service. Blindly, most of the time. So why the hell had he compromised his own position to help her?

Her footsteps faltered. What if he had been setting her up? He hadn't been shy in acknowledging the esteem in which he held Patient Peter.

Unsure and irritated, she scuffed a hand though her new raggedy crop and curled her shoulders against the chill skirting in off the sea.

Deep in her pocket, her phone vibrated. A text.

She messed up her stride and cannoned into a group of tourists. Head down, she mumbled an apology and quickened her step, but not to a degree that would draw attention. The last thing she needed was them puzzling over a crazy woman who might have the look of someone vaguely familiar.

Only when well away from the hustle of the promenade did she dare sneak a peek at her phone. *"Where r u?"*

Uncertainty sliced through her gut, nearly bending her in half. She tightened her grip around the device to keep upright and moving forward. She didn't recognize the number. No reason why she should. But Jack had been quite specific. He'd said he'd *call*. No mention of a text. Anyone could be on the other end. Was it a trick? Dare she respond? What if it was Jack? What if it wasn't?

She flung a glance over her shoulder. The crowds had thinned. She added speed to her step, and gave herself a mental pat on the back that, despite the fear slicing through her stomach, she'd had sufficient wit to turn off the phone. They might be monitoring the signal.

It took an hour of walking against the bitter chill of driving rain—that lashed, just to make her day—before she found sufficient confidence to throw a lasso around her paranoia and bind it tight.

Taking a deep breath, she let her thumb hover over the call option, then closing her eyes, she depressed the button and raised the phone to her ear.

"Damn it, Lowry. Where the hell are you?"

No question at all about *who* was snapping at her. "Ballentyne, you stupid man, you scared me half to death."

"Which is nothing to what I'll do to you when I get my hands on you. Why didn't you respond to my text immediately?"

"You said you'd *call*." She waited for him to compute what she meant. She heard a deep, exasperated sigh.

"The phone's safe. It's got an anti-tracking device built into it. You can talk freely. I'm in Bangor. Give me your position."

For some reason, it annoyed her that he should be so supremely confident that she'd follow his orders without resistance. "No, I'll come to you. There's an open area, a small garden adjacent to the pier. I'll meet you there."

"When?"

"When I get there." She could do snappy, too.

"That sounds suspiciously like you still don't trust me."

"Why would I, Jack?" she asked coldly. "As I recall, the last time I came to you for help, you handed me over to the very people I believe are complicit in trying to kill me."

"Not all of them, Lowry. A lot of good people work at

the Cube."

Her palm suddenly felt clammy against the casing of the phone. She swapped to using her other hand—not that it helped. "Yes, but who? You're the one who broke ranks, secreted me away on that Godforsaken industrial site, and then let me escape. Why?"

"I don't know, but I'm beginning to regret it. You need to know your lack of trust verges on the insulting."

She narrowed her eyes and not in defense against the weather. She wasn't up for light banter, though from the change in his voice, he was. "I'm wanted for a murder I didn't commit, Jack. And someone tried to kill me while I was supposedly under the protection of the Service. Only three people knew where we were. Will, who didn't shoot himself, me, and you."

"I helped you get away, Lowry."

No, he had not liked what she'd implied.

"I know, but I'm no longer sure that was such a great idea. Have you seen the papers? Have you any idea what it feels like to have your face plastered in front of the entire nation? I wouldn't wish it on my worst enemy, Jack, not even you."

Hand trembling, she disconnected the call. Anti-tracking device be damned, he could be lying. He was a Service man through and through. It defined him, allowed him to be who he needed to be with minimal restriction. She had no idea why he had helped her escape. It didn't make any sense, but until it did, she'd take nothing for granted.

She tipped her face to the rain, relishing its icy sting. She could pretend to Jack, but she couldn't con herself.

Her anxiety about meeting up with him had less to

do with trust and more to do with her reluctance to face him. They'd shared a kiss so hot she'd actually climbed his damned body. She'd wanted him, and if he hadn't pulled back, she was pretty damn certain she'd have had the shirt off his back and her fingers at his zipper.

The rain practically sizzled as it collided with the sudden heat scorching her cheeks. She'd lost control. Jack hadn't.

Oh, God, he had probably already it worked out that if he had allowed that torrid moment to continue a second longer, she would willingly have laid herself before him naked and given her body freely. What the hell did that say about her? About the rape? What the hell kind of woman was she?

. . .

It took thirty minutes of close observation to convince her that Jack was indeed alone—and also, for her to pluck up the courage to face him.

He cut a lonely figure, seemingly oblivious to the elements. The rain might have stopped, but the wind blowing in across the turbulent white-crested waves was still cruel.

Anyone other than Jack Ballentyne would have sought cover in one of the cheerful blue-, green-, and orange-glazed shelters dotting the small gardens. Not Jack. He'd opted to lean on the promenade safety rail, his attention fixed on the angry, gray swell of the Menai Straits.

She sucked in a deep breath, drew back her shoulders, and willed her vertebrae to lock tight. She'd pretend nonchalance if it killed her. So what if she'd made a fool of herself? It wouldn't be the first time, and it wouldn't be the last. But, if she could just keep it together, Jack need never know how crucifying this first post-kiss meeting would be for her.

Measuring her approach, keeping it slow, she braced herself against his first scathing remark. "Hi, Jack."

"Lowry." He kept his attention firmly fixed on the distant horizon.

She willed him to turn around and to get it over and done with.

He didn't, not immediately.

Which gave her just long enough to remember the radical change she'd made to her appearance.

She was fully clothed, so why the hell did she suddenly feel so damned newborn naked? She clenched her fists to her side to kill the almost irresistible compulsion to reach up and fiddle with her new, short black crop with hideous slashes of pink.

He turned his head and immediately jerked upright. "Bloody hell, what have you done?"

Chapter Ten

God alone knew what made her do it. Especially after she'd already crashed and burned pulling a similar stunt at the god-awful factory back in London. But, rather than duck his incredulity with a modicum of dignity, she tilted her pelvis forward, planted one hand on the curve of her hip, and threw back her shoulders in classic model pose. "I decided it was time I embraced my inner devil."

And her bravado might have worked, except for the crack in her voice and the suspicious sting of moisture threatening her eyes.

Then he surprised the hell out of her. He leaned in, brought his mouth close to her ear. "It suits you," he said, his voice lilting with humor. Nice humor. Teasing. Not laced with ridicule. "Any piercings or tats I should know about?"

"Scared of needles," she muttered unnecessarily, pushing him away when he started to laugh.

"Come on, I've never been too proud to let a woman

buy me a coffee."

"Jack, in case you missed it, my face has been plastered all over the media. I'm currently doing my best to avoid all human interaction," she pointed out.

Head tilting slightly to the left, he trapped her in a long, hard stare.

A heat, volcanic in proportion, built under her skin and pushed to the surface. Then, just when she feared her spinal cord would snap and she'd collapse at his feet, he again surprised the hell out of her by reaching forward and ruffling her hair. "Lowry, your own father wouldn't recognize you."

The words tripped from her lips before she could swallow them. "No change there then. Even before this," —she sketched an air circle to frame her changed appearance— "I very much doubt he could have picked me out in a line-up."

Realizing how resentful and pathetic that must sound, she bit her lip and screwed up her face. "Forget I said that. Put it down to brain freeze." She waited a moment, opened her eyes, and dared him to comment.

He dared, his eyes narrowing to sharp blades. "You're very quick to write people off, Lowry. It's a bad habit of yours that you might want to examine sometime. That sky-high pedestal on which you isolate yourself is likely to get very cold and very lonely if you don't."

Her chest contracted. Had she blurred the line between fierce self-reliance and complete social withdrawal, to the point she could no longer distinguish the difference?

She frowned and wrapped her arms tight across her waist. Just because she kept her distance from anyone with the power to hurt and betray her, it didn't mean she ceased to care. That she didn't long to matter to those she couldn't help loving.

She heard Jack heave a sigh. Felt his fingers curl around her elbow.

"Christ, you're soaked. No wonder you're shaking. Skip the coffee. Where are you staying?"

Arm out straight, she pointed. "Across there."

His brow furrowed, he turned his head to stare across the Menai Straits to the rural island hovering in the gray distance. "Anglesey? Christ, Lowry, I thought I told you to stay in Bangor, where you could blend in unnoticed."

She dragged in what she supposed might just qualify as a breath; surprised at the effort it took. "I didn't exactly have a choice," she mumbled.

Eyes lowered, she waited for Jack to demand an explanation. He didn't, but she could have sworn she heard him grinding of his teeth.

"Okay. My bike's parked round the corner."

Forty minutes later, she wished they were back on the seafront where she'd at least had room to breathe. Changing out of sodden jeans left little dignity at the best of times. In the cramped, two-man tent she'd pitched within the ruins of an isolated farm building, with Jack taking up too much space, not to mention most of the oxygen, what little was left of her pride whimpered and slunk away.

Flat on her back, wriggling her hips, embarrassment got the better of her. "You could have the decency to look away," she told him.

"I'm trying. See, eyes shut. But it's not helping. I can still hear you, and I've got a dirty mind."

Unable to work out whether his tight laugh was meant to lessen the tension or unnerve her even more, she muttered a series of clench-toothed threats of what she'd do to him if he peeked and increased the fervor of her efforts. Damn, but did denim grip tight when wet.

"Just ask if you need any help. Dirty mind, but clean hands."

His offer, laced with laughter and more relaxed, sent a slow, hot flush across her skin. Gritting her teeth, she kicked the sodden mass aside and gave thanks when, with a quick flick of her hips, the replacement, a short black kilt, slid into place easily.

Her head knocked canvas when she sat up to haul on a T-shirt.

She flopped back down, felt around for the edge of her sleeping bag, and tugged it into place across her body—for self-protection, as much as for warmth. "Done."

He opened his eyes, a friendly blue for a change. He shifted and shuffled his big body to accompanying huffs and curses, then reclined and settled on his back beside her.

The sales woman had assured her that, despite its compact size, the tent had been designed for two. Lowry decided the bitch had lied.

She flinched at the press of Jack's shoulder—perfectly carved, and solid with muscle—against her own. Her automatic recoil, a residual reflex left by the rape, was as instinctive to her as the need to breathe.

With a filthy curse, he jerked sideways.

Although she considered it his fault that his shoulders should take up so much room, she couldn't stop an embarrassed apology escaping her lips. "Sorry. It's not you. It's me."

She sensed his whole body lock. The lack of oxygen

became more acute.

Long, agonizing minutes passed before he relaxed sufficiently to shuffle his shoulders to fit the limited space without touching her. What the hell was wrong with *him*? She was the one behaving like a scorched cat. He, hard bastard that he was, was supposed to be immune to excruciating atmospheres.

"Lowry, you ever apologize like that to me again, and I'll...I'll...forget it," he said, his voice gruff. The canvas sides of her pitiful shelter almost billowed with the depth of his sigh. "Why a tent? I gave you easily enough money for a B&B."

She hated to admit it, but she felt oddly disappointed at the return of his clipped tone. "Yes you did," she said softly. "But, I had to check out. Aside from the sudden need to keep a very low profile, the owner... Well, let's just say, he had a problem with his hands—he couldn't keep them to himself."

The long silence pressed her flat, the underneath of her thigh finally locating the stone that had jabbed her uncomfortably through the previous night. She tried not to fidget.

"I'm sorry. You shouldn't have had to go through that, not after... If I asked for his name and address, would you give it to me?"

She smiled, shook her head. "Jack, I'm not that fragile. You can say it, you know. The word rape. I'm not going to freak out if you do."

"Thank God, for that. But don't make light of the assault, Lowry. It sickens me just to think about it."

"Oh."

"*It*, not you, Lowry. Note the distinction."

Inexplicably, a lump clogged her throat. When it came to what had happened to her, she didn't doubt his horror. Nor his ill-disguised anger that it continued to haunt her and governed the way she interacted with others.

For a man who shrugged at violence and the brutality of life, for a man she'd faulted for having the empathy of a rock on more occasions than she cared to remember, his attitude to the rape raised more questions than it answered. Some easy. Some hard. All of them confusing.

She hastily returned her attention to the sloping canvas ceiling. Funny, but with Jack lying here beside her, its flimsy offer of protection didn't seem to matter. He exuded heat, the promise that all was secure.

She turned her head to the side and snuck a look at him beneath her lashes. He had his eyes shut, his arms folded across his chest, his long fingers entwined. His shirt had ridden up, again revealing several inches of tanned skin, the hard muscles beneath creating an intriguing range of curves and dips.

Naughty palpitations throbbed her body. She jerked her eyes away. She was an idiot. A man like Jack wouldn't want her. Once, maybe, but not anymore. She was too damaged, and Jack couldn't abide weakness. She tried telling herself it was relief she felt, which failed to explain away the extraordinary pain slicing her in half.

She snuck another look at the man stretched out beside her, needing to burn the image of his untamed physical perfection into her mind for the lonely life of nights ahead of her. Only she didn't see beauty, she saw death. Jack would lie like that, laid out in his casket. Because of her. Because of the danger she'd brought to his door. Patient Peter would never tolerate the risk that she might have confided in Jack.

Her heart skipping beats, sweat chilling on her skin, she jabbed him with her elbow.

"What now, Jack? I can't do this forever. Run. Hide. Nor can you."

"I'm not hiding, not in the way you mean. And I don't know yet, but I'll figure something out."

"Better make it fast. It's not much fun being on the most-wanted list, let alone having that psycho after me. When do you have to get back?"

By now, she should have been use to his sudden silences, but this one had her pulse skidding to an abrupt halt.

"Not for a while, I'm on indefinite leave. And, before you jump to the wrong conclusion, it has nothing to do with you."

She jack-in-the-boxed, flapped at the irritating restriction of canvas, and twisted onto her knees. "Oh, God, who'd you hit?"

He dipped his head in salute of how accurately she'd read the situation. "That bastard, John Smith."

For a moment, she could only stare at him in horror. "My father's personal attaché? His right-hand man? For God's sake, Jack, haven't you ever heard the expression 'keep your friends close but your enemies closer'?"

"You weren't there to hear what he called you when I reported your escape. And I didn't much like his tone when he questioned how you and I must have passed those long, boring hours together at the factory. The man's got a dirty imagination and an even dirtier mouth. Besides, he had it coming. He's had a hard-on for me for years."

He wasn't wrong. The enmity between the two men had provided fodder for gossip when she'd worked for the Service.

"True, but we're talking about your career here, not who'll win some ridiculous dick-swinging contest."

The groundsheet of the tent rustled under the friction of him shrugging his shoulders. "Don't worry about it. This enforced leave is just a rap on the knuckles to keep me in line. The Service needs me, and they know it."

It took just about everything she had not to hit him. "That arrogance will get you killed one of these days. Trust me, the Service will burn you, Ballentyne, if it suits them."

"They're welcome to try, but it's a bit late for that. I didn't appreciate the reprimand. I resigned my commission. With immediate effect."

She wasn't sure what her face showed—appall, shock, concern, because she felt all of that—and judging by his scowl, he resented her reaction.

"I have no regrets, Lowry. Besides, your father stuck his foot in the door to stop it slamming closed completely. He's asked that I take some time out to reconsider my position... and you can take that look off your face. I've already told you, none of this is your fault."

"Actually, Jack, I rather think you'll find it is. Does my father know you're with me?"

He gave her one of his looks, the one that suggested she'd parted company with her brain.

"You can't just walk off into the sunset, Jack. Though an asset, you're also a threat. You only get to go on their terms."

Oh God, they'd probably tracked him here. The minute that sickening realization hit, she spun on her knees and scrambled wildly toward the tent flap.

A tight grip fixed around her ankle and yanked her back. She kicked out in panic. She was still flailing when a heavy weight fell upon her. She instinctively opened her mouth to scream. A hand clamped across the lower half of her face.

"For God's sake, Lowry, I took precautions," Jack hissed in her ear.

He eased back slightly, lifted his palm from her mouth, but kept her wrists fixed with his other hand.

"I caught a flight to Rome, came back a different route under a different identity. Why the bloody hell do you think it took me so long to get to you? A friend of mine is currently denting a few of my credit cards across Italy, so no one is likely to make the connection I'm back in the UK."

It took an eternity for her mind to compute what he was saying. She searched his face for any hint of a lie. "Get off me, Jack."

He didn't, not immediately. Not until his eyes drifted to the rapid rise and fall of her breasts, then he couldn't extricate himself fast enough.

He shifted his weight, propped himself on his side beside her, but continued to hold her wrists. His hand tightened as she tried to tug them free.

"Let me go; you're hurting me."

He relaxed his grip, but didn't release her. His eyes drifted, slowly skimming her body as if he had no choice. Blue-blue darkened, odd glints flashed, his eyelids closed, his expression suggesting he was shutting out pain. "That hair trigger, more flight-than-fight reflex of yours, is going to get you killed one of these days, Lowry. What the hell gets into you?"

She had to wonder what the hell had got into him. Why did he feel it necessary to talk through clenched teeth?

She tugged and squirmed. This time he let her go. She brought her wrists down and rubbed at them to get the circulation going. And also to make the point that he should feel guilty. "I know it's an alien concept to you, Ballentyne, but I believe it's called fear."

"Huh, paranoid distrust more like. I can protect you, Lowry. I'm confident about that. But what I've never been able to do is save you from yourself."

"So why bother?"

He gave her a long, hard look. "Because this isn't just about you. I want answers. And, the families of the men who died unnecessarily that night at the warehouse deserve some answers too."

She refused to let him tickle that guilt. She'd asked enough questions and met with a brick wall. If they'd wanted, they could have checked her suspicions. And maybe, if she kept telling herself that, as she did practically every goddamn day, the nagging doubt that she'd failed in doing her best would leave her alone. "They may not appreciate what you uncover."

"That's not the point. At least they'll see that when things go wrong, we do our damnedest to put them right."

"Who's *we*? I thought you'd resigned your commission. Turned your back on the Service. Why should you care, Jack?"

His lips quirked into a lazy smile. "If you're hoping for a hero's statement, sweetheart, you'll be a long time waiting. It's not that I care; it's that I don't like being played for a fool."

Sweetheart? Her blood chilling in her veins, she gifted him an equally lazy smile, let her eyes warm and soften in an invitation for him to draw just a little bit closer. An invitation he accepted.

Her timing was perfect. Her hand snaked to the small of his back, her fingers curling round the butt of his gun. She brought it around fast, the barrel coming to rest bare millimeters from his temple. "Oh, you're a fool, Jack. For underestimating me. This is your last warning. Call me 'sweetheart' again, and I swear to God I'll—"

"I won't. I give you my word. Not if that's what *he* called you."

He snapped the gun from her hand and returned it to its natural resting place in a move that was faster and slicker than hers could ever have been. His fury, silent but palpable, slapped against the confining canvas.

She blinked wildly, her chest once again falling into that ridiculous speed push-ups action. She couldn't believe she'd pulled a gun on him and waved it in his face. She couldn't believe she'd done so and survived.

"That's what he called you and more besides, isn't it, Lowry? Now, because of it, every endearment, any term of affection, reminds you of him."

She nodded reluctantly.

"Then why the bloody hell didn't you just say so? Why do I have to repeat everything I say to you? The shame is that fucker's to carry, not yours."

She waited breathlessly while he re-caged that part of his temper she suspected few had witnessed and lived to tell the tale.

The brutal harshness adding a cruel edge to his features

faded, but not his intensity. His eyes still burned with a raw lawlessness. His jaw remained stubbornly firm, though the corners of his mouth softened into a half smile.

She froze when, with his forefinger, he traced an agonizingly slow line from her temple to the corner of her lips.

"Spirited, quietly fierce, you're a beautiful woman, Lowry Fisk. Don't let what happened diminish you. He'll have won if you do."

Had she not heard it for herself, she would never have believed Jack capable of speaking with compassion, of allowing the hard shell that encased him to open wide enough to reveal that some things did matter to him.

"Get some sleep," he ordered tersely. "We're leaving tonight. I want you fully rested. We've a long ride ahead, given the number of detours I have in mind, and the last thing I need is you falling off my bike in exhaustion."

She was too intimidated by his inexplicable snarl to ask where, and she didn't want to know the answer to why. If Jack sensed any type of danger, she was happy to follow his lead. She might not trust him fully, but she'd never doubted his instincts when it came to a fight.

• • •

Sitting at a sticky table in a less-than-salubrious truckers' café, Lowry made little effort to hide her foul mood. Jack dumped a cup of muddy coffee and what she thought might be a bacon sandwich—though she wasn't certain and poked it with suspicion—in front of her.

"Wait here. I need to make a call. And for Christ's sake,

stop glaring. You're attracting attention and putting us both in jeopardy."

She let her eyes tell him precisely what she thought of his reprimand. And "for Christ's sake" right back at him. She just spent five hours "riding bitch" on the back of his motorcycle. Her arms wrapped around him, pressed so tight to his back that he'd likely carry her imprint for life, unable to relax, ever conscious of each muscle he'd flexed controlling the damn monster machine in a too-fast, too-cold ride through the dark of the night.

He arched his eyebrows, tried to look innocent, failed abysmally, and grinned. Yup, he knew full well how she felt about that hellish ride and clearly found it hilarious.

He was a lot less devil-may-care casual when he returned from making his call.

He'd turned up the collar of his jacket, the winged tips disguising the outline of his jaw, and now wore a scruffy beanie hat, tugged well down on his head to hide the outer contours of his face.

He thumped into the seat opposite her, the blue of his eyes violent with fury.

Fear curled her spine, the fine hairs on her body lifted to high alert. She hooked her ankles around the legs of her chair and anchored her fingers to the edge of the table against the irrepressible impulse to flee.

He snapped his hand around her wrist as if he knew exactly the compulsion she was under.

"What the hell is it, Ballentyne? What's wrong?"

Instead of answering, he hunkered forward, his shoulders forming a barricade. He slapped down a newspaper, flicked the fold so the front page fell fully open, and swiveled it so that for her, it was the right way up. Then he stabbed his forefinger down on a photo.

"Oh my God, Jack. Oh my God!" She dragged her eyes away from the image. Words failed her. What could she say? What could ever give him back what he'd just lost? It was bad enough the paper had profiled Jack, detailing his history, his background, his military exploits, and every damned commendation he'd ever received, labeling him "number one bachelor worth the chase." But to publish his picture? He'd never be allowed to work undercover again. Not for the Service.

She edged her hand across the surface of the table, her fingers climbing the bone-white knuckles of his fist. He snatched his hand away as if bitten by a snake.

Her vision narrowed, her skin couldn't breathe. The smell of burned coffee beans churned her stomach. She should have stayed disappeared. First Adrian, then Will, now Jack. Around her, people got hurt.

This cruelty bore the hallmark of Patient Peter. A man gifted when it came to identifying what would give maximum pain.

"Get the hell away from me just as fast as you can, Jack, because Patient Peter is not going to stop. He wants me, and God help anyone who gets in his way. I can run. I've done it before. This time I won't stop. That way no one else will get hurt."

"And how, exactly, will that fix this?"

She had to cool him down, another savage jab on the photo like that, and he'd likely crack the table. "I'm sorry. Really, really sorry. Maybe you could — "

"What, Lowry? Find a woman, fuck off back to the

family estate, and grow crops? I don't think so."

His fury lashed at her, the whip marks burning hot enough to give her third-degree burns.

"I was going to suggest you return to London," she said softly. "You can still be effective. The Service is in trouble, Jack. Maybe you can help clean it up from the inside."

He glared at her from beneath the ridge of his brow, his eyes rapid-firing death shards. "The hell I will. The Service was complicit in this betrayal, if only through negligence. Every fact, most of it classified, came from my personnel file, the photo, too. They *could* have stopped this. They *should* have stopped this. If it's a war they want, they've bloody well got one."

Chapter Eleven

She wished to God she'd never pointed out that the Service would not just let him go. She should have left him to believe. Believe they'd act with honor. With integrity. That the leak had been caused by someone unconnected.

"You start a war, Jack, and people will die. You included. Because, trust me, you'll lose. You can't fight what other people can't, or don't want to see. And no one wants to see Patient Peter Forsythe for the man he really is."

He leaned in close. "Well, thanks for the show of confidence," he said bitter-sweetly, ever the master of causticity. "So what do you suggest? I give up? Sorry, not a chance. I am not about to turn my back, ignore this,"— another savage jab at the newspaper, and the table groaned alarmingly—"and just walk away."

She swallowed, or tried to. "The way I did, you mean?"

He nodded, though the tight little lines at the outer edges of his eyes appeared to soften.

Her head went down.

"I know things must have looked pretty bloody bleak, Lowry, but could you not have hung on a little longer? Fought a little harder? You could have challenged the court marshal. I half expected you to."

She couldn't imagine why he should sound pained. As if her giving up had hurt him more than it had her. "I was tired, Jack, and everything just seemed so damned…pointless."

She hadn't just been tired. The fight for someone, anyone to listen to her warnings had exhausted her. The laughter and ridicule to which she'd been subjected for being "that crazy conspiracy theorist" had rocked the corridors of the Cube. Every. Single. Day.

Did Jack not realize how much courage it had taken for her to stand up to the mockery and scorn? "Bet you didn't know that I used to vomit every morning before turning in for work, Jack. So, yes, you could say things had gotten pretty damn bad."

His face gave nothing away, but his fingers did seem to grip his mug of coffee just that little bit tighter, and the rise and fall of his chest not only deepened, but also quickened.

Freeing the breath cramping her own chest, she lowered her gaze and started tracing the smoky scorch mark left by a mug on the sad wooden table with her forefinger.

"Jesus, Lowry. I should have realized the initial good-natured teasing had crossed the line into bullying and put a stop to it. For that I'm sorry."

Her head jerked up. Jack Ballentyne never apologized. She hated the strain on his face. The regret paling the blue of his eyes. Without thought, she held out her hand. "Truce?"

Now she really had shocked him. If he continued staring

at her hand in that way, it would drop off. Then his gorgeous mouth slipped into a half-cocked grin. "You going to cringe if I shake that, Fisk?"

She shook her head.

His grip was firm, his hand engulfing hers. A strange sensation travelled her arm. Hot and sudden, like a mild electric shock. The heat spread to other parts of her body. Private parts of her body. "Okay, you can let go now, Ballentyne."

He snorted what sounded suspiciously like a laugh beneath a cough, and released her. "You're getting there, Fisk. You're getting there."

Damn, but his approval felt embarrassingly good. Was she glowing? Sure felt like she was. "You sorry for getting me kicked out of the Service, too, Jack?"

His expression hardened to stone. "No."

She waited, her body temperature cooling.

She waited some more. He'd elaborate. He was just organizing his thoughts.

Silence.

What? That was it? No explanation? What the hell was he hiding from her? "I think we may have to put that truce on hold," she told him, her tone tight, the words hard to get out.

"Too late. We've already shaken, and right now we have bigger things to worry about than your hurt feelings. Like how we retaliate for a start."

"I'm not hurting, I'm annoyed," she corrected acidly.

"Defiant upward tilt of the chin, color loss except for the faintest tinge of pink high on your cheekbones, gray bruising out the green in your eyes, right side of your bottom lip nipped beneath teeth—you're hurting."

"Made quite a study of me, haven't you, Jack?"

He shifted in his seat. "I'm trained to read body language," he muttered in a way that made her wonder just who he was trying to convince. Himself or her?

Then he dragged himself back on track. "Bugger the Service, Patient Peter's going down. And don't look at me like that. As if I'd just tased you. Yeah, I'm a convert," he flicked the newspaper in disgust. "Can't think of anyone else who would have had the gall to pull this bullshit."

"Which is why you can't just up and go after him. He wants to provoke you. He'll take any excuse to have you shot dead."

"So what do we do, Lowry, given you appear to have such an excellent hold on the situation?"

She ignored his biting sarcasm. Emphatically preemptive in nature, Jack wasn't used to being out-maneuvered. Besides, her solution was likely to provoke something far worse than a little acerbity. "We retreat. Hide while we wait for him to make *his* next move. What else can we do, Jack?"

She waited for the nuclear explosion. Instead, his stare was akin to a full body exfoliation with the blunt blade of a rusting axe head. When he did look away, it was to hunch his shoulders. An unspoken warning to her not to dare trespass.

She suspected the full magnitude of who, and what, they were up against was finally hitting home.

Reaching out to him with weak platitudes, even if she could breach the barrier he'd erected against her, wouldn't help. She doubted there were words adequate enough to appease him, either about the situation or to numb the sting of the criticism she'd leveled against him.

Jack knew the score.

If he returned to the Service, he would be anchored to a desk, and to a man of action like Jack, directing operations—his men—from the comfort of an office chair was unthinkable. He led from the front. A backseat, no matter how powerful, wouldn't do.

In stripping him of his anonymity, they'd found his Achilles' heel. Hanging back would slowly destroy him.

And there wasn't a damn thing she could do to put it right.

She stared at the muddy dregs at the bottom of her mug, gave them a brief swirl, and tried not to think about the source of the greasy film that had settled on the surface of her coffee as it cooled.

Dare she unfurl her fist, reach out and cover his hand, crossed-hatched with old scars, with her own? Would he appreciate her gesture of support? No, like before, he'd most likely take it as an insult and recoil. It wasn't sympathy he was looking for. It was revenge.

That's what made them so different. When beaten, she preferred a grateful, and very thorough, retreat. It was enough for her to have survived. Jack, on the other hand, would insist on going down fighting. He'd concede nothing. He'd strike back even as the last breath quit his body and, even then, it was unlikely the stubborn bastard would stay down.

She glanced at him from beneath her lashes, her throat tightening.

In need to something—anything—to do, she sighed and pushed to her feet. Skirting tables, she made her way to the service point and ordered two fresh coffees. She grabbed a handful of sugar packets for Jack.

Head down, she threaded her way back to their table, the mugs scorching her fingertips, and edged back into her seat. She nudged one mug in his direction.

He didn't say a word.

Nor did she.

She wished she'd had the foresight to forget the sugar. Returning for it would have given her an excuse to escape the oppressive weight of his detachment. Even if only for a few moments.

Instead, angling the top half of her body across the width of the table, she kept her voice low, barely above a whisper. "I know I said that they would never allow you to walk away from the Service unpunished, but my father would never have sanctioned your exposure. He could help, Jack."

"Yeah, right. Why the hell do you think he's the Commander of the Service? What he doesn't know about a political two-step can't be taught. Bet he recites, 'the ends justifies the means' every night before he goes to bed, and every fucking morning when he wakes up."

"But…" She bit her lip, slumped back into her seat and dropped her gaze to the sticky table surface to avoid his stony glare. If looks could kill, she'd be lying prone at his feet.

"Lowry, do me a favor and wipe the look of guilt off your face. We both know who's responsible for this, and it certainly isn't you or your father. But that doesn't mean I'm about to forgive him for letting this happen, any more than I can forgive myself. Come on. We're leaving. We've been here too long as it is." He thrust upright, scrapped back his chair, and headed for the exit.

He didn't check to see if she followed.

By the time she caught up with him, he already had his phone fixed to his ear. He pointed a finger at her to stop her from drawing too close and gave her his back.

Her own temper flared.

She was ready to accept full blame for stupidly bringing danger to her own door. Proving she'd survived and done so splendidly, like a phoenix rising from the ashes, had been naïve, vain, and arrogant. If she hadn't agreed to the exhibition and the headline publicity, this hideous chain of events might have been averted. Adrian would still be alive. Jack would not have been compromised, and she could have continued to heal quietly. Privately.

She'd made a huge mistake miscalculating the risk of her assailant recognizing her, and she'd carry the regret and shame of that failure to her dying day. But she had not invited the attention of the Service, and she hadn't asked for Jack's stubborn protection. This was not her fault. Not entirely.

Her mind made up, she waited while Jack put the phone back into his pocket, then stalked over to him. "If that call wasn't to my father, then it should have been. It's not in your nature to run, so go back to London, Ballentyne. Sort out whatever is going on from there."

"Brilliant advice, especially coming from you. Or are you offering to accompany me? You're a fugitive from the law; I'm duty bound to take you in. You prepared to walk back into the Cube and just hand yourself over? No, I didn't think so." He flayed her with a scathing look. "Funny how it's okay for you to have trust issues, yet you deny anyone else the privilege."

"I have reasons not to trust, as you well know."

"What, and you think I don't?"

She hated the bite in his tone, but she refused to back down. "Things are different, Jack. You have people who will believe in you and back you to the hilt. Will, Marshall, the rest of your team. And my father, you *can* rely on him."

"Can I, Lowry? You didn't."

"For God's sake, this is not about me."

"Keep your voice down," he snapped, stepping close. "And you're wrong. This is *all* about you. It started with you, and it will end with you. Who else knows about Patient Peter Forsythe, aside from me? And don't bother lying, Lowry. You're silence protects no one. Lives are at risk."

She shook her head helplessly. "No one else knows. Who'd believe me, Jack? Who'd take the word of a conspiracy-crazy, ex-operative against that of a respected member of the Establishment? That's why you have to go back. I don't have the credibility to fight him. You do."

"Undercover agents with their identities blown aren't exactly in hot demand. No, that fucker Patient Peter has effectively isolated us both. You're wanted for murder. I'm neutralized. I'm not even authorized to carry a gun at present. Not with my resignation still sitting on your father's desk. With Will incapacitated—yes, that's who I called—I've haven't got anyone on the inside able to schmooze a way past John Smith to retrieve it."

She damn near stamped her foot. He couldn't just give up. "So what do we do, Jack?"

His frown lasted long enough for her to worry that it might have become permanent. "We stay out of sight until Marshall clears you of Wainwright's murder. Then we use you. He raped you, Lowry. File a civil suit—your word against his."

It took her a moment to absorb his words.

Then, ribs crushing her chest, a horrendous roaring in her ears, she spun away. Only to have her wrist clamped tight. "I'm not in the mood to chase you down. Get a grip."

"I won't testify, Jack. I'll be ripped to shreds. Find another way. I'm not going public about the rape. And, don't you dare try and guilt trip me with a lecture about stopping him so other girls don't have to suffer what I went through."

He released her wrist, and dug untidy furrows in his hair as his fingers raked. "I wasn't going to. You're not, and never have been, responsible for his actions. So scrape off the guilt. You've been through enough. What I meant was Patient Peter has no way of knowing you won't testify. He daren't risk the public exposure a lawsuit would bring even if he manages to get the case thrown out of court. He needs you dead now, and the longer we keep you alive, the more desperate he'll become. And desperate men make mistakes. We wait him out."

Excellent. He was laying a trap with her as the bait. "And how exactly do you plan on keeping me alive? His reach is monumental, Jack. Look at what he's done to you. If you need a reminder, revisit that newspaper piece. He has help. He's got minions. Highly placed minions. How do you protect a person, who I might add has zero credibility, against a force as powerful as that?"

He thrust his hands deep into his pockets. "Actually, your father gave me the answer to that when he, somewhat dangerously, raised the subject of my family before I took you into protective custody. I can't believe I'm actually going to do this, but I think I know the perfect place for us to take cover."

. . .

Harrick Hall was as imposing as it sounded, and he knew Lowry was intimidated, not least by its size.

In the falling dusk, his inheritance hunkered like a beast in the shadows of the hills rising behind it. Four stories high, the elegant sweep of Georgian window frames lining each level did little to soften its mathematically precise lines. That two wide, equally splendid wings flew east and west from the main manor only added to the architectural statement that the Hall had been built by the very best for a powerful family, extraordinarily rich and cresting the highest social echelons, a masterpiece of its time.

And it had been a damned eternity since he'd been back.

He shot a glance at Lowry. The visor of her helmet up, her lovely eyes had never looked wider. Serves her right for taunting him about his title. From her shocked expression, the reality of who and what he was, a viscount and the heir, by a bare five minutes, to this ancient pile and the surrounding land that stretched as far as the eye could see, had never fully struck home. She also looked terrified.

"Come on, we'll leave the bike and helmets here, skirt the tree line, and duck in through the rear courtyard. Stick to the shadows. I don't want to alert anyone to the fact we're here. The Hall might be under surveillance. It's unlikely, but I don't want to take the risk."

He placed one hand on her shoulder not just to ensure she stayed down, but also to steer her through the dark. Her reluctance bucked beneath his palm. He firmed his grip. When she turned her head to protest, he tried to scowl her into submission. As unusual, it didn't work. Never had with her.

"I'm not taking another step, Ballentyne. Not until you tell me what's going on. What are we doing here? Surely this is the first place they'd look for you."

"Hardly. I haven't been back in damn near a decade. And it's well known my family and I are…distant."

"So what the hell are we doing?"

"Frankly, I'm not entirely sure. All I know is you'll be safe here."

"And what about your family, Jack? How safe are they going to be?"

"Let me worry about that."

He firmed his fingers around her shoulder to stop her from retreating back into the copse through which they'd just crept. That flight instinct of hers had reared its ugly head.

"Who exactly lives here, Jack?"

"My parents and Richard, he's my twin. Maybe a couple of my other brothers who use it as a bolt hole when on leave."

He caught her as she stumbled on a hidden root.

"What, you don't know?'

He heaved a sigh. Would she never stop with the questions? "It's been a long time, and I may have understated the distance I mentioned earlier. It's complicated, Lowry." Another understatement. He was about to confront an anguished past he'd sworn never to revisit.

"You don't have to do this, Jack," she said gently.

Gently? Oh, Christ. He did not need her reaching out to him with…with…well, *that*. Whatever the hell "that" was.

His feet stopped moving. The hit of adrenaline instant—the gush of blood through his veins, his pulse struggling to catch up. Very occasionally it kicked in when a mission went to shit and an urgent retreat was in order. He waited for the icy calm that usually followed to take hold. "If you've got something to say, say it."

"Just that I know about running, especially from yourself. You don't have to do this. Not for me."

More of *that*.

"Your expertise in running has never been in question, Lowry. Christ, you wrote the bloody book. But don't presume to know me. That sense of tragedy I can see glinting in your eyes is insulting."

He gave her a nudge to get her feet moving. He wasn't looking forward to this anymore than she. His dread was as strong as hers, probably stronger, but at least he had his I-don't-give-a-fuck mindset to fall back on. "Stop worrying. While I can't rule out a certain amount of growling, I very much doubt anyone will bite. And certainly not in front of you. We Ballentynes are known for our social graces and impeccable manners."

His attempt at some levity worked—well, kind of worked. From the incredulous look she gave him over her shoulder, she clearly believed something had gone dramatically wrong with his education in that field.

He grinned and moved in front of her to take the lead. If he had to do this, confront his family after all this time, face Richard in particular, there was no one he'd rather have by his side than this somewhat crazy, hugely exasperating, and totally complex woman. Because, without a doubt, he *knew* she'd have his back.

An admission he wanted to pull his gun on and shoot. He'd let her down in so many ways, he'd lost count. The last thing he deserved was her loyalty. He'd felt the tug of something beyond simple lust, days into her joining his team. Something dangerous. A need to connect that had him wanting to beat his chest and shout *trust me, let me take care of you.* After what had happened to Richard? Not. A. Chance.

So he'd pushed her away.

And the "need" had only gotten worse when she stubbornly refused to quit. Even though he'd subjected her to the harshest training regime he could think of, scoffing when she got things wrong.

Finally, he'd taken to ignoring her and all she had to say. Well, not entirely, he'd listened, he just hadn't responded in the way she needed. So she'd flown solo. Unprotected. Which had resulted in her getting raped and then him shooting her, for fuck's sake.

A scar he would carry with his others. Those he'd earned for each harsh word, each betrayal he dealt her over the years to ensure he kept his distance — and she bloody well kept hers.

Lying beside her in that tent had damn near killed him. Lying across her moments later to prevent her flight had been agony. He had put her off-limits years ago, the one decent thing he'd done for her, but with her beneath him, soft, curved, slowly calming, he'd damned near broken and given in to temptation.

He'd had to resurrect his hard bastard persona fast. But God, she was resilient. In her own way, Lowry didn't know *how* to give up.

And he couldn't wait to introduce her to his parents.

He halted abruptly. She ploughed into his back.

When the hell had introducing her to his family taken on significance? He wasn't out to please them. He'd burned those bridges years ago. Why should they care? Why should he? *God, he hoped they liked her.*

Completely felled by the ferocity of that last thought, furious that, despite his efforts, she'd snuck past his defenses, he swung round and snarled, "Damn it, Lowry, a brass band would be less conspicuous. Concentrate."

"You concentrate. You're the one who stopped without warning. You're the one who looks shell-shocked. Don't blame me."

Muffling a growl, he seized her elbow, steered her to the front, and gave her a gentle push to drive her forward.

A few yards on Lowry stumbled. He caught and yanked her upright, his eyes fixed on the high brick wall that encased the Hall's vast kitchen garden.

Fuck. He'd have to hoist her up. And right now, he didn't trust himself. Not the twitchy state he was in. Not when all he wanted was for her to climb his body and hang on tight. Like armor. Which he needed, given what he was about to walk into.

Trouble was, judging by how she'd reacted last time he'd lifted her, providing armor wouldn't be on her mind. Too-long suppressed need, passion hungry to be released—and Christ, he'd tasted her searing brand of passion—would see her flare out of control like a wild fire. And, God help him, he wasn't sure he'd be able to pull back. So he'd take a long soak in an acid bath before he let that happen.

No, they'd go the long way around, avoiding the wall.

Entry from the terrace would be more conspicuous than through the kitchens, but if it meant he didn't have to touch her, it was a risk he'd take.

In a rare showing, nausea rolled his gut. Through the beveled panes of the high, glazed double doors leading in from the terrace, he took a moment to watch his family at dinner. More were present than he had anticipated—all four of his brothers were in attendance. They, like his parents, looked to be enjoying a convivial evening. Something he feared his sudden appearance was about to ruin.

Too late now, though. This wasn't about him. It was about Lowry. About keeping her safe.

Sucking in a deep breath, he knuckled one window pane and, when his knock failed to gain attention, thumped more insistently.

Mouths froze mid-conversation. Heads swung in his direction.

He pressed his face close to the glass so they could see it was him.

Seb, his youngest brother, moved strangely fast to let him in.

He dragged Lowry to his side, stepped into the dining room, and waited in silence while Seb re-secured the door behind them.

His heart pounding hard enough it was a wonder the crystal chandeliers didn't shake, Jack reached for Lowry's hand and intermeshed her fingers tightly with his. "I need help." Fuck, he'd never thought he'd hear those words fall from his lips.

Chapter Twelve

A tall woman, willowy, her face quite, quite beautiful beneath a cap of gray curls, rose from her place at the table and approached them. "You must be Lowry," she said with a smile, side-stepping Jack. "Welcome to the Hall." She extended a narrow, pale hand.

Regal and supremely self-contained as the woman was, the suspicious shine in Jack's mother's eyes alarmed Lowry. Oh God, if this was going to be a tearful reunion, Jack would likely pull his gun.

Forcing her feet to remain exactly where they were, Lowry tugged at his hand insistently. How on earth was she supposed to politely accept the offer of a handshake if he refused to release her?

He looked at her blankly, then scowled when he glanced down and saw her fingers wrapped in his. As if burned, he dropped her hand and buried his own deep into the pockets of his battered leather jacket.

She resented that her cheeks should be the ones to tinge pink. Holding hands had so not been her idea. She wished now that she'd resisted when his fingers had brushed, then curled tightly through her own and he'd hung on tight.

In what she hoped would be interpreted as an I-am-not-in-the-slightest-bit-embarrassed gesture, she notched her chin higher to make eye contact with the men in Jack's family. And felt her blush immediately deepen—probably to puce. Each of his brothers wore a wide, we-just-caught-you-mooning-over-a-girl grin. His father, too.

She looked up at Jack. Brows drawn tight, he was death-raying the men with a warning, laser glare.

Christ, she hoped she wouldn't have to step in and referee.

Jack's mother drew her firmly toward a spare space at the table. Oh God, she didn't do people. She certainly didn't do families. She'd never understood them, wistfully envied them, yes, but never understood them. They scared her half to death.

Especially this family.

"Don't bother looking at Jack for help, my dear. His manners were always appalling, though I tried my best to civilize him. Left to him, you'd starve and die on your feet with exhaustion. Sit. Sit. Jack has an excellent memory, I'm sure he remembers his place, though I'll concede it has been a good number of years."

"I'm not sure we can stay," he warned, ignoring the gentle rebuke.

Lowry froze.

"Well, I am," his mother said firmly. "And, of course you're staying, at least for the night. This poor child looks exhausted."

Lowry grimaced at being described as a "poor child" and her jaw nearly dropped when Jack obeyed without further argument. She shot a glance at his mother and realized she, too, would not have dared argued with that fierce expression. All grace and favor on the outside, this woman hid a core of solid ebony every bit as unbending as Jack's. She guessed that his mother would forgo making a scene, pretend he hadn't been absent for nearly a decade, he'd told her—so long as he sat the hell down.

Two of the younger men high-fived each other. "Told you he'd be back... Eventually."

A plate of stew with an accompaniment of perfectly formed new potatoes materialized in front of her. A glass of wine appeared on her left.

She snuck a nervous glance toward the other end of the table, where the most senior of the men sat. Jack's father winked at her.

It was enough to confirm she'd entered a parallel universe, the realms of the surreal.

Bizarrely, no one seemed particularly fazed by their sudden appearance. Once the initial shock had worn off, his family returned to whatever they'd been chatting about. As if the unannounced return of the prodigal son, with an odd Goth-punk-looking woman at his side—one wanted for murder, at that—was an everyday occurrence. This was the English aristocracy at its politest—and most disturbing.

She was too distracted by the effort of trying to remain invisible to hesitate when Richard, Jack's twin, offered to show her to her room. Mumbling her thanks to Lady Ballentyne for the meal, she pushed upright, grateful that, for once, her knees weren't going to shame her. Steadfastly avoiding all eye contact with anyone other than Jack—who just shrugged unhelpfully—she followed his twin as he guided his wheelchair from the room into a vast, columned foyer.

Decidedly uncomfortable, she eyed the wide sweep of the grand staircase that rose from the center of the magnificent entrance hall. A hand brushed against her hip. She stared down into a grin, the mirror of Jack's when he knew he had the advantage.

"There's an elevator back here. Jack ordered it installed, though the architectural heritage police gave him merry hell."

Hoping against hope that her blushing would subside, she followed Richard as he wheeled his chair across the tessellated black and white marble floor to a wood-paneled door.

They were midway down a long, wide corridor on the top floor when he dropped his bombshell. "You're with Jack in his old childhood room. The west wing's being re-wired, so his usual quarters are out of commission. The bed's probably narrower than he's used to these days, but I'm sure you'll both cope."

It was as if she'd been doused with icy water. Her feet took root in the wide Persian runner lining the honey-colored floorboards. Heart pounding, her instincts screamed at her to turn and flee. The scent of lemon floor wax, which only moments before had delighted her, now turned her stomach. "It's not like that between us...me and Jack...I mean..."

His laugh alone told her he didn't believe her. "No need

to be coy, Lowry. I still have friends in the Service. They kept me current on what Jack was up to, and things got a whole lot more interesting when you joined his team. The whispers about you two kept me entertained for years. In fact, life became rather dull when you left the Service. And I lost a shed-load of money on the bet I placed."

"What bet?"

"That Jack was smitten. I can't tell you what a shock it was when I heard he'd not only shot you but insisted on you being court marshaled. My bank account's still in recovery. What the hell did you do to him, anyway? Sleep with someone else?"

Patient Peter's cold, cruel face flashed before her. "In a manner of speaking." God, was that her voice? She waited for her mouth to moisten, her throat to relax. "But, just so we're clear, there never was and never will be anything between Jack and I. We're not even friends…and if you lost money in that disgusting bet, you can take it from me, a shed-load wasn't nearly enough."

She willed herself to keep rock still as Richard turned his chair full circle and slowly wheeled himself back along the corridor toward her. His face was as implacable as Jack's, and his eyes, the same deep blue and just as mesmerizing, calmly held her glare.

"My mistake," he said, without a hint of apology. "The guest room's just next door…if you're sure."

"I'm positive, but then you already knew that. You just wanted to test me," she accused softly.

"Yes, I did. I sounded out Will and Marshall when you, then Jack, made the headlines. We all went through training together. I was curious to know why the notorious Lowry

Fisk, wanted for murder, appeared to have my indefatigable brother in a spin—again. I felt the need to double check what I'd been told. It's not like my brother to look a gift horse in the mouth, certainly not one as pretty as you, sweetheart."

The floor lurched beneath her feet, ice shot through her veins. Tilting from the waist, she braced her hands on either side of him on the armrests of his chair and stared her anger directly into his eyes. "Well, next time you feel the urge to check on something about which you're not certain, do so at someone else's expense, not mine."

She shifted upright, desperately aware that any moment now, the suspicious sting in her eyes would give way to a flood. She stepped around him, moved further down the corridor, and stopped beside what she hoped was the correct door. Her hand around the spherical brass handle, she paused before twisting. "Is this the guest room?' She hated that her voice caught on a tremor.

"Yes. And I didn't mean to upset you."

"Actually, I think you did. You're just like him. You'll do whatever it takes, because the end justifies the means. But what's really depressing is that no matter how long you've been free of the Service, you still adhere to that. And I'm not upset; I'm pissed off."

"Who said anything about my having left the Service? But you're right. I am like him. In as much as I'm fiercely protective of those I love. Hurt him, and I might have to consider shooting you myself…and you are upset."

"Upset about what?"

Terrific, when the Fates decided to have a little fun at her expense, they did so with malice. God alone knew how much of the exchange Jack had overheard, but from the whip-like tone of his voice, it had been more than enough.

With the floor threatening to give way beneath her feet, she turned and cursed them both. "Go to hell, Ballentyne. Go to hell the *both* of you."

She didn't slam the door. There was no need. If either of them failed to understand the emphatic *click* of the key turning in its lock, they didn't deserve to live. Which they wouldn't. Not if they tried to follow her.

· · ·

Jack exhaled a deep breath, before turning on his brother, his brow arched in question.

Richard raised both hands in a poor attempt at innocence. "Don't look at me. How was I supposed to know you'd lost your legendary touch? That there existed a woman who is immune to your good looks and charm, and who would take umbrage at the suggestion she share your bed?"

He squeezed his eyes shut, the resulting creases, he suspected, deeper than those on a busy whore's bed sheets. Maybe, if he couldn't see his twin, the violent urge to lunge at him and inflict bodily injury would pass.

"You have my permission to hit me, bro. Don't worry; I won't break. And, God knows, you've wanted to beat the crap out of me since our little foray up the facade." Richard slapped the sides of his aerodynamic wheelchair. "Don't let this little baby stop you. I didn't. I got on with my life. It's just a crying shame you haven't. Not in any meaningful way."

He opened his eyes. Stared hard at his brother—the once strong, vital man with unquenchable energy—now confined to a wheelchair. The wheelchair Jack had put him in. All because of a dumbass challenge from which neither one of them had been prepared to step back.

A man he couldn't face. A man he would avoid all he could, until able to get the hell away from the Hall.

But he wasn't about to let Richard off the hook for what he'd just done to Lowry. "You could always be counted on to put your foot in it. You called her 'sweetheart.' You're bloody lucky you're not sprawled on your ass right now. Last time I made that same mistake, she pulled a gun on me."

Richard barked a laugh. "Smart lady. And I'm not sure it's particularly sensitive to tell a man who can't walk that he just put his foot in it."

"No less insensitive than what you just did. If you've spoken with Will and Marshall, I presume you know the score. About Lowry. About what happened to her at the warehouse. The animal who raped her called her sweetheart, and probably a whole lot of other sweet nothings that now turn her stomach when she hears them."

"So you did overhear everything," his brother said quietly. "Look, I am really sorry if I caused her further pain, but you would have done the same. And, like I told her, I needed to double check a few things."

"Apologize to her, not me," he growled. "In the meantime, we need to talk about her safety, and I only hope your computer skills are half as good as they're reputed to be, because two lives are depending on it. Lowry's and mine."

Richard nodded, suddenly deadly serious. "Okay, your room or mine?"

He glanced at the door through which Lowry had disappeared. And locked. He doubted she'd appreciate him breaking it down to check she was all right. "Neither. We'll use the alcove at the end of the corridor. I want to keep an eye on her. First, I'll ask Seb to stand watch on the terrace. I wouldn't put it past her to try and make a run for it."

"She's on the top floor, Jack."

"That didn't stop us." He scowled at yet another of his brother's laughs. "And it sure won't stop her. Not if she's scared. And, right now, I suspect she's bloody terrified. Staying here is going to be a huge leap of faith for her. Make that any harder on her than it needs to be, and I'll toss you off the roof myself."

He threw a final exasperated look at her door, clenched his fists, and turned abruptly on his heel. "I'll be back in five," he promised. "Don't disturb her. Your apology can wait."

After he got Seb situated, it took a little over an hour for him to brief Richard and answer questions. And Jake and Gid, who elected to join them in the alcove for the war talk. His mother and father, too, had steadfastly refused to be excluded. All that had been missing, he thought sourly, was a rug and a basket of sandwiches. They could have enjoyed a family picnic.

He'd gotten through the briefing with the help of the better half of a bottle of whisky, but drew the discussion to an abrupt close when Richard, true to form, delved too deeply into the subject of Lowry and why he, Jack, felt the need to flush away his career, and everything that defined him as a man, over a woman he apparently didn't even like.

"You're letting that mammoth guilt complex of yours get in the way," his twin told him straight. "Damn near ten years you've paid for what happened to me, and now you're risking what's left of you for a woman who, from what Will and Marshall tell me, is dangerously unpredictable if pushed to the extreme. She's more than capable of taking care of herself. In fact, from what I hear, she prefers it."

"What's your point, Richard?"

"Just, that it's about time you learned to allow others to take responsibility for their own damned mistakes."

"Except Lowry hasn't made any mistakes."

Richard snorted. "Yes she has. A whole heap of them. She should have trusted you from a start. She had a responsibility to convince you that her suspicions about the Service had foundation. Instead, she went maverick and damn near got herself killed. You didn't rape her, Jack, and she's damn lucky you did shoot her. So get over it... Although why the hell you had to then go and get her court marshaled, I'll never understand."

Ignoring the sudden hush that followed Richard's disclosure about what had happened to Lowry, and keen to escape, he dropped a kiss on his mother's cheek and beat a fast retreat on the plea he needed sleep and that he'd catch up with them all in the morning.

His brother had it wrong. He didn't regret shooting Lowry. And he wouldn't hesitate to do so again if it saved her life. He felt no guilt about recommending her discharge either. The Service had been slowly poisoning her. Of those two things, he was certain.

It was the rest that bothered him.

The fierce need to protect her, when he was foolish enough to stare deep in the misty-gray shadows of her eyes in search of the green depths below. The way his fury surged when he caught other men scoping out her body. And, most of all, the fear he hadn't been able to rout or master. The gut-wrenching, heart-stopping, brain-numbing fear that she'd end up trusting him, and he'd fail her. The way he had his parents.

Their unspoken clemency for his part in Richard's injury, and his subsequent brutish behavior toward the family since it happened, had knocked him on his ass. It had also planted a nag of unwanted questions in his brain. Would Lowry ever forgive him for all he'd done to her? Would she ever again trust him? Doubtful. No man got to escape the crimes of his past, twice. A future, his future, with Lowry at the heart of it, wasn't something even he was arrogant enough to imagine as a possibility.

And…standing guard outside her door like a lost, love-sick teenager wasn't doing him any good. Richard had assured him the alarms would be set, that the dogs—the family wolfhounds—would be left to roam free. His brothers, all fully trained men with Service experience, would patrol and were more than a match for any intruder.

Resigned that there was little more he could do, he moved onward to his own room. Maybe a shower would ease the tension threatening to rip him apart? Because the whisky sure as hell hadn't helped.

The shower, a hot and powerful torrent, did indeed ease his muscles, but not his mind. When sleep still wouldn't come, he gave up.

By way of distraction, he stripped and cleaned his gun—twice—while running his plans for keeping Lowry safe through his head, testing all the angles, probing and countering the "what ifs."

When finally sleep let him in, he entered with his fingers curled tight around the pistol grip of his Sig tucked beneath his pillow.

Which is how he damn near shot her for a second time, when she slid between his sheets.

Eyes fixed to the ceiling. Teeth gritted tight. He gave her a second warning when, by his own edict, he only ever gave one. "I told you once, Lowry, that I'd take what was freely given. You've got exactly ten seconds to come to your senses and shift that sweet behind of yours back to where it belongs. Next door!"

He heard the sheets rustle.

"I'm sick of being afraid, Jack, sick of the fact he has power over me. Four years of flinching when a man brushes against me. Four years of running when a man shows interest. It's time to exorcise that bastard and what he did to me. And you're going to help."

There was no quiver to her voice. She sounded certain. But the gravelly hush with which she spoke revealed her fear.

His six-pack knotted into a twelve-pack. Cursing fit to make hell blush, he propped himself on one elbow and wished he could see her face. Read her true expression. "Do I get a say in this?"

"Only to say no. But you owe me, Ballentyne, give me this, and I promise we'll be quits."

She was trembling. This close, he could feel the vibrations. And her words were more a plea edged with desperation than a demand. She was sweating, the heat of her skin strengthening her scent. Light and fresh, a little wild, more herbal than floral. *Delicious.*

He tried not to inhale, breathing through his mouth rather than his nose. There was only so much torture a man could take. Reaching across her, stilling a nanosecond at the sudden hitch in her breathing, he flicked the switch of the small lamp on the cabinet beside her.

He wanted the advantage of light. Better that she read his message in his eyes than just hear it. She'd believe him better that way. "Then I say no. I won't settle any debt this way."

As he'd predicted, she was up and at the door in a lightning flash.

But he was quicker, reaching the door ahead of her to close the foot-wide gap through which she'd intended to make her escape.

Chapter Thirteen

Jack looped his free arm around Lowry's waist and gently pulled her flush against him, her spine rigid against his chest. He waited for the skip of her pulse beneath his fingertips to calm, for the rapid rise and fall her breasts to settle to a more even pace as her panic retreated.

The delay damn near skinned him.

He dropped a lingering kiss on her exposed collarbone — *so smooth, delicately sweet* — felt her heart skip again and blew on the imprint to cool and soothe. He lifted his hand from the doorframe and let it join the other on the sweet curves of her body, skimming silky smoothness with a tender reverence he'd never have believed himself capable. Not with flames licking his skin and vicious need riding him into the ground.

He felt her quiver, a tiny ripple that — *thank you, God* — carried away some of her tautness in its wake. "I said no to the settlement of a debt," he murmured, his mouth a whisper away from her ear. "I'd be out of my mind to refuse the rest. I'm not sure I could, even if I wanted to. Unless you want to leave."

He pulled her closer, unashamed of his red-hot erection from hell. He wanted—needed—her to know it was for her. That no man could possibly make her any less desirable in his eyes.

Christ, he'd waited an eternity to hold her like this. A few precious moments. Of barriers down. Of exquisite intimacy. Of being the man he wished he could be. Sensitive. Tender. Gentle. Because that's what this was going to take. It was going to take *everything* from him.

He moved his lips away from her ear, returning them to the oh-so-delectable curve of her shoulder, this time using the tip of his tongue to trace the outline of fine bone, filling each shallow dip along its length with the heat of his breath. God, she was soft, so sweet.

He forced his hands to still and pulled away. He owed her one last chance. "You sure this is what you want?" he asked. Jesus, when had he ever sounded that husky? When had his cock *ever* been this hard?

His temperature kicked up into the danger zone when she turned to face him and nodded, her gorgeous eyes wide, brave, and unrepentant. His stare drifted to the pulse throbbing dead center at the base of her throat. He wanted his lips there, and fast.

He hauled at his self-control. No ravishing. He took another step back, extended an arm, his hand palm upward in invitation. "Then after you."

This, he swore, would be her last reprieve. If she declined and scooted out the door, he wouldn't blame her. But if she accepted and climbed back into his bed, then she was his.

At least, for the remainder of this night.

He sucked in a breath when she moved toward his sheets. Sucked in another and damn near swallowed his tongue when she trailed the nail of her forefinger across his chest, one nipple to the other, as she passed close in front of him.

No doubt, her way of warning him that in what was to follow, she didn't consider herself a victim. Brave woman, his Lowry.

And f-u-c-k, if she didn't have the sexiest spine he had ever seen. Damn, if he didn't want to fall to his knees and swear undying worship.

Swallowing an agonized groan, he followed her onto the sheets and stretched his full length beside her. Close, but not yet touching, his weight propped on his elbow. "You've taken my side of the bed."

"It's still warm—and closer to the door."

He smiled. It amused the hell out of him that her little paranoid idiosyncrasies embarrassed her not a bit. "Light on or off?"

She took a moment to consider. "Off."

He reached back and clicked off the light. He didn't mind not seeing her. She could give up her secrets to his fingers, his mouth, his tongue.

He found her in the darkness, trailed a lazy finger from the pulse at her throat that beat so enticingly, to her sternum, then lower still to her navel. Her skin was baby soft, cool, and smooth. He needed to feel more and flattened his palm, fingers splayed wide across the level plane of her belly. He sought her lips, nipped gently, and encouraged them to open with a gentle press of his tongue. Christ, he'd have to take this slow, resist with every fiber of his being the maddening need to ravish and slake.

He was careful to hold his weight from her, staying on his side beside her, his shoulders angled toward her, his lips gentle, caressing. He kept it slow, let her trust unfurl. He'd give her no excuse to panic.

But when she touched her tongue shyly to his, inviting him in for a deeper taste and her hand lifting to his bicep, her fingers curling so her nails scored his skin, he nearly lost his mind and unleashed the hunger raring inside him.

He deepened the kiss, his fingers smoothing the contour of her breast, a perfect handful, firm but at the same time soft, as only women's bodies could be, and gently squeezed, his senses on heightened alert for any sudden recoil.

She didn't retreat, just dug those nails a little deeper, one arm slinking round his neck to bring him closer.

He prayed there was enough blood left to keep his brain functioning, that it hadn't all rushed south. Who would have thought that picking a way though a minefield where one false move might spell game over could be so damned sexy? And such agony.

He left the pleasures of her mouth, needing to taste more, skimmed his lips across her breasts, before fastening firmly on a peak, hard and defiant. *Pure unadulterated bliss.* As close to heaven as he had ever been. As close to heaven as he deserved to get.

• • •

On a gasp, Lowry arched, shocked and at the same time

empowered by Jack's need to feast, the thrill that he wanted to savor, and not just slake his greedy appetite, set her senses aflame. And he was hungry. She could feel that against her thigh. Rock hard and impatient. Hand sliding lower, pausing to explore knots of tight muscle and intriguing dips, she smiled when she reached her goal and swiped her thumb across the tip of his head, the telltale pre-cum assuring her this was no imagined, out-of-body experience.

She swallowed a moan as his fingers grew bolder, more urgent, tickling, teasing, tracing. Advancing, retreating, tuning into her. She bit her lip. She wouldn't beg. He couldn't make her.

"Please, Jack…" Not her voice, not that feverish cry. She lowered her eyelids, saw stars, lost her grip on reality, too desperate to sense him nudge her thighs apart, too lost in white-hot need to be aware he'd covered her, his weight hot and heavy.

Hot and heavy. Over her. She couldn't move. She couldn't breathe. Those stars, just moments earlier brilliant and mesmerizing, exploded into red hot sparks. Her eyes flew open; she lost the battle against the rising terror and widened her mouth to scream.

He swore, then fastening his mouth over hers, his hand firm behind her head. He carried her with him, twisting so that he lay flat on his back and she sprawled on top of him.

He set her free, lifting his hands from her to tighten in a death grip round the cool brass bars of the antique bedstead.

• • •

Through gritted teeth, he gave her his promise. "I'm all

yours; take what you want. I swear on all that's…" Hell, he wished his mind would clear. Urgency had numbed it, almost shut it down. What could he swear on that would soothe and convince? "I swear on all that's England, I won't touch, I won't *move*, without your permission."

A lesser man, less confident, might have been alarmed at her sudden fit of giggles. Not him. He found them sexy as all hell, the sound electrifying, tantalizing. He tightened his grip on the bars.

Damn, he'd actually exorcised her fear. Succeeded— finally—in making her laugh, taste exhilaration. He wanted to throw back his head and roar while beating his fists on his chest.

Now to gain her trust. He'd given his word not to touch, not to move. Somehow he'd endure the flames, the fire coursing through his veins, suffer the torture of her lips on his chest. The lead was hers to take. For once, he'd relinquish that role and follow instead.

He lowered his eyelids, tried to concentrate. He knew his knuckles must be glowing white. Hot damn, was that her tongue circulating his nipple, her teeth that were nipping, her fingers that had fastened tight around him? Stroking. Squeezing.

His eyes crossed. Much more of her hand to his cock and he'd come. *Bugger not moving.* He raised his knees, widened his legs and flattened himself to the bed to stop his hips… lifting, seeking, gyrating. *Fuck.*

She added a naughty twist to her wrist action.

He groaned. Pin-pricks of moisture broke across his upper lip.

He heard sheets rustle, felt her slide. Down. Down. The

heat of her breath against him, pulling his balls tight.

Oh, God, no licking. Please, no licking.

Her lips closed around him. Her tongue pressed.

Lights, white and searing, fired behind his closed eyelids. *No sucking, definitely no sucking. Holy, sweet fucking torture.*

She shifted, he felt the burn of her slow kiss-climb up and across his stomach as she positioned to straddle him, her knees tight against his hips. He growled when she took him in, inch by agonizing inch, deeper and deeper, tighter and tighter. *Fiery hot. Sweetly wet — bliss. Heaven. Hell. Paradise. Everything.*

Agony. Exquisite. Need to be in charge. Right Goddamn now.

Muscles straining, he tightened his grip. The bedstead groaned, one bar buckled.

Her breasts brushed his chest, and she whispered in his ear, "Now, Jack, I release you from your promise. I give you my permission."

On a shout, he thrust upward, his hands falling to her hips to grip tight. His eyes shot down to where they joined. His balls tightening at the excruciating thrill of watching her take his heavy length deep, again and again. He refused to release, not without her leaping from the cliff with him. Releasing one hip, his fingers delved, found, strummed.

With speed and wild fury, they rode each other, each daring the other to surrender first. He recaptured her mouth at the last moment, his arm supporting her arched back as she fell first with him in fevered pursuit, thrusting hard, thrusting deep.

That he was able to give his little firebrand five sweet orgasms, with his mouth and his body, through the quiet of the night was a pleasure-privilege he'd hold in his soul for the rest of his life.

Though that might not be too long.

• • •

Lowry awoke to find herself in a ridiculously comfortable sprawl. On her stomach. And alone. Spread almost diagonally across Jack's bed, the sheet rumpled around her hips.

She did not want to move. Wasn't sure she could.

A heavy languor held her leaden and replete.

But where was Jack? And why hadn't he woken her?

Sunlight streamed through the window, the shadows of the separated frames repeating in the gleam of the wide, polished oak floorboards. The sun's gentle heat, magnified by the glass, warmed her naked back.

She opened up her mind and poked at it cautiously. Wasn't embarrassment supposed to consume her? Shame? Guilt? The tiniest flicker of remorse? She felt none of those, not even a tickle. Instead, she felt weightless, elevated, liberated.

In-bloody-vincible.

Hauling the sheet around her, she thrust upright in glee, draping its folds toga-fashion. Her knees gave slightly as she wobbled, the mattress undulating beneath her feet. She'd done it. Actually done *it*. With Jack Ballentyne. Man-god and gorgeous, once tormentor of her dreams. No more recoiling. No more revulsion. No more shakes and shudders of the bad kind. Sex was good—no, sex was terrific. Bye-bye fear…hello, liberation.

She bent her knees, sprung upwards, one fist punching

the air. She landed, bounced, her laughter bubbled forth. Lifting her knees in turn, the sheet clasped tight between her arms and sides, she gyrated a victory dance, turning round and round. She was free. Free. Free. Free.

A stifled cough, more a swallowed laugh, interrupted her jubilant, and very private, celebration. A fierce heat immediately slapped her face. She locked her legs against the rebound of the too-well-sprung mattress, staggering ungainly when it threatened to catapult her onto the floor.

Jack, his shoulder propped against the doorframe, a neatly folded bundle of clothing held against his chest, shook his head slowly. "And to think I once accused you of not being a morning person."

The heat consuming her from top to toe flared to a white-hot intensity. "Oh," she croaked. That was as much as she could manage, her stupid tongue having turned to stone.

"Bathroom's through there." He gestured with his head. "Breakfast will be on the table within forty minutes. My mother rustled you up some clothes. She's about your size, so they should fit."

Something wasn't right. Jack's voice scratched like gravel caught between panes of glass. Lines of tension thinned his lips. The blue depths of his eyes flickered silver splinters.

The fire licking her bone-deep extinguished as abruptly as it had flared, a brittle mantle of frost shrink-wrapping her skin.

Instinct screamed for her to run. Jump through the window with only the sheet for a parachute. Her lungs straining, she locked it down.

He moved to the bed. She took a shaky step back. He dropped the pile of garments at her feet.

He regained the threshold of the door before turning to pin her with an arrow-direct stare. "Last night was a one off, Lowry, never to be repeated. You got what you wanted. You've exorcised Patient Peter—what he did to you. Take that. Move on."

She locked her knees. No way would she fold. Her mind incredulous, begging as to how the hell she was supposed to just move on from the most incredible, exhilarating, experience of her life, she asked, "And what about you, Ballentyne? What did you get out of last night's little escapade?'

His smile was strained, more a grimace. "I finally got to scratch an itch that's been irritating me for the longest time." Then he closed the door quietly against her.

. . .

Discordant white noise deafening her ears, Lowry allowed her knees to fold, then scooted to the floor when she realized she was kneeling on the bed where they'd...where she'd... where Jack had...

Stupid. Stupid. Stupid. She had no business feeling hurt. Mortified maybe, by her own shamelessly brazen behavior, but not hurt by Jack's body-slam of a rejection.

She should have known. Known that Jack would never stick. Not with her. Christ, he'd ditched his own family for damn near a decade to avoid feeling...anything. What the bloody hell had she expected?

It had just been sex. Admittedly hot, definitely raw. Indescribably sublime. But that's all it had been—sex. She'd used him to exorcise a small part of her past, and he'd used her, "to scratch an itch." They were both consenting adults. No big deal.

So why, damn it, did her heart feel like he'd plucked it from her chest, tossed it high, and shot it full of bullets? And why did she suddenly feel...?

Swinging on her heel, she scrambled to the bathroom.

Fifteen minutes later, an icy sweat still coating her skin and her stomach muscles on fire from the dry retching convulsions she'd feared would never stop, she yanked on the borrowed jeans and a pretty, jade-colored cashmere V-neck. Knees still not quite steady, she turned to face herself in the freestanding, full-length antique mirror standing in the corner of Jack's childhood bedroom.

Her breasts were fuller than his mother's. The hem of the jersey fell shy of the hip-hugging jeans, leaving an inch of her lower midriff exposed. *Bloody marvelous.* It was bad enough she could still feel the mild scratch of the beard rash he'd left behind, without having the evidence of the full and thorough exploration to which he'd subjected every inch of her body on open display.

Heaving free a resigned sigh, she lifted both hands and ruffled her hair, still damp from the shower she'd snatched. Hacked short, bangs uneven, nightmare black. Though the pink steaks were fading. Christ, small wonder Jack had beaten a hasty retreat. She looked ragged, oddly unfinished, damaged even. She hardly resembled one of the gorgeous, urbane sophisticates usually favored by Jack. Funny how, for the first time in her life, she actually gave a damn. Who knew that one little slip into vanity could possible hurt so much?

She threw her arms wide then let them flop to her sides. What the hell did it matter what she looked like? The bastard had made his indifference more than clear. Still hurt though, like a sharp blow to the sternum with the claw end of a hammer.

Suspecting any further delay would result in someone coming to find her, she cast a longing look at the window. She'd have climbed out on the sill and down the façade if the sheer distance of the flagstones far below hadn't unnerved her.

Returning her gaze to the mirror, she schooled her face into a nonchalant mask and prayed she'd be able to hold the mask in place. Jack wasn't going to enjoy hearing what she had to say, but then she wasn't exactly going to have a ball facing down his family—who had to be wondering what had driven Jack to bellow so loudly during the night—six bloody times!

Five minutes later, chin not as high as she would have wished, Lowry realized she should have followed her instincts and stayed hidden in his bedroom. The all-too-knowing looks she received from his brothers as she entered the dining room pricked at her skin.

A wave of heat swept through her, made its way to the surface, and refused to subside. She bit her lip and scuttled to a spare place at the table.

"Are you quite well, my dear? You looked terribly flushed."

Lowry slid into an empty chair and with a tight smile, assuring Jack's mother that she was fine, maybe just a little tired—which invited a less-than-discreet snort from Richard.

Lowry flung him her fiercest glare and was alarmed to see Jack doing the same. Great. A row. Just what she needed. Not.

She took a half-hearted bite of her toast and nearly choked as it caught in her throat, rough like sharp gravel, dry as dust. She saved herself with a swift gulp of coffee, instantly regretting it when heat scorched her taste buds. The start to her day had been an unmitigated disaster, and yet, she suspected, it was about to get a hundred times worse.

She was familiar enough with the feeling to recognize her own fear. Jack was not going to react well when he heard what she had to say.

That's why she'd decided to use this public forum rather than telling him in private. Even he wouldn't kill her in front of his parents. "Jack, I'm going back to London. I'm turning myself in. I've spoken with my father. He agrees it's probably for the best."

The sudden silence was deafening.

"Care to tell me how you contacted him?"

With studied care, she set her cup back on its saucer. Oh boy, that tone was all too familiar. How many times in the past had it reminded her of a bullet chambered, waiting for the percussion that would release it to create mayhem? "I still have the cell phone you gave me. Don't worry, I didn't tell him I was here, and yes, I flushed the SIM card."

"Smart move, though unnecessary. Richard's got this place wired so no calls, in or out, can be traced. What arrangements did you make?"

She ignored the chill that beckoned for her skin to abandon her, her focus more on the cadence of Jack's voice. Unnaturally calm. Too precisely measured. She'd expected him to erupt, his words to spew over her like molten tar. Instead, he was spitting ice shards. Never a good sign.

"I'm meeting him at Victoria railway station at three."

"Trains from near here go into Euston."

"I know. But I wanted him to think I was coming from the south, not the north." She'd lied to protect Jack and his family. It was the least she owed them.

"Quite the little secret agent, aren't you? I'm almost impressed. But I'm afraid your father's going to have a long wait. You're not going back. Not until I'm convinced it's safe for you to do so."

"That's not your decision to make, Jack," she warned. "It's mine. I'm done with hiding. I'm done with running."

His eyes lethal, he pulled at his lower lip. "You sure about that? Given your impeccable timing, I'd venture a guess you're running from what happened last night."

She realized her forefinger was beating an ungoverned rhythm on the table, fast and furious, jigging to a tune all of its own. She forced both her hands out of sight beneath the table and threaded her fingers tight. "Don't flatter yourself."

"I never do. Last night was a one off. You're not the first woman I've had to remind—"

"Jack!" His father accompanied his sharp verbal intervention by bringing down the flat of his hand on the table with a loud slap, making her jump. "Respect—you'd do well to learn a little. Lowry, what do you intend to do when you reach London?"

She raised her eyes to meet a piercing blue stare, like Jack's, less hardened but just as sharply intelligent. "I'm going to give a taped statement under oath. I can't guarantee anyone will believe what I have to say, but at least I will have tried. Then, when I'm cleared of Adrian's murder, I plan on getting as far away as possible from this hideousness, and any reminder of it. I'll disappear. I've done it before. Second time round should be even easier."

The older man nodded sagely. "Well, the first part seems eminently sensible to me. I have some well-placed contacts within the government. They might prove useful witnesses. I'll contact them if you like."

"The hell you will," Jack exploded. "You know she was raped, but you have no idea as to the power and reach of the man who did it. What she's proposing goes beyond a simple whistle-blowing event. It's an open declaration of war against some extremely dangerous men, only one of whom she can identify. They will retaliate. Violently and brutally. You'll be giving those contacts of yours each their own personal body bag…"

Her coffee cup became two and blurred before her eyes. *Oh my God, he'd told them, he'd bloody told them. They all knew about her sordid violation. She was sitting surrounded by his family, for Christ's sake. They had to be looking at her. Imagining. Not believing. Judging.*

Chapter Fourteen

"You told them, Ballentyne. You bloody told them. What happened to me was private. Intensely personal. How could you? Of all the mindless, heartless…"

The hoarseness of her voice, barely above a whisper, peeled back Jack's skin. He pushed his chair clear of the dining table, wood scraping against wood, ready to tackle Lowry with a full body check, should she try and bolt.

He couldn't disagree with a single one of the slurs she spat. He *was* cruel, brutal, pitiless, and all the other dark adjectives she stormed. Confirmation, as if he'd needed it, he was not the man for her.

Not the way he'd failed Richard—the guilt of which a flood of Noah's proportion could not wash away. Not the way he'd already failed her. His decisions, his actions, so fucked, they'd endangered her in a way that had gotten her raped and shot.

Rejecting her the way he had had been the right thing to

do. Tact would have been lost on her. Lowry only ever heard what she wanted to hear.

And he wasn't sorry for the rejection itself. She'd made him feel…well…things. Dangerous things with the power to weaken him. Like the weird deep inner peace that had lit the darkness inside him last night. Like the feeling of excruciating tenderness that had narrowed his throat, making it all but impossible for him to swallow. And fear. He'd do well not to forget the fear. A gut-wrenching fear that if anything happened to her, if he lost her, he'd lose himself. Christ, he'd never felt so fucking vulnerable.

Him, a hardened killer, for Christ's sake. Stained with the blood of evil men who were taking too bloody long to die by any natural means. That was his job, and change was not, and never would be, in the cards. Not for him.

But he had *not* breached her confidence about the rape.

"Jack's right," Richard said quietly, cutting the torturous hush that had fallen. "You can't go back while you're still wanted for Wainwright's murder. Forget getting within a hundred yards of the Cube, because you will be shot dead on sight. And, what's more, you'll take others with you—your father, Jack, his men—because they want the same thing that you do, Lowry. The truth *and* the traitors. And they'll lay down their lives for it."

A hand fixed around Jack's wrist, the long, narrow fingers squeezing. His mother, silently warning him to hold his tongue. To let Richard have the floor.

Tendons straining to the point he wasn't sure there would be sufficient elasticity left afterwards to hold his muscles in place, he yanked back on his anger. He'd concede for now, but one hint of further distress from Lowry and, wheelchair or not, he'd pin his twin to the ceiling.

"...And what will that achieve?" His brother continued in a flat tone, his facial expression hard and unforgiving. "A whole cluster of funerals for too many good men. You were an agent for long enough, Lowry, to learn rule number one: know your enemy, find his weak spot, and, only then, take him down. And, Marshall, not Jack, told me what had happened to you. *I* shared that with the family. They had a right to know. Just as we all have a right to know the name of the man who stupidly believed he could violate you and get away with it."

"Patient Peter Forsythe," Jack intervened quietly, sparing her from the lie of telling them she didn't know.

A different kind of silence descended, one of shocked disbelief, and broken only by the tick of the carriage clock on the mantelpiece.

"You have got to be kidding me," Richard eventually heaved with a strained laugh.

Lowry, her eyes wide with indecision and panic, had paled to the color of smoked ice. Jack shifted his eyes to her chest, needing to see movement, needing the reassurance she still breathed. "Take a look at her face, Richard. Think she's joking?"

His mother dug her nails into his wrist in fresh warning. She knew his temper well. If she wanted to avoid blood spill, she'd better hold on tight.

"Far from it." Richard protested. "But, damn it Jack, you should have called and told us who you were up against when you first found out. You're as bad as her. Keeping secrets. A counter attack needs to be put in place and fast. Oh, please, don't tell me the reason you haven't shared is because you plan to go up against that bastard on your own. No chance, bro. No. Bloody. Chance. We've only just got you back."

Jack ignored him. He kept his eyes fixed intently on the woman sitting opposite him, toast discarded, uneaten on the plate beside her, head bowed, her arms wrapped round her midriff. Those should be his arms holding her tight. Reassuring her. Begging her forgiveness because he'd screwed up. Taken what little trust she had in him and stomped on it.

He watched the one woman who had never taken any of his shit, who'd always stepped forward to meet his surliness, rather than stepping back like most others, slowly cave as she computed what Richard had to say. The blame she took all upon herself, draining away her earlier show of resolve. No. He would not stand by while she just gave up. Not again. "Lowry, you're right; it is your decision to make. If you want to return to London, I'll take you myself. My men can lock the area round the Cube down tight. Marshall can sit on Patient Peter, so we'll know if he makes a move."

"And the streets of London will run red with blood. Brilliant idea."

"Shut up, Richard, and stop being so bloody melodramatic. She could do without the guilt," Jack snapped. "She—"

"She," Lowry interrupted quietly, "will make her own damned mind up about what to do. What's your interest in the Service anyway, Richard? I thought you quit a long time ago."

"You're father brought me back in. Four years ago, shortly after you left—"

"I was dishonorably discharged," she reminded him dully.

"Whatever."

His hand curling in to fists, Jack promised himself that if his brother dared dismiss Lowry like that one more time, he wouldn't be responsible for his actions. She was hurting. Couldn't his brother see that? It was blatantly obvious to him.

"Your father approached me and asked me to establish a hush-hush electronic surveillance center, tasked specifically with monitoring any suspicious activity at the Cube. No one knew, not even Jack, who was working the case, just from a different angle."

He thought he'd kept his growl under his breath. Obviously not. Lowry shot him a perplexed scowl. "I think you might want to shut the fuck up about that, Richard."

Richard ignored him. "Jack believed you, Lowry. He trusted your instincts. Pity you didn't hang around long enough for him to prove it, and an even greater pity that I haven't been able to trace a single lead...until now."

Jack's heart damn near cracked at her brittle laugh

"So, why the hell didn't Jack tell *me*?" Lowry said. "I *would* have come forward, if I'd thought for a moment he—"

"He knew you'd already written him off, and he wanted you safe. Out of harm's way. He trusted you enough to look after yourself. It wasn't easy for him, Lowry."

Jack watched as indecision and bewilderment swept her face, then she nodded, her shoulders slumping. "And still, after all this time, Patient Peter's running free. Okay, so how do I help?"

"For a start, you accept that until your name is officially cleared, you remain in Jack's protective custody. Do anything stupid, and it reflects on him and your father. You'll stay here at the Hall, while Jack and I work on a plan."

Up came that little chin of hers. He recognized that look. Richard was about to find out why he referred to her as Lowry-*bloody*-Fisk.

"While *we* work on plan," she clarified. "Or I'm on the first train back to London, regardless. This is my fight. It always has been. I…I should have settled it years ago."

Jack had heard enough. She was fading again. Christ, he wished she'd stop flickering like a candle caught in a draught. He doubted his heart could take further strain. "*Our* fight. If you are in any doubt that I'm in this with you up to my neck, re-visit the newspapers. But arrangements can be made to get us out of here, Lowry, if you don't feel safe, and yes that 'us' does include me. Where you go, I go. No argument. I'm not letting you out of my sight until that bastard's neutralized— dead preferably. The least I owe you."

Head rising, she locked eyes with him, all signs of her earlier distress gone. "You cleared all outstanding debts last night, Jack. Trust me, the slate's wiped clean."

Had he not heard it for himself, he would never have believed she could sound so…disengaged.

Around him, throats cleared, silverware clumsily clinked against fine porcelain, bodies shuffled. He ignored the sounds of deep discomfort and pushed all thoughts but the duty to protect from his mind.

Peter Forsythe, for all his patience, must by now be writhing in frustration, making him more deadly, but also more open to making a mistake. The longer Lowry stayed beyond his grasp, the more desperate he would become, and the harder he would trip and fall.

Which suited Jack just fine. Once a man stumbled, there

was no guarantee of a recovery.

And he should know. Last night had proven it.

What the hell had he been thinking, taking Lowry to his bed?

Or, maybe that was the point. He hadn't been thinking at all. Not with his brain. What red-blooded man could? When faced with naked legs so long and exquisitely turned, his eyes had near gone blind with pleasure tracing their length. And breasts, like blushing apples ripe for the plucking. Not to mention feline eyes that whispered a come-hither, and a mouth so deliciously naughty, it promised a lifetime of hot and dirty.

But despite all that tempting physical promise, that's not what had felled him. He'd looked beyond the stunning window dressing to the bravery beneath. To the courage it had taken for her to give him her trust. The sweeter seduction.

Sonofabitch, but he wasn't supposed to feel like this. Open to guilt. Consumed by regret. Not to this extent. He never had before. Not even about Richard. Christ, he should have resisted. Damn straight he would in future. Or, at the very least, he'd die trying. Whatever she claimed, he still owed her.

"You want to tell me what those arrangements are, Jack, because if they don't suit, I'm going nowhere with you. I'm suddenly rather choosy about the company I keep."

Her tone made him want to reach for a fork with which to stab his own ear drums.

"And, I can't say I blame you, Lowry. Jack's not infallible, something he doesn't find easy to forgive in himself," said his mother. "And despite the many mistakes he's made, and even worse decisions, I've never before felt the need to apologize to anyone for my son's actions—until now. The way he disrespected you when you walked in this morning made me ashamed of him for the first time in my life."

Words no son wanted to hear from his mother.

It was akin to suffering instant anaphylactic shock. For the first time in his life, heat climbed his neck to settle on his cheeks. He glanced at the males sitting around the table in silence. All had their heads bowed as if fascinated by the blue and white design on their plates, even Richard who could normally be counted on to seize the moment and twist the knife.

Though it damn near snapped his neck doing so, Jack kept his own head upright. He owed eye contact to both the women his behavior had shamed. He wouldn't duck their condemnation.

"But if I know my son," his mother continued softly, raising her hand to still Lowry's interruption, "I very much doubt he's going to give you any say in the matter. He is every bit as arrogant, rude, and overbearing as you believe, and just as insensitive." She fixed Jack with a reprimanding glare before returning her gaze to Lowry.

"But, I fear once he makes his mind up about something, there is no deflecting him. A trait I'm afraid he gets from me. And I've decided that you will both stay here. I'll hear no further argument about it. Besides, no one will dare make another move on any member of my family. The furor I would cause would unseat the government and destroy the Intelligence Service. For good."

"You don't know Patient Peter. He really wouldn't care," Lowry mumbled, shooting Jack a desperate look to intervene.

"We are all aware of the risks, Lowry," the older woman continued softly, "but I don't see anyone heading for the door."

. . .

Knowing the repetitive action would put his younger brother on edge, Patient Peter repeatedly thumbed the trigger of his gold Mont Blanc pen with a double *click*, the nib darting in and out of the tip like a little tongue.

Walter. Walter. Walter. Oh, the things he'd like to do to the self-important, deluded grub. Should have erased the unwelcome smudge at birth—not that he hadn't tried a time or two. And not that he wouldn't have succeeded, but for father watching. Always watching. "Patience, Peter," he'd said with a special smile.

So he'd waited.

And on his twelfth birthday he'd received his reward. Father had shown him how to play. First with mummy dearest—she'd bled deliciously—then over the years with those other girls, younger, sweeter, their screams louder. Walter always in the corner looking on. Graduating from high chair to bar stool to knife of his own.

Poor father had been Walter's first very own toy. Seized without consent. Such an angry teen.

He continued to click the pen. God, how he wanted to stab it into Walter's eye. But who then would serve as his eyes and ears, his paymaster and pusher, within the Service?

"Walter, I believe I've got a plan," said Patient Peter, his thumb still busy. "I'm not prepared to expend further wit chasing that girl round the country. We need Lowry Fisk to come to us. Make sure her father has an accident. Nothing fatal, not just yet, but severe enough to hospitalize him. She'll come. She'll visit. And when she does…well, we'll have some fun. See to it."

"And Ballentyne?"

"I've already warned you, Walter. Leave him be. Poke a hornet's nest, and you'll get stung. Besides, it's not as if he's in any position to threaten us. Not after my little leak to the press. He's gone, and there's no way back for him now. I promised you I'd fix him, and I did. Now, go and arrange some hurt for the Commander. I want that girl here by the weekend."

Hmm, that was not a pleasant gleam in his brother's eye. For a moment there he'd almost looked…dangerous. Insubordinate. The nerve of the little shit. And after all he'd done for him.

. . .

Stir crazy did not begin to define how she felt. Four days into her confinement within the Hall—not trusting her, Jack had forbidden her on pain of death to dare venture into the gardens—and she was mentally pleading for Patient Peter to make his damned move.

After years of social withdrawal she found the Hall, vast as it was, too crowded. Jack's fault. She was never alone. He didn't trust her not to run, so she was watched. Every goddamn minute of the day.

Oh, Jack's brothers were sympathetic and discreet, their expressions at mealtimes oddly apologetic. But Jack had insisted she never be left on her own, and they were just following orders they dared not disobey. Not considering the mood Jack was in.

She'd pull a door closed, and it would mysteriously open to be left ajar.

Every four hours, she'd hear muted whispering. A changing of the guard, she suspected.

And she always knew when Jack was on duty. It was like being stalked by a thunder cloud ready to burst. He made no effort to soften his tread; he didn't care that she knew he was on rotation.

Once she'd paused too long at a window, mesmerized by the view of swans on the lake with the majesty of rolling hills beyond. He'd bawled her out. Loudly. Loud enough for those swans to take sudden flight.

God knows what his parents must have thought.

His sighs of exasperation and huffs of frustration whenever she chose to meander the endless corridors, exploring the Hall—as she'd been invited to do—dogged her every step. She'd walk for hours, the west wing, the east wing, floor by floor, then start over again.

And he'd follow.

She turned it into a game just to annoy him. When it was his turn to shadow her, she set out on her travels. Payback for him all but ignoring her. For being brooding and moody. Taciturn and snappish. Even Richard noticed and commented on Jack's blue funk when around her. "Take yourself off the rotation, bro, if you can't take the strain. We'll happily share your turns between us. We like following Lowry. She's gorgeous to look at, and she's got a great pair of legs, and a cute little behind…"

Jack had sworn. Richard had laughed. She'd pinked with embarrassment.

On day five, a consignment of paints, brushes, and blank canvases arrived.

"Jack's way of apologizing, I suspect, which has to be a first. He knows he's behaving like an ass," Seb said cheerfully as he deposited the last of the boxes in front of her. "Just don't expect to hear him admit it."

"Oh God, he must be out of his mind. Now they'll definitely know I'm here. Who else would Jack have ordered all this paraphernalia for? Stupid, stupid man. I have to get—"

Quick as light, obviously briefed by Jack, Seb slapped his hand round her wrist to stop her flight. "He'll have thought of that, taken appropriate measures. The last thing he'd do is put you at further risk."

"*Exitus acta probat*—the end justifies the means, motto of the Assassins, and Jack's the leader. He wants Patient Peter, Seb, badly enough to use me as bait if his patience is tested. This is him scenting a trail—right to me."

"Let go of her wrist, Seb. She's not overly fond of being touched."

She spun around to face Jack. Why couldn't he have stomped his presence the way he'd taken to doing these past few days?

"It occurred to me you'd be a lot less unpredictable if distracted," he snarled. "Painting seemed an obvious activity. And I'd never carelessly put you, or my family for that matter, in harm's way. Once was enough."

Hostility from Jack was nothing new, but even for him—hands fisted at his sides, his chest rising and falling at an unnatural speed from the sharp breathes he huffed—his reaction was over the top. Skin stretched tight, his expression stormy; she wondered what kind of infraction she had committed now. Then she noticed his eyes, not the vital, fierce blue she'd never get used to—never wanted to, if she was honest—because they represented excitement, life lived to the full, but flat, almost pained. Christ, but for knowing he had the feelings of rock, she'd almost suspect he was hurt.

"Leave, Seb, I'll take it from here," he ordered abruptly. His brother didn't protest. He didn't even hesitate. *Poof*, and he vanished.

Way to go, Jack, let common courtesy hang, keep pushing everyone away. "Try that brand of intimidation on me, Jack, and I promise I'll hit right back."

She bent and hefted up a carton of paints. Balancing the box in the crook of one arm, she flipped open the lid and stirred the silver tubes, each affixed with a neat label donating a different flash of wild color, with her forefinger.

"They the right kind?"

She looked up, surprised. Why should it matter to him? He'd never shown any interest in her art. She'd assumed he'd simply hit the Internet and randomly ordered whatever had shown on the screen. She examined the tubes of paint more closely. These were *her colors*, nothing dark or muted, all shockingly bright—the yellows, the greens, violent reds. And white, lots and lots of tubes of white. Brilliant white, without a tint, her favorite. "I couldn't have chosen better myself. Thank you," she said quietly, her voice a little wobbly.

"Nothing to it."

"Why do you do that, Jack? Abruptly push away? Don't forget, I *know* there are over seventy tints of white to choose from, yet you cared enough to select the right one. That's a good thing. Why hide it?"

For a moment she thought his head would explode. Then he exhaled, and striding past, he crossed to stare out the window, his body blocking the sunlight filtering into the room.

"Because I don't care. I can't afford to. Tried it once, and it three-quarters killed me when it all went wrong."

Well, that made about as much sense as a fish in a tutu. Then it hit her. "This about Richard, Jack?" she asked softly. "You push him away harder than you push me. A lesser man might be offended."

He snorted at that. "Richard's bulletproof when it comes to taking offense. Just a pity that invincibility couldn't protect him from broken bones and a pinched spinal cord... But I should have."

"What happened, Jack? What happened to Richard?" For a moment she didn't think he'd heard her. She hadn't spoken louder than a strained whisper.

Then he glanced over his shoulder. At her, daring her to look hard and see the very worst of him. "I happened."

Her throat constricted.

Jack crooked a tight, mirthless smile, as if he knew she was having difficulty swallowing. He returned to staring out the window, this time propping his forehead against one of the glass panes.

"Always gung-ho, always fiercely competitive, we were both on leave and keen to celebrate the successful completion of our latest mission. We argued good naturedly and with a lot of crude laughter about who had the better shot of one day taking command of the Assassins. Two hours later, tanked to the brim by the best part of a bottle of brandy each, we agreed it would be brotherly for one of us to step aside. But, which one of us? A challenge was in order, to separate the best from the *also ran*."

A terrible sense of foreboding skittered up her spine. She wanted to raise her hand, cover her ears and beg him to stop. Not just to avoid the awfulness she knew was coming but to still his voice. Empty. A lifeless monotone.

"It was my bright idea that we scale the face of the Hall. That the first man to the top would be deemed the winner. The loser would withdraw his future application for the command. Only, as usual, we tied. So, I suggested another race. This time, back down.

"Richard won. He fell the final thirty feet. Smack into the flagstones laid by our ancestors."

"Jesus, Jack. Jesus."

"No, sweetheart. He was absent that day."

She didn't hold the use of that endearment against him. She couldn't. This wasn't the Jack who'd promised never to use it. This was a man lost in a world of pain.

She didn't care that he wouldn't see the gesture. She shook her head. "Stupid. Reckless. But not your fault alone… Not the way you've been carrying the blame all these years. Richard doesn't hold you responsible. He knows he was there too, that he's just as culpable as you. Speak to him, Jack…stop pushing him away. Just speak to him."

He swung around, his breath-snatchingly handsome face, a tear of savagery. "And what the fucking hell good would that do? It's not like one 'sorry' from me, and up he'll stand and start walking again."

Steam replaced the blood in her veins. So much waste.

Too much waste. "No. But it might heal you."

Heart wrenched in two, her chest too tight from the pain of what both brothers had lost, she spun on her heel and quit the room.

Jack didn't follow.

An hour later, sitting on the edge of her bed, the box of paints Jack had bought her on her lap, she realized that she hated being alone. That she missed the presence of someone watching out for her.

A solid series of rapid thumps and Seb, pushing his head around the door he'd just opened, grinned at her. "Urgent message from Richard. He wants us all in the cellars now. He's got Marshall patched through. Any idea where I might find Jack? Richard wants him there, too."

Chapter Fifteen

Jack loved the cellars beneath the Hall. They were where he and his brothers had schemed and played. Where he'd first decided—age nine—to become a cop-spy-astronaut-fireman-rock star. Yes, he'd been overly ambitious, but two out of five suited him just fine.

And it had been years since he'd visited them.

Richard's fancy little subterranean operation put the high-tech facilities at the Cube to shame. Banks of computers lined each wall of the cavernous space. The muted whirl of electronic activity filled the underground area, which was backlit with unholy green light to reduce the glare of data streaming across the many screens.

It annoyed Jack that he hadn't known of this little operation's existence, but then there wasn't much that hadn't annoyed him these past few days. Especially Lowry, who'd taken to pretending he didn't exist.

In fact, she was annoying him now. Standing there in the

doorway, bottom lip tight between her teeth, clearly reluctant to enter the enclosed, windowless space. Steadfastly refusing to catch his eye.

Richard rolled his wheelchair aside to make room for Lowry at the main console. "Come on in, Lowry, Marshall's got something to tell you," his twin coaxed. "I'm switching to speaker mode, so we can all listen in."

She hesitated, her eyes darting nervously across the bank of screens, then stepped forward and crossed to stand beside Richard who, much to Jack's disgust, took her hand and dropped a kiss of encouragement on it. She didn't seem to mind. She even managed a weak smile.

Jack narrowed his eyes and folded his arms. He'd be having a word with his brother about that later. He and Lowry might not be on speaking terms, but Richard needn't think he was about to get away with taking advantage. Brothers had rules. You did not hit on another brother's woman. Not unless you wanted full-scale war.

"You're in the clear, Lowry. I've finally got irrefutable proof that you couldn't possibly have killed Wainwright," said Marshall, his voice echoing loudly from too-great amplification.

Richard leaned forward and flicked a few switches to adjust the volume.

"You got lucky. We found the disc drive from your surveillance camera during a random security check of the drains beneath the Cube. Water damage has compromised a lot of the detail, but from what the techies have managed to pull, you can't possibly have been the killer. You're too slight. The absence of drag marks on the floor, and no evidence of abrasion on Wainwright's heels, suggests he was carried.

A physical impossibility for a woman of your stature. And nor, to the best of my knowledge, do you possess a sick sonofabitch giggle that registers within the male vocal range. The warrant for your arrest has been lifted."

The high fiving and jubilant banter from his brothers had Lowry waving her arms for shush. "Can you run that past me again, Marshall? I'm not sure I heard you right."

Marshall did as asked. This time laying out every detail as to why she was no longer the prime suspect in the murder of her friend. He closed his account with, "By the way, Lowry, Will sends his love. He mentioned something about footing the bill of a wild spending spree in a lingerie boutique of your choice. On condition he gets to accompany you, and watch while you try on whatever you fancy. His words, not mine."

Her snort morphed into a giggle from which she appeared unable to recover. Tears, silver in the dim of the cellar, traced her cheeks. Happy tears.

Jack clenched his fists. Shit. He loved that giggle. Not sweet and shy, but cheeky. Naughty as all hell. The way his heart flipped in his chest was a little alarming, but not unpleasant. And the layer of tingly warmth lying just below the surface of his skin felt extraordinary. He could have done without the cockstand though, given what he would have to do—rob her of an all too rare moment of carefree frivolity—because he seemed to be the only one struck by the bloody obvious. That Lowry could now do what she'd told his father she would do once cleared of the murder. Up and vanish again, believing she'd be safe.

Only she wouldn't be.

Patient Peter would not stop until she'd been silenced.

Not even if successfully brought down and locked up for life. He'd want vengeance. And Christ alone knew the true length of that bastard's reach.

She could kick all she liked—and fuck, was she likely to kick—but he wasn't standing his protective custody down. He'd lock her up. Down here in the cellar, if he had to. She'd hate him. But at least she'd be safe.

Chest clamped in what felt like an ever narrowing vice, he waited for her to push her chair clear of the console and stand to accept the wide grins and warm hugs his brothers were all too ready to give her. She was more comfortable accepting displays of affection now—too damned comfortable, in his opinion.

Oxygen peculiarly sparse, he sucked in as deep a breath as he could find. "This proof of your innocence changes nothing, Lowry. As a known threat, Patient Peter is going to come at you hard. And God help anyone who stands in his way. *Now* you can be afraid. Fucking terrified. And not just for yourself. Family, friends—he's going to mow them all down to get to you." His words, sharp, abrupt, and deliberately cold, had all heads turning toward him in shock.

As dampeners went, his brutal observation was a killer, just as he'd intended. No way would he sanction her thinking she was safe. Not even with the Service now, discreetly, going after Patient Peter's ass. She wasn't the only one to have doubts about the integrity of the Service. He had them, too.

One look though, at her suddenly straightened lips, drawn so tight they'd tinted blue, and the sight of silent agony fleeting her eyes, and he crumbled like a wall built of sand and held together by spit alone.

He relaxed his fist, dragged a hand over the curve of his

chin, making a surreal mental note that he needed a shave. "That was unnecessary. I'm sorry. Neither Patient Peter nor any of his minions are going to get anywhere near you, Lowry. You, or anyone important to you. Blood oath."

The force of her anger as she approached and got in his face caused him to take a step back. She didn't say a word, just stared him down, before shoving past him, her elbow precisely targeted and timed, jabbing him deep in the ribs.

One foot braced on the first step of the flight of stairs leading to the floor above, she paused, and again caught him dead center in the crosshairs of her smoky-greens. "Get over yourself, Jack. It's not in your power to give me that guarantee. And if I thought for one moment that you were capable of regret or remorse, I'd accept your apology. But you're not."

She paused, stared at her feet. Her body shook with temper. No one intervened. No one dared. He sensed his brothers draw a collective breath. And hold it. His lungs were still seized from her jab to his ribs.

She blew out a series of little puffs, before continuing.

"You're right, Jack, you don't care. You're every bit the hard, driven, ruthless, clever bastard everyone says you are, but don't take that as a compliment. Others may revere your reputation. Personally, I find it tragic. You and Patient Peter? You may have chosen different paths to follow, but scratch beneath the surface, and the two of you are fundamentally the same. Both empty shells...dead on the inside."

He didn't much mind her insults. He deserved them— except the Patient Peter comparison, which he'd take up with her later. Her tears, though, horrified him. He'd made her cry, and not pretty little silver ones of joy.

He made a move toward her. To hold? To comfort? To shake? Hell, he didn't know. He just wanted her tears to stop.

"Not another step, Ballentyne," she warned, swiping at her cheeks. "And don't you dare follow me. Because I won't be answerable for my actions if you do."

Before he'd had time to blink, she'd dashed up the stairs and was out of sight. He listened to the muffled thud of her sprinting above. Only releasing his breath when he heard her mount the staircase to the upper floors. From the sounds of it, she was taking them two at a time. For a moment there, he'd feared she'd head for the front door.

"And to think I once envied you for your skill with women. Not such a lucky bugger now, are you, Jack. I wouldn't want to be in your shoes, not even when she calms down."

Jack glued his arms to his sides to stop from ripping his brother's head off. "Thanks for that, Gid. Just what I needed to hear." He snagged his brother's shoulder hard with his own as he moved past him to follow Lowry. To say what, when he caught up with her? He didn't have a clue.

Richard rolled forward to block his path. "She didn't mean it, Jack. What she said. She was upset. Frightened. Give her some time. And for God's sake, don't do anything stupid like going after Patient Peter on your own. She won't be impressed."

"I'm not looking to impress her. I just want her safe… and with me. Goddamnit."

It had been one thing to have that stray thought skirting elusively the darkened corners of his mind, quite another to hear himself admit it, out loud. And in front of witnesses. It felt like a trapdoor dropping away beneath his feet. Shocking, breath-thieving, heart-stopping. And terrifying. Because he couldn't tell when his fall would finally bottom out.

"Then tell her that, bro, or if you can't find the words, show her, because if you don't, you will lose her. And, though you're the most stubborn, hardest bastard I know, I doubt even you could survive that."

Jack looked at his twin. "That had better not be pity I can read in your eyes."

"It isn't. It's incredulity. For a supposedly intelligent man, you can be amazingly thick sometimes. She's more than halfway in love with you, Jack. Any idiot can see that. The question is, are you *brave* enough to see if you can take her all the way?"

He wasn't. Sure that is. About his ability to take her "all the way," but that poke at his courage hadn't sat well. Which is why, hours later, and wounded from the mental lashing he'd given himself, he now stood dithering outside her room, Richard's dig still ringing in his ears, and his hopes of resolving things with a woman it choked him to admit he might care about, slowly ebbing away.

He'd undertaken lethal missions in the past, faced down and lived shoulder to shoulder with the most brutal terrorist cells before rendering them stone dead, but his gut had never clamped this tight. He'd never tasted uncertainty and hesitated before. He'd never felt so damned exposed.

Sucking in a breath, he raised a knuckle, deliberately forgetting he'd planned a softly-softly approach, and rapped sharply on her door. He'd intended to wait for her permission to enter but…to hell with that. He wasn't about to give her any opportunity to send him away. He pushed through into her room, ditching the charm offensive he'd had planned. He'd used it on other women, and it had never failed. But Lowry wasn't "other women." She was…more. Besides which, it would only make her suspicious.

Lowry, her eyelids too worryingly tinged pink for his liking, unfolded herself from the bed and went to stand in front of the window. Just about as far away from him as she could get. "What do you want, Jack? If you're here to start another fight, then—"

He held up both hands, palms facing her. "How about a truce? No more fighting. I even have a peace offering for you."

Those impossibly long lashes of hers fluttered like a moth trapped. "Now I'm really scared," she confessed, her eyes darting to the door he'd left open. "What's going on?"

"Get some shoes on, and I'll show you."

She held herself absolutely rigid—not even breathing, as far as he could tell—while she took a moment to consider his offer.

The tank parked on his chest, dug deeper with its solid metal tread. A bead of sweat tricked between his shoulder blades.

"Okay, I admit I'm intrigued," she finally conceded, slipping her feet into a pair of sneakers. "Lead on."

A few minutes later, though his mind it felt like the passing of millennia, she paused long enough on the threshold of the French doors leading onto the terrace to throw him a questioning look.

He tried to shrug, but his damn shoulders had frozen. "Thought you'd appreciate a stroll in the Walled Garden, a chance to re-acquaint yourself with the great outdoors."

Her face lit up. "Seriously? On my own?"

Jesus, not yet one foot outside and he already faced disappointing her.

"No. Thought I'd tag along." Grimacing, he rubbed his lower sternum with the heel of his hand. Bet she'd given him an ulcer.

"For protection?"

She did not sound happy.

"Not exactly."

She did that rolly thing with her eyes. Once, way back when, it had triggered his temper faster than a lightning strike. Now, he found it oddly…cute. Cute? *Fuck.* Should have brought his gun. The way his mind was misfiring he might need to shoot himself. "Got a couple of things I need to say. Come on, we'll probably both find this easier if we walk."

They'd almost reached the farthest corner of the Walled Garden, the silence between them far from companionable, when she heaved a sigh deep enough to scatter the last of the evening songbirds into the dusk. "For someone with something to say, Jack, you're not exactly chatty."

"It's complicated, and no matter which way I try and shuffle the words, my brain flashes 'prize A-hole.'"

"Smart brain," she muttered.

"Smart mouth," he countered before he could stop himself. *Shit.* Some peace offering. He softened his tone. "Don't give me a hard time, Lowry. I'm following up on something Richard said, and it isn't easy."

"You spoken to him yet? You know what about."

He pursed his lips and shook his head. Disappointment number two.

The look she gave him suggested she fully endorsed

his brain's A-hole assessment. "I'm going back." She went to sidestep him. His arm shot out across her front, his hand coming to rest on her far hip.

She stared at his hand then raised her head, eyebrows arching.

"Please… Just hear me out."

The pressure against his arm didn't increase, but then nor did it lessen. Slowly, cautiously, he inched sideways until fully in front of her then, shoving his hands into the back pockets of his jeans, he took a step back. "Drives me crazy. The thought of you being in danger. Makes me say things and behave in ways of which I'm not exactly proud. Like ruining your moment when you'd just found out you were in the clear for Wainwright's murder. Like making damn sure you got kicked out of the Service, because I was so bloody pissed at you for putting me in a position of having to shoot you. That moment: me squeezing the trigger, watching you go down, my hands slick with your blood, your eyes dulling, your pulse barely flickering, it's on permanent loop up here." He tapped his temple. "Never stops. Same with Richard's fall. Two short clips of time that never leave me the fuck alone.

One corner of her bottom lip disappeared behind a nip of white ivories. He noticed her hand twitch as if to reach out, then fist tight at her side. Neither signals of uncertainty because her chin stayed high, but more a suppression, he guessed, of the urge to interrupt.

The tightness in his chest eased a little. She was giving him a chance.

"You survived six months of physical and mental annihilation on one of the toughest selection processes ever devised, Lowry, and there wasn't a commanding officer at the Cube who didn't respect the hell out of you for doing so. But that didn't mean a single one of us wanted you on their team. Not after the instructors had already flagged you as a handful."

Oh fuck, he recognized that scowl. He pushed on quickly before she could protest the label and they ended up in a fight.

"And you and I didn't exactly get off to the most auspicious start, remember? Still riding the glory of having survived basic training, and a bare couple of hours into your induction day at the Cube, you decide it's time to meet your new commanding officer. So you track me down to the male locker room, sashay in, slam your papers against my chest and, smile wide as the sky, proudly announce that your request to join the Assassins has been accepted. My very naked chest, I might add, given I was still toweling off after a shower, having just got back from a truly horrendous mission in Pakistan. I yelled at you to show a bit of respect. You yelled right back that I'd have to earn it first. Our first public fight. In front of six other commanding officers, all splitting their sides with hilarity."

Oh, she remembered. Her hand flew to her mouth, but not fast enough to cover a spurt of laughter. He was even less successful at hiding a reluctant grin. "Never had a recruit give me as much trouble as you did, Lowry. There I was, supposedly the hardest bastard in the Service, having rings run round me by a sexy as all hell subordinate who alternated between finding me either amusing or annoying."

"That's because you made me feel a little hysterical, Jack. You'd glower at me, even when I hadn't done anything wrong…but had I known it was because you found me sexy—"

He shook his head. "Don't go there, Lowry. Not when we both know that if I'd set aside the fact I was your superior officer, crooked my finger, and beckoned, you'd have been on my lap faster than a scorched cat."

Her lips pushed into a pout, her cheeks glowed a pretty pink. Both had an atrociously instant effect on his groin. "We're getting somewhat off topic here," he muttered, sobering, at the same time removing his hands from his back pockets to ease the tight strain of his jeans.

"And my sanity might just have survived you, Lowry, had you not started kicking over rocks and poking in dark places with a too-short stick. Yeah, you heard the laughter and suffered the ridicule of demanding answers to questions *no one* wanted to hear. But you were deaf, dumb, and blind to the anger and fear you were dredging up which, given the type of men you knew worked out of the Cube, was just plain stupid."

Oh. She did not like that. If he didn't rein it in, and fast, he'd balls this up and his apology wouldn't be worth shit.

In a pincer like movement, he squeezed the tip of his forefinger toward the tip of his thumb, the gap he left barely able to fit a cat's whisker. "You were this close to taking a beating, Lowry. But for my protection, and the reputation of the Assassins when I was in the field, woman or not, you'd have found yourself hauled down a dark alley and taught a lesson."

Eyes suddenly wide, her lips parted. A barely-there gasp escaped. No, she'd been unaware of the danger. Oblivious to the smoldering animosity, the raw resentment of increasingly scared men whose lives depended on trust, not wanting to look in the mirror she'd held high. Thank fuck he'd done something right during the months she'd gone through hell.

"You were protecting me?"

He rubbed his jaw with his fist. "Someone had to."

"So you believed my warnings that rot had set in at the Cube?"

He wouldn't lie to her. "No. Incensed, I went to your father and demanded an investigation to prove you were wrong. His response was to ground the Assassins in London indefinitely with the order that *I* look into the possibility of you being right."

She blinked. Slowly. "My father believed in me?"

She sounded so damn bewildered, so damn lost all of a sudden. Not trusting himself to find the right words, he just nodded.

Even nature held its breath in the long pause that followed. He resisted the urge to reach for her as she struggled to assimilate what he'd said, her fingers clenching and unclenching, her rib cage visibly going through an extreme work out. "One of you should have told me," she whispered hoarsely, then more strongly, several octaves higher. "It would have made a difference. Just to have known one goddamn person was on my side—" She slammed her fist into his chest. Followed it with the other.

The only way to stop the pummeling was to wrap her in his arms and hold her tight. "I'm sorry. So fucking sorry." Odd how easily those words rolled off his tongue once he dared voice them. Eyes closed, he kept up the litany while she sobbed against his chest, his mind reeling at how the hell they could have moved at whiplash speed from awkward silence to blunt truth, dangerous flirtation to fury and heartbreak, over the course of a bare fifteen minutes.

What he didn't time, because he didn't care to, not with the weightiness of his own heart threatening to crash through to his boots, was how long it took for her crying jag to slow into a series of little sniffs and hushed gulps. But when she did eventually quiet and he felt her settle more deeply against his chest, he relaxed his arms from around her and, taking her by the shoulders, gently eased her to arms length. "Not done with everything I've got to say yet, Lowry. You okay to go on, or do you want to head back?"

"Best get it over and done with," came a somewhat thick, muffled reply from behind the heavy curtain of hair. "But maybe we should make our way back at the same time."

He hated that she wouldn't look at him. He tightened one arm around her, tucking her close to his side, momentarily stunned that she fitted perfectly, and that holding her like this felt so damned right. "Has it ever occurred to you that I'm always at my worst when around you?"

"Yes," she answered with conviction, her head rising. "And it confirms I irritate you, exasperate you, make you want to reach for your gun and shoot me."

He grinned, relief flooding his veins that having been knocked down, she'd stood right back up. His kind of woman. "All true, but you left out disturb, frustrate, and drive insane. But the point I'm actually trying to make is that—"

"That you're not the callous bastard I accused you of being. That you understand fear and doubt, guilt and regret, though it would kill you to ever admit it? I'm sorry I said you reminded me of him—Patient Peter."

He pulled her to a stop. Turned her toward him and

waited for the sudden tension that held her stiff to ease. Then, he waited a bit longer. Until she was ready to raise her eyes to meet his own.

When she did, he continued. "Actually, I *am* every bit the brutal bastard you called me, especially when someone important to me is threatened. Now do you think you could shut up for a minute, so that I can finish what I need to say? This is the really hard part."

God, he loved it when she nipped at her bottom lip that way, only he preferred to be the one doing the nibbling. But not until he'd said what he had to say. "The point I am trying to make is that the feelings I have for you...ah...spook the hell out of me."

Her response wasn't instant, it wasn't even fast. She took her time to consider what he'd said. He resisted the urge to take a savage kick at the pea gravel beneath his boots. *Fuck, he had left it too late. Too late for what, he didn't have a clue. Something was there, he just couldn't get a hold on it.*

"Then I guess there's hope for you yet, Ballentyne."

Had she not given a soft husky laugh, he might have left it at that. Taken it slow and settled for just holding her in his arms. But that sound, tantalizingly wicked, invitingly naughty, put paid to the caution he'd promised to show. "Don't mock me, woman. I'd rather face down an army of raging Taliban fighters than have to make a declaration like that again."

This time he didn't wait for her follow through, he chose to drink in and swallow her laughter, his lips hitting hers. He'd only take a sip, he promised himself, then he'd step back and allow her to get her head around the fact that, if he cared for her, that could mean she'd never be free of him.

• • •

She had to admit, it was her fault things spun out of hand. He held back. She figured what the hell; it felt like she'd waited half a lifetime for this. A declaration from Jack that he felt something for her. Even if it "spooked" him.

So she pushed past his guard.

She poured her heart and the heat for which he had only himself to blame into the kiss. Sharing her hunger, letting *all* her barriers down. And, when that wasn't enough, she climbed his body, granite hard, strong, in no doubt that he'd hold her safe.

She looped her legs around his hips, lengthened her spine, buried her fingers into his hair, and tugged his head back. Then she used the advantage of that superior position to gift a second kiss, long and deep, giving and trusting and wanting. Wanting it all.

And, with a grunt, he did hold her tight. His stance widened, the pea gravel scraping beneath his boots. One large hand slid down to cup the curve of her rear, the other, with fingers splayed, firm at the back of her head.

She caressed him, her wet heat rubbing tight against his hardness, urgency whipping tender and slow into desperate gyration. His hands, all of a sudden under her skirt, his fingers slipped the hem of her panties, his thumb pressing, circling. Two fingers deep, deep in her wet heat, sliding, thrusting.

She tightening her thighs and threw back her head to extend the vulnerable length of her throat. Wanting him to suck, to mark her. White heat flared inside her…so close, so close, so—

He held her tight while she came down. Her body a ripple of aftershocks, not breathing—gasping.

From a distance she heard him order her—it was a command, a simple request would not have gotten through—to unclasp and drop her legs. Hands biting into her hips, he steadied her when her feet found the ground. Her sole consolation, through the daze misting her vision, was that his breathing was every bit as rapid as hers, and as jagged.

"Jack—?"

"That's Richard calling. We'd better go. Even he wouldn't dare disturb us unless it was critical. At least, it bloody well better be critical or I'll…"

Shaking his head, his fingers deftly re-fastened the buttons on her blouse that she hadn't even realized he'd undone.

Cheeks flaring like two beacons lighting the night, she raised her hands to help him.

He nudged them aside. "I'll do it. Your fingers are shaking too much."

She looked at his, watched them fumble over one stubborn fastening. "Yours are hardly rock-steady."

His laugh was low, but rich, smooth like hot honey. "We'll return to this later. I hate unfinished business. Hurts."

Then, he leaned close and whispered the filthiest suggestion she'd ever heard, about what he meant by *business* and what he meant by "to finish."

She clamped her thighs against the intimate rush of heat, the clench of her womb shocking her with a fast, mini-orgasm.

Jack grinned. She blushed.

"Later," he promised.

...

Though he did so surreptitiously, it did not escape her notice that when they quit the relative safety of the Walled Garden, he again maneuvered himself to take up position on her exposed side. He really couldn't help himself, she realized. He was as much a victim of his determination to protect as she'd been of her need to run. And though she never wanted to flee again, she knew *he'd* never change.

Her knees tangled. But for his sharp reflexes, she'd have stumbled into the one-armed, moss-covered stone statue of some ancient god.

The glow that had warmed her from the inside out stuttered and died. Goose bumps dimpled her skin. She rubbed her hands up and down her arms before folding them tight around her midriff. They didn't have a future. Not her and Jack. There'd never be a happily-ever-after for them. They were too different, their views on how to survive too divergent. She wanted peace and to hide from the ills of the world; he *needed* to attack.

If she tried to change him, it would hollow him out, and she'd lose him. If she allowed him to be what he must be, she'd lose him. Because he would go back to the Service in some capacity or another. He'd find a way to make it work. And she needed the Service, every taint, every blight of it, the hell out of her life. Too many bad memories. To forgive, she needed to forget.

"What's wrong?"

Numbness creeping her veins, she forced a smile, praying the darkness would disguise its lack of conviction.

"Nothing," she lied.

Richard was waiting impatiently for them on the terrace. He didn't bother sugaring his words as they approached. "It's your father, Lowry. I'm sorry. Despite the enhanced security around him, someone got to him."

She raised her hand to her throat and squeezed. *Patient Peter.*

"Lowry, did you hear what Richard said? Your father is going to be okay."

She was only dimly aware of Jack balling her shoulders with his rock-steady hands and giving her a gentle shake.

The giant fist that had punched through her chest found her heart and squeezed hard. Her father—always strong, unbreakable—was hurt, lying in pain, maybe even dying. Her fault.

Her father who didn't communicate. He didn't know how. But is his own silent way, he'd loved her. Back at that wreck of a factory, Marshall had said that learning about the rape had broken him. Richard has said her father believed her fears about corrupt manipulation within Service, and had set up a surveillance operation, a hugely expensive surveillance operation, because he'd trusted in her. Something Jack had confirmed.

That man, whose attention she'd fought for since childhood, *had* noticed. He'd heard her, he'd believed in her, and in his quiet, quiet way, he'd stood firm in her corner. She'd urged Jack into making amends, finding his peace with Richard. Could she stomach being that much of a hypocrite not to put her own ghosts to rest?

She shrugged away Jack's hands. She ignored the concern reflecting in his eyes—concern he wasn't supposed to know how to feel. She'd thought the same about her father and been wrong. Two men, men she loved, hurting because of her. She had to put that right. Starting with her father.

"I heard, Jack. My father's going to be okay. Sure, he's got a cracked sternum, fractured ribs, and he's currently hooked up to a monitor to ensure his heart keeps beating, but, hell, everything is going to be just fine. But, as I've already told you, you can't give me a lifetime guarantee. Not while Patient Peter is free to stride the corridors of Whitehall unchallenged."

Still out on the terrace, night closing in, she swung to confront Richard. "Have they arrested him? Made any attempt even to take Patient Peter into custody? Or are they all too fucking preoccupied putting in place a damage limitation strategy to protect the reputation of the Service?"

Chapter Sixteen

She caught the save-me look Richard shot Jack.

"Lowry—"

"Forget it, Jack," she said, holding up a hand to ward off his excuses for an administration so Machiavellian, *doing what's right* had been forgotten. "And don't even think about going after him on your own. Not for me. Not when you will stand unsupported, no official authority to cover your back. Promise me, Jack. Give me your word right now that you'll leave Patient Peter alone."

"I can't do that. Playing by the book isn't working. I—"

"Not ten minutes ago you were telling me how much you care for me," she yelled. "Goddamnit, you showed me with damn near everything your body had to give. I'm calling you on that, Jack. Promise me, promise me right now, you'll stay out of it." She sucked in a breath. "And while we're on the subject of the problem you seem to have with 'caring': Talk. To. Him." She stabbed a finger in Richard's direction.

The stone-clad look on his face was enough. He wouldn't be making any promises tonight. And he certainly wouldn't agree with her need to see her father.

Which left her no choice. She stepped past both men and retreated through the terrace doors. At least, she hoped they'd read it as a retreat. She bowed her head and slumped her shoulders to convince them. Both men had to believe in her defeat.

She felt no hand on her shoulder, heard no voice calling her back. Jack didn't follow her. She hadn't thought he would. Nor was she surprised when he didn't check on her later that night. In fact, she'd counted on it. Jack didn't make promises he couldn't keep, or explain his actions to anyone, so he'd avoid her. A mistake he'd just have to live with. Because she owed her father a visit. She owed him so much more. She owed her father some daughterly solace. He deserved to know she loved him. Too important a message for anyone to relay on her behalf. She'd be careful, though Jack would likely never forgive her, but she was London bound.

• • •

His feet locked to the flagstones of the terrace, Jack couldn't remember ever feeling this cold. Maybe the breeze drifting the terrace hadn't realized it was supposed to be spring. Or maybe, he'd just forgotten that up here in the Lake District, everything seemed more extreme. The beauty. The weather… Damn it, the drama.

"I'm not sure what that was all about, but I'm betting you couldn't do it? Lay yourself wide open and trust that she'd accept all that you are. Bet you fluffed your way through some half-assed declaration about 'maybe having some feelings.' Why, Jack? What the hell are you so afraid of?"

He turned to face his twin, his eyes fixing on the ever-accusatory wheelchair in which his brother was confined. "Do you really need to ask?"

"Fuck you, Jack." Richard thumped his fists on his nerve-deadened thighs. "This was not your fault. I *never* blamed you. Nor did the rest of the family. But you suck, nevertheless, because you denied any of us the chance to prove it. You were too damned busy shouldering a blame, the weight of which would have shamed Atlas. Damn near ten years of self-imposed exile. What the hell were you thinking?"

"That it should have been me." His bellow echoed against the facade of Hall, shocking them both.

Richard was the one to eventually break the frozen tableau. "*Could* have been, not should have been, Jack. We were equally drunk, equally determined, equally stupid. It was a *joint* decision. And I'll tell you straight, I'll take this chair over the misplaced guilt you've been carrying any day. I lost the use of my legs, but you, you lost yourself. Lowry was your way back, yet it looks like you screwed that up again. Why?"

Jack scoured his face with both hands. Time to come clean. "Self-protection. Found out the hard way that getting too close, caring too much, can result in a shit load of hurt. Not sure I'd survive if I have to go through it again."

"Never had you pegged as a coward," his brother said, shaking his head. "You know that old saying about no pain, no gain? Looking at you, seeing the man you've become, no, the *half man* you've become, I've got to figure it to be true. Love is supposed to hurt, Jack, how the hell else are you supposed to know it's real?"

Well…and didn't those quietly spoken words, from a man who had allowed nothing to diminish him, just shame the hell out of him.

· · ·

With her hair newly stripped back to its natural color, sandy blond with pale streaks of platinum, and wearing green scrubs she liberated from the hospital's laundry room, Lowry reckoned she made for a passable junior doctor.

She was here to make her peace.

The dark shadows smudged beneath her eyes, and the fact she was harried had to lend an authenticity to her disguise. So, too, the stethoscope she'd pinched and draped round her neck, and the pair of those weird white clogs with rubber soles favored by medics.

Head upright but avoiding all eye-contact, she did her best to look confident and purposeful as she traipsed the disinfectant-scented corridors of the sprawling hospital in search of the private wing where she'd find her father.

The harassed Ward Manager, thin lipped with a bloodless pallor, didn't deign to look up from her screen when she asked where she might find Harry Fisk. "Corner room, down there. Room 228."

Lowry frowned, anxiety quickening the flow of blood already gushing her veins fit to blow a geyser. Security around her father should not be this slack. He was a target, and Patient Peter and his minions were still out there.

As for the two guards posted at the doors to her father's room? Boredom appeared to have rendered them lifeless. Damn it, anyone could get to her father. Anyone. This security was piss-poor and tantamount to downright negligent.

Ducking her head, she pretended absorption in her clipboard and, muttering something incoherent about angina and blood tests, thrust into her father's room. She closed the door firmly behind her.

"Bloody incompetents," she breathed.

She waited for her anger to subside before approaching her father's bed. The monitor to which her father was attached beeped rhythmically.

Her breathing fell into step with the sharp little sound. Someone had dimmed the lights and closed the curtains. He seemed peaceful. Bruised, horribly swollen in places, with butterfly strips sealing the lacerations to his face, but peaceful.

Too peaceful.

In a rush of panic, she crossed the room and placed fingers that shook against her father's neck in search of a pulse.

His eyes flew open. She stepped back in fright, her heart fluttering uncontrollably. He shot a hand out to steady her. "Lowry? What are you doing here? And where the hell is Jack Ballentyne?"

"I don't know. I'm not his keeper, and neither is he mine." Relieved as she was that her father was alert, she couldn't stop the same old mutiny coloring her tone. It had always been the same. Her father automatically put her on the defense. His disapproval had been a constant in her life, and so too, her responding need to defy.

She tried to wrest her wrist free. Coming here had been a huge mistake. She should have listened to the reassurances that Richard had offered that her father, though his injuries were extensive, would be fine.

Her father's fingers tightened around her wrist. Such strength from hands upon which the skin looked paper-thin. "You need him with you, Lowry. It's not safe. For God's sake, what were you thinking?"

"That you might be relieved to see me—maybe even a little pleased." Christ, how many voices did she have inside her that she didn't recognize? This one was brittle as ancient bone.

Her father tugged her closer, close enough that she had to hitch her hip onto the edge of his bed. "Never, ever doubt I'm pleased to see you. But I'm also concerned. Patient Peter wants you. I trusted Jack Ballentyne to keep you safe. To keep you away."

Her father wheezed a weak cough.

She squeezed his hand lightly, trying to hide her mounting anxiety.

"He doesn't know. He'd never have let me come. And I had to. You and I, we've already wasted too much time. I needed to say I'm sorry and that I want to put that right, before it's too late."

"I thought it was already too late when I found out what had happened to you. That you hadn't felt able to come to me when you needed me most. I would have understood, you know, about the rape. I would have taken care of you, helped you, had you just given me the chance." There was nothing reprimanding in her father's tone, just a deep regret and sadness.

The lump in her throat thickened. "Not the easiest thing in the world to confide," she tried.

"And since when did you ever do easy?" her father asked gently.

She chanced a half smile. "True, and probably not since mum died. That's about the time you and I stopped connecting."

"Connecting yes, but I never stopped caring. I just didn't know how to show it. Still don't. You were a precocious six-year-old, but I should have tried harder. Found a way to reach you."

The marked pain adding a harsh breathlessness to her father's voice, thickened the lump riding her throat. "As I remember it, you did try. I was just…too angry to listen. With you, with mum for leaving me."

"Yes. And I'd never missed your mother more. Where you were concerned, I relied on her to steer me in the right direction. Suddenly she wasn't there to do so anymore. It was easier to bury myself in the job, as far as possible from the pain of knowing I was failing you."

"And the more you pretended I didn't exist, the harder I fought for your attention. I only joined the Service to get on your nerves. I wanted you to notice me, to be proud of me. Pathetic, really."

The grip of his fingers around her wrist tightened again. "There was never a day that passed when I wasn't proud of you. I still am. Fiercely so. But I will admit to an intense sense of relief when you followed a different path. Your art, Lowry. Now *that* would have made your mother very proud."

The lump in her throat morphed from a stone to a

boulder. She managed an embarrassed, "Oh."

"But you can't be here, Lowry. It isn't safe," her father said urgently.

"Maybe not, but this, what we're doing, talking—makes the risk worth it."

"Damn it, Lowry, I'm not about to lose you now. Get hold of Jack. He's the only man I trust to keep you safe."

The monitor bleeped alarmingly.

She raised her hands, placed them gently on her father's shoulders—a man she hadn't seen in four years, a man she hadn't touched or comforted in two decades or more—and eased him back against the pillows. "Dad, knowing Jack, he's already coming after me. Just get yourself well and back where you belong. Heading up the Service. I've a feeling Jack is going to need your support there in the not too distant future."

She waited for him to settle, whispering silly things about the good times they'd enjoyed when they'd still been a family. Before her mother had died. She waited until his eyelids grew heavy, finally closed, and his breathing steadied to the even rhythm of deep sleep.

She edged her hip from the bed, dropped a kiss on her father's brow. Yeah, having found this peace with her father, she *dared* Patient Peter to come after her.

She had been that bastard's victim long enough. Now she'd make her stand. Her skills might be rusty, but once she'd been good. With Jack's help she would match and return anything Patient Peter threw at her.

When she stepped into the corridor outside her father's darkened room, the harsh brightness blinded her for an instant.

That's why she didn't notice him until he fell into step beside her. "Hello, Lowry."

She kept her eyes dead ahead. "Jack."

"Want to tell me how you got out of the Hall without it being detected?"

Trust him to cut to the chase. "Not particularly. You'll only yell."

He held a door open for her, following through behind her as if they were two co-workers casually engaged in light chitchat and chivalry came easy to him.

A complete lie!

She could sense his anger strumming just below the surface.

"No, I won't. I'm so far past yelling, I've crossed six horizons. I am, however, curious to know how you managed to get passed Seb. He was adamant he didn't fall asleep."

"If he says he didn't, he didn't. But I bet you bawled him out anyway. You'll have to apologize to him."

They'd left another two corridors behind them and had just stepped into the late afternoon sun outside the hospital's main entrance before he spoke again.

"Even knowing what happened to Richard, you climbed down didn't you? Four *fucking* stories!"

She didn't think an answer was merited.

She paused at the head of the short flight of stairs leading to the sidewalk, closed her eyes, and tilted her head slightly to catch the sun. "Do me one last favor, Jack. Arrange for the security detail protecting my father to be replaced. This lot are hopeless. Next to useless."

"I'm still *persona non grata* with the Service, Lowry. Or had you forgotten?"

"No, I hadn't forgotten," she said softly. "But you have contacts, and you'll soon be back. Everyone knows that."

"Everyone might be wrong."

"Please, Jack, if you don't want to use the Service, give me the name of a private firm I can contact—a good one. The best."

She opened her eyes, turned her head, and looked up at him. Jack Ballentyne had been a huge force in her life, destructive in so many ways, and yet also oddly healing. He'd lent her a fearlessness she'd never again hoped to possess.

"Replacements are already on their way, Lowry. This lot will be stood down as soon as they arrive."

She smiled. "So you are back with the Service?"

He shrugged. "Either that, or those contacts you referred to came in handy."

"You're being deliberately evasive," she pushed.

Something almost uncivilized tightened his face. "Which, coming from you, I'll take as a compliment."

Exercising every ounce of restraint was costing him dearly, she suspected. If his lips narrowed any further, they'd disappear.

They were blocking the way. People navigated round them, some showing their displeasure by jostling as they brushed past. Lowry fired an apologetic smile at the exasperated doorman and continued down the short flight of steps. She took up a position that avoided the worst of the foot traffic.

"You may not have yelled earlier, but I can feel you building up to a rant now."

He wasn't listening. He wasn't even looking at her. His eyes were skimming the rooftops and frontages of the buildings opposite. Somehow, without her noticing, he'd nudged her deeper into the recess provided by the rise of the stairs and had angled his body so that he now stood between her and the rest of the world.

Apparently satisfied with his visual scan of the area, he turned to her, reached out, and smoothed away a stray lock of hair that had fallen across one of her eyes. "I'm glad you got rid of the black. I think I prefer you blond. And I'm not going to rant, I'm too fucking relieved to see you in one piece."

"Don't be nice to me, Jack. Because—"

"Because you're afraid. Well, so am I. I didn't ask for this," he waved his forefinger to and fro between them. "If I'd known how badly it could hurt, and what a jerk I'd be when trying to push the risk of any pain away, I'd have had Richard strangle me in the womb. But, I'm not going to run from it anymore, Lowry. And nor are you. I won't let you."

"Excuse me?" Jack could be obtuse at times, but he'd lost her at the finger waggle.

"Spoke to Richard. He's somewhat of an expert at calling a prick, a prick. That would be me. Should have told you when we were in the garden. Might even have done so, had that twin of mine not interrupted."

His eyes had flickered back to scanning the skyline; suddenly, he fixed them on her, staring intently. "I've a horrible feeling…" He paused, an almost desperate look on his face.

Fascinated, she watched his Adam's apple vibrate, then dip as he hauled in a deep breath.

"Actually, I've got a *great* feeling I'm…well…ah… shit… Okay, I'm in love with you. And yes, you best take that as a warning. I have it on good authority that I can be insufferable…at times. And never more so than when I allow my heart rather than my brain to dictate. And you, Lowry-bloody-Fisk, have been playing with my heart as if it was a yo-yo, for years."

Her heartbeat stuttered. Her breathing tightened. The noisy environment around her faded to mute. Jack might not easily speak the word "love" out loud, but he had made up his mind. Nothing would sway him now. Arguing with him would be like counting every grain of sand in the Sahara—not just pointless, but impossible.

He loved her.

He wasn't going to let her go. Unnaturally calm. Deceptively even. Precisely measured. She was all too familiar with that particular tone of him. The hesitation and awkward stumbling over words was new, though.

Not that it brought her any comfort. What was she supposed to do now? Yes she wanted him. With all her heart. But not his future. That she couldn't embrace. Not if it involved the Service. How to tell him that, without forcing him to choose?

Chapter Seventeen

Jack had barely crossed the threshold of the Commander's house when the horrific cat started on him. Hissing, spitting, arching its back. Had there been a gallon of water at hand, he might have been tempted to use it, but Lowry wouldn't have approved.

And he needed her on his side. Just long enough to find out what the bloody hell she had in mind. He'd promised himself he'd keep his temper in check, avoid confrontation and coax it out of her instead. So far he thought he'd done a pretty good job. Though, admittedly, he'd nearly lost it when she'd all but confirmed she'd scaled the facade of the Hall.

He'd made that descent himself, experienced the agonizing muscle spasms of clinging tight. That's why he'd laid into Seb. His mind had refused to compute what she'd done. She was right; he'd have to apologize to his brother — once he finished imagining the many punishments he wanted to bring down on this crazy woman he had no desire to live without.

He considered giving Claude the Cat, who was now nestling in his mistress's arms and purring up a storm, a stroke and swiftly rejected the idea. That would definitely be pushing it. He and the damned cat had a history, and it wasn't pretty.

Besides, it would mean getting close to Lowry, and he was finding it hard enough to keep his hands off her. Whether to strangle or to hold and kiss the living day lights out of her, he wasn't certain. But either way, it was as frustrating as hell. A feeling he suspected he'd have to get used to if things worked out for them as he intended.

But until then, he'd made himself another promise: No touching. No cajoling her with his body. He didn't doubt she'd respond. He'd been there each time she went up in flames. She hadn't been able to save herself. She was like a rampaging wild fire when he kissed her and, despite his asbestos shield against relinquishing control, he'd invariably joined her.

An abrupt double knock on the front door cut across his thoughts. Snapping his attention to Lowry, he lifted his eyebrows in silent query. Was she was expecting anyone?

When she shook her head, he gestured for her to retreat from the wide hall into the drawing room and, pointing a finger at her, whispered an order for her to stay out of sight.

He reached for his Sig. He didn't have to test its balance in his hand; it fell naturally into place. Home sweet home.

His body angled to the side, he flicked on the small screen beside the door, recognized the face, and cursed.

He couldn't stand John Smith, the Commander's personal attaché, but then the feeling was entirely mutual.

He was tempted to leave the man standing on the front doorstep, but if John Smith was sniffing around Lowry, he wanted to know why.

He released the heavy-duty door latch and stood aside to allow the man entry. He didn't re-holster his gun. He wanted the slimy bastard intimidated. The bruise he'd dealt to this man's jaw appeared to have healed. *Pity.* But sight of his gun would remind Smith not to fuck with him, because he wouldn't hesitate to put him on his ass again.

"What do you want, Smith?"

"Some papers the Commander left. I wasn't expecting anyone to be here."

He wanted to shove his fist into the man's mouth so he wouldn't have to listen to that obsequious voice. "So why knock?"

"Because it's good manners to do so. Polite."

Was that a pointed dig at his own lack of finesse? He grinned and let the insult slide. It was accurate enough.

"But I have keys, should I have needed them."

Smith jangled a set in his face as if he held the keys to the universe.

Jack's resolve to remain civil slipped. He hauled it back. Lowry was just next door. She wouldn't appreciate the violence.

Annnnnd, speak of the she-devil. As insubordinate as ever, Lowry stepped back into the hall. "What papers, John? My father never brings work home."

"How would you know, Ms. Fisk? It's been at least four years. Things change."

Jack wanted to rip the man's head off for talking to her like that, faultlessly polite, but with the edge of a sneer. He settled for releasing the safety on his weapon.

The *click* was warning enough. Smith stepped back, a bead of sweat swelling on his brow.

The man was a complete dick.

Never more grateful for his reputation of shooting first and *not* asking questions afterwards, Jack laughed.

Lowry fired a hot look of warning at him to behave. He did his best to look contrite. She sighed and shut her eyes for a beat, clearly unimpressed.

"You'd better come into the study. If my father brought papers home, they'll be in there," she said.

. . .

She had never liked John Smith. The way he looked at her made her flesh creep. But he was her father's trusted aide. She could hardly deny him access to the official papers he'd come to collect. She drew the line at playing hostess though. She'd offer no refreshments. The sooner the man retrieved what he'd come for and left, the better. Jack, she could sense, was itching to have a go at the man, and Smith had sufficient influence to make Jack's return to the Service problematic.

Her stomach clenched. She tried to thrust that thought aside. Jack's return to the Service was inevitable, and it would remain an insurmountable barrier between them. One she'd promised herself she wouldn't even try and scale. It wouldn't be fair. Not to him.

A desk job might kill him, but at least he'd have a purpose. He'd find a way to make it work. Leaving the Service just because she hated it would destroy him. What would he do as an alternative? She couldn't see him running the family estate. Exchanging his boots and sneakers for Wellingtons, his gun for a hoe.

So Jack would be the last thing the Service ever got from her for free. Her one unselfish act. Still hurt though; her heart felt as if it had been cleaved in two. God, she loved him. Enough not just to let him go, but to push him out the door, if that's what it took.

She folded her arms tight to dull the agony wrenching her chest and watched while Smith shuffled and sorted through the papers on her father's desk.

"You do realize that whilst you've been cleared of Wainwright's murder, Ms. Fisk, a statement from you is still required. It won't take long, and I could have Marshall ready to record it if you accompanied me back to the Cube. I imagine you want to put the whole unfortunate business behind you. It would certainly ease your father's mind to know that the investigation had been put to bed, at least, as far as your involvement is concerned."

She glanced at Jack. What Smith suggested made sense.

"She's not going anywhere. Not without me."

She glared at Jack, ready to argue the point on principle alone. Smith intervened before she had a chance.

"I don't believe that's your decision to make, Ballentyne. Besides, your clearance has yet to be reinstated. You won't even get into the Cube. I appreciate you have continuing concerns about Ms. Fisk's safety, but I went through the same rigorous training as you. I'm just as adept with a firearm. I also have a driver outside who is a fully trained operative. Jameson. You might know him? She'll be quite safe...Ms. Fisk?"

If he called her Ms. Fisk in that snide tone one more time,

she'd use Jack's gun to shoot Smith herself. Remembering she had a higher purpose, she sucked in a calming breath. "He's right, Jack. I need to file that statement."

"Then file it here. Smith can take it. I'll act as witness."

"Which would render whatever she has to say completely meaningless," Smith smirked. "You and her? Tongues always wagged, and the witness has to be impartial."

She shot her hand out to restrain Jack. The muscles of his chest rock hard and unforgiving beneath her palm.

"He's right about that too, Jack, and I'm not prepared to make the statement twice. With the questions they'll ask, once will be hard enough."

"That's right," Jack snarled, never once taking his eyes off Smith. "It's likely to get brutal, and they won't spare your feelings. You'll have to relive every minute of the rape down to the most intimate detail, which is why you need me with you."

She dropped her hand and took a pace back. She'd hoped to push him away in private, but she'd suffer an audience if it proved more effective. "No, Jack. I don't need you. Not now, not ever. Remember what you told me that morning? About things being a one-off, a never to be repeated experience? Well, you were right, and the last thing I need in my life is a man like you."

Smith smirked again.

She stepped forward to block Jack's path, her eyes never leaving his. "Don't, Ballentyne. I'll go hand-to-hand with you if I have to. I'll lose, but you're the one who will have to live with the fact you hurt me unnecessarily. And not even you are hard enough to get past that unscathed."

It took an age for his jaw to unclamp. She stood her

ground, but not easily.

"Don't make the mistake of underestimating me, Lowry, not where your safety is concerned." Jack shifted his stare, suddenly all dead and flat, to Smith. "Fine, she can go with you, but I'll call Marshall myself. I want her covered at all times, or I'll hold you personally responsible. And, Smith, believe me, I'm every bit as dangerous as people say. I presume the windows on your vehicle are bulletproof?"

"Naturally. It's the Commander's car. I've requisitioned it for a while," Smith said, pretending to admire his manicure.

She had to wonder what kind of man required a manicure when he spent his life behind a desk.

"I just bet you have," Jack growled. "But don't get too comfortable, Smith. The Commander's going to want it back."

"That may not be his call. One or two of his decisions of late have been called into question. Like rejecting your resignation in favor of a leave of absence."

This time she had to push hard against Jack's chest to prevent him from going after the man. "If we're going, Smith, we're going now," she insisted quickly. "I want to be back in time to visit with my father again this evening."

Her breath held so tight, razors slashed at her lungs, she quit her father's study without sparing Jack a glance. She needed him to take her dismissal as final. Releasing him was the hardest thing she'd ever done. Why the hell did love have to hurt so damned much?

Crossing the hallway, she checked to see that Smith was following. He was, and she couldn't suppress a shiver. The man made her skin crawl.

She'd reached the flagstones fronting her father's house

when Smith decided he needed the last word. "Watch your back, Major," he tossed back at a glowering Jack standing in the doorway. "You never know who's behind you. Friend or foe, ally or enemy."

The unnecessary taunt froze the blood in her veins and had spiders tap dancing the length of her spine.

Wasn't premonition a bitch?

. . .

Slumped deep in the cushions of the Commander's green silk sofa, his long legs stretched out, his ankles resting on a low, red-lacquered antique travelling chest that served as a coffee table, Jack was engaged in a staring contest with Claude the Cat when his cell vibrated. Without relinquishing eye contact, he dug into his pocket and worked free the device. "Ballentyne."

"Jack. Tell me she changed her mind. You've got Lowry with you, right?"

"Damn it, no, Marshall, she's supposed to be with you." He was on his feet and heading for the door before finishing his sentence.

"She hasn't arrived, Jack. Even allowing for traffic, she should have been here by now. Hang on a minute, a report's just coming in…"

The crack of his phone's casing warned him to relax the muscles in his hand. Smith was with Lowry. She'd be fine.

"…Jack, the tracking device in the Commander's car shows it as stationary about a mile from you. Bridge Street. Gunfire has been reported in the vicinity. Units are on their way. I'll send a car, a blue and white. The sirens will get you through the traffic."

"No. It'll be quicker on foot." He was already racing west, his feet eating sidewalk. At a full sprint, he could cover the distance faster than any damned car trying to negotiate traffic, sirens blaring or not. Shoving his phone into his pocket, he worked his elbows and legs.

What the hell had gone wrong? Gunshots? Lowry? He picked up his pace, screaming at pedestrians in his path to get the hell out the way. He vaulted a pedestrian barrier into the oncoming traffic. Slammed his hands down on the bonnet of a car that almost stood on its nose in an effort to avoid him. The driver hurled insults and gestured foully. Jack didn't attempt to pacify them. He didn't have time.

He hurled himself into the adjacent streams of traffic, multiple lanes. He dodged, skirted, leaped one vehicle's hood and rolled across another. He freed his gun, ready to blast the next obstacle daring to get in his way.

He arrived on scene at the same time as Marshall spilled from a car. The investigator yelled for the rapid-response unit to stand down, with a warning to them not to get in Jack's face, that one agent was already down—the driver, a bullet to the head—and that he didn't plan on losing anyone else.

Bent forward, his hands locked on his knees, Jack ignored the agony splitting his chest. If his lungs didn't fill soon, he'd pass out. "Find me an eye witness. I want a status report," he rasped.

"Already on it," Will replied. "But put your gun away, Jack. We've got enough petrified civilians as it is, and I've barely got the response team in check. With an agent down, they're on a knife edge."

Through willpower alone, his spasming lungs filled with air. "Just find me a fucking eye witness right now," he roared.

A few moments later, Marshall returned, hustling a rotund man in front of him. "Newspaper vendor. He saw the car-jack go down." He nodded to the man to relay what he'd seen to Jack.

"White van came out of nowhere, forced the Jag straight into the railings. Next thing, there's a man lying dead on the pavement, and the shooter's trying to bundle some girl and another bloke into the back of the van. Girl clipped him one though, with her foot. Looked like he hit her with the gun to knock her out. Nothing I could do. The shooter was firing madly into the air, no telling where he'd have aimed if challenged."

Tight lipped, he nodded his thanks to the newspaper vendor and turned away, his rage decamping abruptly. Calm took its place.

Tonight, that son of a bitch, Patient Peter, would die. No judge. No jury. No forgiveness. No mercy. That psychotic freak had a one-way ticket to hell, and Jack was going to punch it for him.

Marshall dropped a firm hand on his shoulder. He looked at it and then shook it free.

"Come on, Jack, from the sounds of it, Smith's with her. He's good. Better than good. He'll take care of her."

He grunted and dug his phone from his pocket. "He'd bloody better be, or he's going down, too."

The investigator didn't argue. Few did when he was in full execution mode. Wise men got the hell out of his way.

"Richard? Pick through every morsel you've got on Peter Forsythe. He's got to have a hidey-hole somewhere…

Then run the fucking program again, cross-reference every detail, his boxer size to his socks. And after that, run it again, and again, until you find something. The bastard's got Lowry. Call me back."

Jack had barely disconnected when a freight train smashed into his chest pounding him to the pavement.

He couldn't move. Pain lashed through his body, but it was nowhere close to the agony of knowing he was supposed to save Lowry, and he was letting her down. He let the pain crest, rode it for a moment, then seized it to devour its power. He struggled to rise to his feet, only dimly aware of the yells around him. He *would* harness that power. It would get him to Lowry.

He still hadn't relinquished the gun in his hand.

"Lie back down Jack; you've been tased." Marshall's voice.

"Who's responsible for this god-awful cock up?" Still Marshall. And he sounded livid. He vaguely computed the investigator tearing the leader of Unit B, Special Arms Division, a new one. The fact that something had finally shaken Nick Marshall's resolute calm made Jack grin. Or, he hoped he was grinning. Might have been a wussy wince. But at least he hadn't been shot. He could still get to Lowry. Damn it, he had to get to Lowry. If he could just get his body to bloody cooperate.

Chapter Eighteen

Clawing her way through darkness, thrusting shadows aside, Lowry tore and ripped her way toward full consciousness. Instinct demanded she open her eyes and scope her surroundings. She kept them firmly shut as she tried to piece together what had gone wrong.

Oh God. Patient Peter had come for her. In person. She recognized him at the same time she'd accepted she'd never stood a chance.

Cautiously, surreptitiously, she tested her muscles, her breath clamped tight in her throat against the possibility of searing pain. No pain, at least, nothing she couldn't handle. A few bruises wouldn't hold her back. She'd fight.

She tested her psyche. It was just about holding up, too, though she could taste the edge of panic at the back of her throat.

Jack's voice whispered through her mind recounting, as he'd done during her training, what she must do. Strangely, it calmed her, providing her with an anchor.

Pin down what happened. Assimilate as much information as you can. About your assailants, about your location. Stay calm, be ready to fight.

The lump on the back of her head throbbed. She vaguely remembered the car being plowed into, gunfire, yells, and screams. Fighting. Fighting for her life. Yelling for Smith to help her, as she was dragged toward a large van. A blow to the head, pain, then…nothing.

Lying on the steel floor of the van into which she'd been bundled, trying to brace herself not to roll under the momentum of the vehicle each time it hit a turn, she recognized the tang of sour sweat. Never a good thing. It suggested fear, and a panicking captor could be rash and violent. How many captors? Who was driving? Who was in the back with her? Because someone was. She could hear breathing and a soft, weak whistle. A tune, vaguely familiar, but which she couldn't quite place. The notes repeated, aimlessly, over and over and over. What was that damn tune? Who was making that sound? Not Smith, why would he be whistling? Someone else. Where was Smith? Was he dead or alive?

Her fear jumped. She could handle one man on her own, possibly two. But more?

She measured the odds.

Her entire left length was numb from lying on her side. The smell of oil and the unmistakable stink of blood, old and fetid, continued the assault on her nose. Nausea threatened, and her head ached, but otherwise she was fine. She could fight. Though it wouldn't be pretty.

She clung to Jack's voice. Ran through the close combat

moves he taught her. In her mind, she heard him yelling when she got it wrong. Heard him mocking when he'd put her on her back. Heard his order, his insistence that she learn to attack, because although defense might buy her time, it wouldn't save her life, nor anyone else's.

She sped through the chorography of kicks, grips, choke-holds, and blows he'd forced her to learn. He'd been a brutal teacher, and she was ready to use every one.

Her body bounced and jolted against the hard metal floor, the terrain suddenly uneven. The van was slowing. She kept her body limp, unresponsive when hands yanked on her ankles and dragged her toward the sudden burst of fresh air. She needed the advantage of surprise.

She readied to attack.

Didn't get the chance.

A plastic bag was dragged over her head and down across her face.

· · ·

Back at the Cube, Jack smoldered animosity. He knew none were brave enough to approach him. They'd give him a while. The bastards had used a specially adapted stun gun on him. One favored by the Service because it incapacitated for hours and hurt like a sonofabitch. It also left bruises the size of cartwheels, but in his case, at least his ribs were intact.

The leader of Bravo unit had protested that the order to zap Jack on sight had come down from HQ earlier that morning. And it had not been countermanded. Not to his knowledge.

Marshall had immediately stood the entire Bravo team

down and added the incident to his growing list of internal investigations to be pursued.

Too little, too late for Jack. By the time he'd recovered sufficiently to be able to walk unaided, the opportunity to pick up Lowry's trail had been lost. He was now totally reliant on his brother coming through with information about where Patient Peter might be found.

And the waiting was killing him.

Christ, if this is what it felt like to be stuck behind a desk rather than leading from the front, and if this is what the future held for him, he'd shoot himself.

But what about Lowry?

She'd likely blame herself, and he wouldn't be around to bully her into believing otherwise. Double Christ, he hoped she was hanging on. She had to know he was coming for her. She had to trust him that much. And if she had doubts? Well, he'd fucking spend the rest of his life proving he was worthy. He'd handcuff her to his side and lose the bloody key if that's what it took.

The alert put out on Patient Peter brought him little comfort. It had come too damned late. That was the problem with having to wait for proof and evidence: it caused unnecessary delays. He should have followed his own code. Act first, worry about the questions later. Patient Peter was now in hiding. And *goddamnit*, he had Lowry.

His cell phone slow-danced across the low coffee table in front of him. He snatched at it, his other hand rising to hold the bruising on his chest, which kicked like a mule in protest against his too sudden movement.

"Richard. What you got?"

"A private property on the outskirts of Henley registered

to a Mr. Alan Dawes who, oddly enough, doesn't appear to exist. No national insurance number, no nothing, and yet our Mr. Dawes is shown as having called Peter Forsythe's office on fourteen occasions in the last year alone."

"For fuck's sake, is that all you've got?"

"No, and you need to calm down. Forsythe's secretary remembers the calls because on each occasion he'd suddenly clear his diary and disappear for forty-eight hours. He expressly forbade her to contact him during that time. Jack, you should know the timeline fits for the abduction and brutal killings of several young women. God, I'm so goddamn sorry, Jack."

The tick from the clock on the wall filled the abrupt silence, each tock ratcheting the temperature of his blood to a hotter degree. "Just give me the address."

"12 Priory Walk. It's a private gated estate. It's a long shot, Jack. But it's all I've got...and I think you need to hurry. Those poor women—"

The pain in his chest forgotten, Jack disconnected and thrust to his feet. His bellow for Marshall rattled the windows.

"I need a motorbike now, and some extra clips for this." Jack waved his Sig in the investigator's face. "Got a lead, I'm going after her."

"You know I can't allow that."

He crossed to his friend, got right in his face. "I know you can't stop me. Every second counts."

"You need back up."

"Granted, so put out a call, but I'm not waiting. It's going to take you at least fifteen minutes to get clearance for an op and another ten on top of that to scramble a task force. I'll meet you there. 12 Priory Walk, Henley. Please, Marshall, I need to get to her. Right now."

Marshall stared at his shoes for a moment, his conflict obvious, then raised his head to meet his impatient glare. "Okay, Jack, but if this goes tits up, the Commander will kill me himself. You mate, will already be dead. The bike will be out front in three. I'll get you those clips."

. . .

She focused on her breathing. Each inhale and exhale had to be even and controlled. The bag they'd placed over her head had small perforations, but if she panicked and sucked in air too rapidly, the fine plastic collapsed across her mouth and nose, and she risked suffocation.

She may have lost an opportunity to strike back, hard and fast, but she would hang on tight. There'd be another. She had to believe that; it was all that was keeping her terror at bay.

Her wrists were bound, her ankles, too. She gave up battling the bitter chill gnawing on her skin. Let her teeth chatter. Let her body shake as if gripped by illness. Maybe it would put Patient Peter off.

When he'd tied her to the chair, his hands had brushed, his fingers had wandered, and for that trespass alone she'd kill him. To hell with legal process. Sometimes justice couldn't wait.

She heard bolts being thrown, the snick of a door opening, the hideous *rasp* as its foot scoured concrete— maybe tile.

"It's been too long a time, sweetheart, since you and I

last met, but I have never forgotten. Not you. Certainly not our delicious little interlude all those years ago."

She wasn't sure what was more terrifying. Not being able to see him because of the bag over her head, or the fact that any moment now, he might raise it, and she'd once again be forced to stare into his eyes.

"But you were a mistake, and I don't like mistakes."

The wave of nausea swelled in her stomach and threatened to overtake her. She clenched her muscles against it. She would show no weakness. No fear. She clamped her teeth together, sealed her lips. Nor would she respond.

The bag on her head was pulled up and free. Strands of her hair rose with it, caught in the static.

She blinked furiously, then let her eyes do the talking, her glare defiant. She punctuated her revulsion, her loathing, with an exclamation mark of disgust.

"Temper, temper, girlie. Though I confess it will be interesting to have you more responsive this time. In fact, it almost seems a shame to destroy that spirit. Are you ready for a repeat of the fun we shared, Lowry Fisk?'

She held herself stiff and swallowed the impulse to recoil when he traced his forefinger down her cheek. Which must have angered him, because he seized and squeezed her chin tight, twisting her lips.

"I wouldn't count on maintaining that stony silence, my dear. I wouldn't count on it at all. I *will* hear you whimper. I *will* see you weep. I *will* relish every scream, and I *will* make you beg."

Lowry willed his fingers to edge closer to her mouth. She wasn't unarmed. She had teeth. For a man who didn't make mistakes, he was remarkably careless. She clamped down hard on the fleshy part his palm with her teeth and closed her ears to his wild bellow.

The pain of him bunching his fingers into her hair and yanking her head back hard barely registered. She spat and started laughing. He'd think twice about touching her again. His lesson for the day: underestimate *me* at your peril.

Her cheek flamed, and her lip split under the open blow he dealt to her face. She was still laughing when a heavy thud to the side of her head ignited a starburst and then plummeted her into darkness.

• • •

Jack throttled back and held the bike to a more sedate hum. No need to alert anyone to his arrival. He coasted fifty yards more toward the shadow of a large copper birch, then hit the brakes.

He paused to assess the darkness before kicking at the bike's stand and dismounting. He unfastened the strap beneath his chin, lifted his helmet clear, and scoured the area once more.

He'd already rejected parlaying with the guard on the gate. No time. The fifteen-foot wall would be easy to breach. If the privacy and the security of the residents were so important, they should have insisted the perimeter of their exclusive existence be cleared of trees.

Dropping his helmet to the ground, he launched himself upward, his hands catching hold. He swung one leg up and over and hauled himself into a seating position astride the branch. Alternating toe and handholds, he edged higher. Gaining his balance, he walked the length of the thick bough stretching clear above the wall.

He dropped, his legs folding to absorb the impact as he hit the ground.

The pseudo-mansions had been built in a crescent line, sweeping drives to the front, sprawling lawns to the sides and rear. He'd go in though the back. Use the gardens for cover. All he had to do was count off eleven dwellings. Lowry, if she were here, would be in the twelfth.

He tossed a handful of gravel against the darkened window, hard enough to trigger the alarm if one was set. He'd work with chaos if necessary, though he'd prefer the element of deadly surprise.

The heavy silence stayed unbroken. No lights flicked on. Excellent.

He withdrew a tiny canister from his jacket pocket and sprayed the surface of the window, then jammed his elbow against it in a sudden short, sharp jab. Heard the crack.

The adhesive plastic held the pane in place. He peeled at a corner, drew the covering down, squares of the fractured glass clinging to its surface. He knocked free the few stubborn strays still embedded in the frame. Made a mental note to endorse the recently developed material for further use by the Service.

His spine folded, he fed himself backward through the window and dropped to a crouch. The silence didn't unnerve him; the eye-watering stench of disinfectant did. Damn, but someone had a heavy hand when it came to cleaning up. He crooked his arm, used his elbow to protect his nose and mouth.

It took him less than ten minutes to establish that the ground floor and two upper levels of the house were clear.

Were it not for the God-awful stink of cleaning product, the place would be a veritable show home, inhabitant-free.

But Lowry was here. No one made the hairs on the back of his neck twitch like her. No one had the ability to fire his instinct for potential danger quite like her. She had to be close.

He ran his fingers through his hair and forced himself to think, then checked his watch. Fifteen minutes, he estimated, before reinforcements arrived en masse, sirens blaring, lights flashing.

Panic would make Patient Peter unpredictable, doubly dangerous, and there'd be no negotiating with him.

He had to find Lowry fast.

Where the hell was she? Jack looked at his feet. If she wasn't up, then the only place she could be was down. Logical place for a cellar door—underneath the stairs.

He tried not to imagine why the hell anyone would completely tile a cellar—the walls, floors, and ceiling. Or why the space should have been converted to hold six stalls, each big enough to accommodate a metal autopsy table. Three brass-headed faucets projected from the wall opposite the sinister compartments, a hosepipe neatly coiled beside each. A dark outline of drains, black and ominous, like empty eye-sockets, pockmarked the floor. He suspected the forensic boys would have a field day.

With the fingertips of one hand tracing the surface chill of the tiles, Jack edged his way along the wall toward a door at the end of the walkway fronting the stalls.

No lock. He inched the door open. His heart kicked. His breathing grew more rapid. He clamped down on both. The sheerest slither of light sliced the foot of yet another door, an arm-length ahead. He prayed he'd find Lowry behind it. There was nowhere else to look.

No matter what sight assailed him, he was going in to negotiate. For the first time in his life he'd try diplomacy, beg if necessary. If it saved Lowry's life.

He tucked his gun away, crouched, and patted his calf to make sure his knife was secure. Dropped his hand lower to double check on the small holster strapped just above his ankle. He might have talked himself into a softly-softly approach, but he hadn't lost his mind completely.

He sucked in a deep breath, held it for a moment, and then expelled it. He raised his hand, curled a knuckle, gave a sharp rap, stepped back, and kicked the door with every ounce of power coiled in his hip.

It took just a nanosecond for his eyes to adapt to the light.

His heart stuttered. He couldn't silence the strangled groan lodged in his throat.

Lowry lay strapped to a double bed, her arms and legs splayed wide, one limb arrowed toward each corner. Someone had wrapped her in a kimono, the same misty-green color of her eyes. Embroidered crimson song birds rose from the hem and took flight toward her breasts. Jesus, but her breathing was shallow.

And she wasn't alone.

Patient Peter, obscene in a blue-striped, button-down shirt, red silk boxers, and black socks held up by a pair of those ridiculous sock-garters, reclined in a wing-chair, one leg crossed, his ankle balancing on a knee.

"Evening, Jack. Good of you to drop by. Walter will be beside himself with delight."

Chapter Nineteen

Patient Peter pointed his snub-nosed pistol not at Jack but at Lowry's head. "Now, start depositing your weapons, Ballentyne. Very, very carefully on the floor."

"Untie her first."

"Oh, I don't think so. She's drugged right now, but when she awakens, which might be any moment now, I'd prefer to avoid the risk of her lashing out." Patient Peter lifted his other hand and frowned at the pristine white bandage binding it. "It never ceases to amaze me how some woman react when I touch them."

Jack hid his revulsion, focusing instead on the rush of warmth as his awe for Lowry's courage hit new heights. This animal had once raped her, terrorized and disabled her, and yet she'd still fought back.

Her lip was split. An angry bruise, discolored and swollen, marred one side of her beautiful face. A spear of white-hot heat gutted him. The bastard had hit her. For that alone, he would die.

"Your weapons, Ballentyne. Don't make me ask you again."

Jack reached to the small of his back, removed his Sig, and slowly lowered it to the floor.

"Kick it over here."

He complied, and the gun spun across the tiles. He tracked its path. He might need it shortly. He also removed his cell phone, subtly setting it to record before sliding it across the floor.

"And the rest."

Jack eased down into a crouch. Not once did he lift his eyes from the pistol Patient Peter trained unwaveringly at Lowry. Not even when she gave a muted groan and tugged weakly against her bindings.

He lifted free his back-up gun, his knife too, and scooted them across the floor, each in a different direction. He noted exactly where each came to rest. If it came to a messy fight, he wanted to know exactly where his best friends were.

"Now kneel. Hands behind your head." Obedience was getting on his nerves, but Jack held himself in check. Were he alone with the deviant, he'd surge up and rain down violence on the bastard, gun or not. But he wouldn't risk Lowry's life just because his pride was offended.

But he would poke, provoke, and distract. Aggravate Patient Peter into launching an attack on him. "Have you any idea how sickeningly ridiculous you look, Forsythe? Those garters do absolutely nothing for your legs. Little wonder the ladies are unimpressed."

The pistol rose a smidgen. Fired. The bullet shattered one tile to smithereens and fractured its neighbors. Acoustically enhanced by the tight confines of the underground cell, the noise was so shocking, he had to glue his knees to the floor to stop from leaping up to shield Lowry's ears.

"Watch your mouth, Ballentyne. Next time it's her head."

Lowry moaned again. The shot must have roused her. "Jack?"

"You okay, sweetheart?" He dropped in the hated endearment to rile her, to remind her that the man with the gun had once called her that, too. Doing so had him wanting to rip out his own tongue. But he needed her furious. He'd even settle for scared, because when he freed her, he wanted her to run and keep running until she was safe.

He didn't want her watching or anywhere near when he took Patient Peter apart with his bare hands. If she were to witness that, she'd never look at him in the same way again.

And he didn't want her viewing him through blood-tinted glasses. God, his chest ached. What if he lost her? What if he never got the chance to convince her that he could be the man she deserved?

"She's fine…for now. Can't answer for how she will be feeling a few hours from now, though. With what's she's cost me, I deserve a little fun, a little entertainment. I like to play."

Jack looked at the man with absolute loathing. "You sick, sick fuck. Why do you do it? Or don't you even know?"

"Because I can. It's as simple as that. And you needn't look so disgusted. You and I, we're not so very different. Both killers and very good at what we do. Both playing a dangerous game, because if we're honest, we need the challenge. The rush it gives us. To feel alive."

"I am *nothing* like you."

"I hunt. I hurt. I kill. So do you. Where's the difference?"

"I don't kill innocents. I don't abuse women. I do what's right. By anyone's definition, you do everything wrong. And, I'm sure as hell not insane."

The vein that dissected Forsythe's temple filled with blood and started to throb violently.

The corners of Jack's lips tipped upward in a slight smile. He'd just found the freak's weakness. Patient Peter was vain. He didn't like it when his sense of superiority was attacked, when imperfection was implied. "You're broken, Forsythe, damaged beyond repair."

The man's laugh curdled his blood. "And yet, I still bested you. Tell me, how did it feel to have your picture in the paper? Was it fun? It sure gave me a kick. All it took was one press of the send button and…whoops, your life was over."

Lowry moaned again, her eyes fluttered open. He made sure to capture her dazed stare and gave the silent order for her to keep still. "Don't add underestimating me to the catalogue of mistakes you've already made, Forsythe."

"Mistakes? What mistakes? You're the one on his knees. She's the one tied up. I'm the man with the gun."

"Killing Wainwright wasn't smart. Nor was framing Lowry for it. And as for failing to dispose of that security tape properly…" Jack laced his laugh with ridicule.

"The security tape was no mistake of mine," Patient Peter rejected coldly. "And Wainwright served his purpose. His death scared the hell out of her, and besides, the pleasure his screams gave me—"

"You evil, psychotic bastard." Jack tensed at Lowry's furious interruption. She sounded ready to spring. Did she have to disobey his every order, even the unspoken ones?

"Tut, tut, tut, my sweet girl. Language. I'll be kissing that potty mouth of yours soon. Please bear that in mind."

The sudden glint in the man's eyes, the way the tip of his tongue shot out to moisten his lips, stoked Jack's revulsion. He had to get Forsythe's attention back on him and away from Lowry.

"Tell me about the other girls, Forsythe. You've done this before haven't you? Brought them here, tied them up, killed them. How many?"

"One or two. Okay, I admit I lie. Make that ten or eleven. Maybe more, lots more. As said, I like to play."

"But not on your own. You had help. Who?"

Patient Peter tapped the side of his nose and chuckled. "Now if I told you that, I'd have to kill you."

The man's laughter at his own wit near peeled the flesh from Jack's bones. Lowry struggled against her restraints. Jack fixed her with an anxious frown before returning his attention to Forsythe. "You mentioned a brother. What's his involvement in all this?"

"He likes to watch first and play later."

"So you two are close?"

Patient Peter made a rude noise. "Hate him, always have, but he had his uses."

"Who's *he*?"

"Oh you'll meet him soon enough, Ballentyne. I'm giving you to him as a reward for services rendered. He'll salivate at that. You actually know Walter rather well, though you know him better as—"

A sharp retort cracked the air.

Jack lunged sideways, rolling fast. He curled his fingers

round his knife and hurled it with deadly precision as two more thunderous shots rang out.

With Peter Forsythe down, he spun, ready to go hand-to-hand with whoever stood in the doorway behind him. And relaxed. "Smith, where the bloody hell were you?"

Not waiting for an answer, he crossed to Lowry and frantically started on her bindings. He wanted her out of here. Now. She seemed incapable of dragging her eyes away from Patient Peter, who lay slumped on the floor, three bullets to his chest and Jack's knife buried to the hilt straight through his heart.

"I was supposed to take him down, Jack. Me not you."

Her whisper wasn't intentional, he was damn sure. It was just all she could manage. "You wouldn't have been able to do it, Lowry." He tapped his two fingers against the left side of her sternum. "This would have stopped you from taking him down, even to save your own life. He didn't change you, because here, in your heart, your sense of due process is pure and too damned strong."

Her eyes flooded, and tears spilled down her cheeks. She buried her face into his chest. "For pity's sake, get me out of here, Jack, before he taints me from beyond the grave. I don't want to fight him and his evil anymore."

He slipped his arm beneath her legs and straightened. Holding her close. Knowing she was safe. This was as close to perfection as he'd ever got. And he was damned if he'd ever let her go. He just had to find a way to convince her to look beyond the temper and bloodstains to see him.

He cocked his head at the faint sound of sirens. "That'll be the reinforcements, Smith. Go be a hero again, and make sure they don't come in guns blazing."

Smith, his face grim, nodded, and then retreated.

Jack followed minutes later. When he entered the hall, Lowry still held tight in his arms, it was already crowded with men made larger by body armor. He snapped at them to put their damn weapons away. Lowry needed no reminder of the violence she'd witnessed.

"There's a drawing room at the end of the corridor. If you take her there, it will be quieter."

He frowned. How the fuck would Smith know that? He dismissed the niggle. If Smith had been able to free himself from wherever it was he'd been held, he'd have cased the joint in his search for Lowry.

· · ·

"Got it, Jack. Forsythe's confession. I take it you deliberately triggered the tape mode as a 'just in case.' I'm keeping your phone. It's evidence."

Jack slapped Marshall on the back and grinned. "It's all yours. But you should know that as a second 'just in case,' I forwarded through a copy to Richard. There's no telling what might happen once that phone disappears into the Cube."

Marshall nodded. "We will get the other rat bastards, Jack. The investigative broom has already started sweeping." He shifted his gaze to Lowry. "She all right?"

Jack glanced over to where Lowry sat huddled on an overstuffed crimson and white striped sofa. And he promptly swore a full spectrum of blues in his head. By now, she should have been packed in a private ambulance and on her way back to central London.

He'd argued with himself that his reason for keeping her at his side was sound. That he hadn't wanted her crossing paths with Forsythe's body when it was recovered from the cellar. He'd wanted to spare her that. But in truth, he hadn't been able to let her go. He was not yet ready to let her out of his sight. He wasn't sure he ever would be.

He looked down and was relieved to see his fingers were rock steady. The way his insides still quivered, he'd have expected his hands to be vibrating hard enough to power up half of London. "She's fine. I'm waiting for a car to take us both back to London. Shouldn't be long now. Is the…ah… clean-up completed?"

"Yeah, but you need to get her out of here, Jack. She's horribly pale."

"She's also got excellent hearing. And, Jack's right. I'm fine." Her voice was stronger. Jack felt his guilt recede. New sensation that—not the feeling of guilt itself, but acknowledging it. Oddly, he found it quite empowering. He doubted it would stop him doing what he had to do, but facing his own demons had to be easier than running from them—as long as Lowry had his back.

"The bruising to your face is fairly horrific, though admittedly you look kind of cute in Jack's jacket," said Marshall, flatly.

"Thanks for the 'fairly horrific' comment. I'll add it to the list of compliments I received from the medics who checked me out. And before you go and interrogate them, no I don't have a concussion, and the after-effects of the drug that bastard gave me are short lived and probably already out of my system."

"Told you she was fine," said Jack, dropping a hand onto

Marshall's shoulder.

Smith joined them. "Your lift is waiting, Marshall, and yours will be here in fifteen minutes, Jack. Was it really necessary to insist on a separate vehicle?"

. . .

Funny that for a man who had shared her ordeal, Smith was remarkably together. He had certainly gotten lucky in the bruising stakes. There wasn't a mark on him.

She creased her brow. God, even now, with Patient Peter dead, her mind was still clouded with suspicion. Jack had insisted good men worked for the Service too. She was inclined to agree. Her father, Jack, Marshall, Will, others she didn't know, but who were probably just as loyal.

But Patient Peter had rallied supporters. Bribing, enticing, blackmailing even. But who?

Her head throbbed; the familiar taste of panic soured the back of her throat. There had been another man in the van, the one who had whistled. Who was he? Where was he?

She shot an anxious glance at Jack, her blood chilling as he reached forward to shake hands with Smith—a man she knew he disliked profoundly.

"I owe you, Smith, for what you did for Lowry, for what you did for me. If ever you want to reconsider giving up that desk of yours for a return to the field, you'd be welcome to join The Assassins."

She pressed deeper into the soft clutch of the sofa cushions. She was being ridiculous. Despite what the medics had said, that drug she had been given was probably still flowing through her blood, making her paranoid. And who wouldn't be spooked and edgy after all she'd been through? Jack was a good judge of character; he had an innate ability to spot the good in men. It was almost as if he sought out and cultivated the very qualities he denied in himself—a respect for rank and order, empathy, compassion, the restraint that came from having a conscience, though he'd likely shoot her before admitting it.

She trusted Jack. If he felt confident enough to extend an open invitation for Smith to join his team—the highest accolade he could give—how irreparably damaged was she still to doubt? Fuck Patient Peter. Yes. Fuck. Him. Because even in death, he still tainted.

She expanded her lungs against the weight bearing down on her chest, the fierce sting behind her eyes, and adjusted Jack's leather biker jacket across her shoulders, pulling the lapels together. Its weight was comforting, and it carried his scent. She'd keep it as a reminder. A memento of what might have been.

Because, if nothing else, it was clear from what Jack had said to Smith that he would be returning to the Service and the life he loved. That he'd find a way to deal with a back row seat, somehow. And she was thrilled for him.

No, she bloody well wasn't! She hated the idea of him going back. Hated the idea of him settling for less than he needed to be. Hated that he'd even contemplate working for an organization that had let him down. But, for his sake, she'd pretend.

Lucky Service. They got to keep him. She'd lost him for good. He might be able to forgive the Service. She never would. It would always be a reminder of the deep trauma she'd been through.

When she looked up again, Smith was at the door, hovering on the threshold as if waiting for something. Jack, standing over beside the fireplace, was scowling at her as if she done something wrong.

"What?" she asked, her vocal cords straining to sound halfway normal.

"Smith said good-bye. You ignored him." That's because she'd been thinking of him. Jack. And steeling herself against the pain she knew would slam into her when she said good-bye.

"Oh. Sorry. Miles away." She shuffled onto her knees, ready to turn and apologize for her unintended lack of courtesy. A soft, thready sound froze her mid-movement. That whistle. Similar to the one in the van. No, not similar. Exactly the same. And that tune…something about two little boys having two little toys, wooden horses or something. Half thoughts collided then crashed into order. Smith: bruise free, his suit still immaculate. His fortuitous appearance. Just in time to shoot Patient Peter dead before he revealed the identity of his accomplice. And that mindless whistle.

She threw at desperate glance at Jack. He immediately straightened, his muscles going taut. Lousy timing, but she knew then he'd never question, never doubt her instincts again. "Smith," she mouthed silently.

His nod was barely perceptible.

She continued to turn around, not wanting Smith at her back. And found herself looking down the barrel of a gun, its appearance made more terrifying by the ugly fat silencer lengthening its end.

"Jack?" she croaked.

"Lowry. Don't move. What the fuck, Smith?"

The man stepped more fully into the room, reached backward, and closed the door. He kept the gun firmly pointed at Lowry, but spoke to Jack. "You know the procedure: lose the gun, the one at your back. The one on your left ankle, too. No need for me to ask for your knife, we both know where that is."

Her heartbeat lost rhythm as she watched Jack follow Smith's instructions. Marshall had left, so too the other reinforcements. She and Jack were on their own.

"Have I ever told you how much I loathe you, Ballentyne? Of course not. You never gave me the opportunity to do so. You rarely deigned to speak to me. In your eyes I was a lessor man because rather than run around waving a gun in the air, I chose to become a desk jockey."

"No, I didn't deign to speak to you because I didn't like you. Still don't."

She gaped. Was Jack crazy? Couldn't he just pretend nice? Just this once?

"And yet, you just invited me to join your team," Smith gloated.

"I never let how I feel get in the way of business. You impressed me earlier. You didn't hesitate to kill. The invitation has been withdrawn, by the way."

Smith smirked at that. "Why would I hesitate? I may not favor guns, but I'm damn handy with a knife. Had a lot of practice as it happens. A little hobby Peter and I shared."

"I labeled your brother a sick fuck. That goes double for you, Smith."

Drawing her brows together, she shot a pointed scowl at Jack. You did not push the enemy when he was the one holding the gun. She angled her body so that she was fully facing Smith, rather than straining to look at him over her shoulder. With the cushions of the sofa soft beneath her, kneeling was awkward, but if she had to, she could spring up and leap the distance to Smith. The force of her body hitting him might give Jack time to retaliate.

"Don't be stupid, Lowry. You're so easy to read. Attack and you die. Now get over here, and no sudden moves, because I will shoot you dead."

"There are still men out the front, Smith," Jack reminded him softly. "That silencer is not going to deaden the noise if you fire. Not completely."

"Oh, I wouldn't worry about them. They're a couple of Peter's players. I recruited them for him, and now with him gone, they'll take their instructions from me. The Service really needs to pay better if they want to ensure loyalty. I gave you an order, Lowry, so get over here."

Her knees buckled a little as she moved to comply. From kneeling, she assured herself as she forced down the fear.

"What did Peter do to you to make you hate him so much, Smith? Steal your toys? Rip the head off your favorite teddy?" Jack asked, his voice now soft. Deadly.

God, she wished Jack would just shut up and stop riling the man. Once she was close enough, *she'd* make a move.

"Not my teddy, our mother. Does that count? I think I was about three at the time. But her passing was a bedtime story Peter liked to tell over and over and over. Paid Father back for his part in her mutilation when I could. Peter's turn was always going to come. For that, and for finding it so damned amusing."

"No one laughing now, John. I can't imagine what you went through with Patient Peter for a brother. The man was sick. A sadistic bully. But this isn't going to help." She wasn't sure talking kindly would help, but she was ready to try every option.

"Do you recall the last time you called me John, Lowry? I asked you to have dinner with me. You declined in the same pitying voice you're using now." He reached out, grabbed her hair, yanked her close against him, his arm fixing across her throat.

Through the mist of pain, she heard Jack growl and felt the cold of the gun barrel cut deeper into her cheek.

"Back off, Ballentyne. Or she's dead on the ground before you get to take another step."

Chapter Twenty

"You won't get away with this, Smith."

"Yes, I will. If nothing else, I'm a meticulous planner. I kill the girl; I kill you. I pin the blame on the two men out there. Of course, they'll have to die, too. I'll say there was a firefight, that I did my best to avert the tragedy. I'm already the hero of the night, thanks to you. I'm as good as home free."

Lowry tried to suppress the shudder. She'd never have thought it possible for a male to giggle like that. Smith must have felt her revulsion, because he tightened his grip.

"Marshall will come after you," Jack disagreed. "He'll turn your story inside out. He knows Patient Peter had an accomplice. It's all on tape. I recorded everything your brother had to say on my phone."

"Yes, but then he'll be looking for Walter Forsythe. Who, thanks to my father, is officially recorded as having died over thirty years ago, alongside Jenny Forsythe, much beloved mother and wife. A tragic boating accident, the bodies were never recovered. To be fair, the real John Smith is dead too…or was until he was resurrected through me. My father was always uncannily good with records and paperwork."

She tried to shut her mind to yet another peel of horrendous giggles. So damaged, so unnatural. So goddamn frightening.

"So Marshall can dig all he likes. Eventually, Walter will be dismissed as just a figment of Patient Peter's crazed imagination," Smith continued. "Something you'll no doubt find amusing, Lowry, having been in a similar situation yourself."

She hoped Jack was ready. She wouldn't get another chance. From the distant wistfulness in his tone, Smith appeared to be momentarily distracted in his own glee.

She pulled her elbow forward and then drove it back deep into the man's ribs, at the same time curling her left leg around his to knock him off balance.

He lost his footing. Her body cushioned his fall, his weight driving the air from her lungs as he pinned her to the floor.

Not quite what she'd planned.

Her surprise body blow to Smith had caused him to discharge his gun, the stray bullet taking out the central chandelier and shorting out the wall sconces in the room.

She gulped in a breath as the suffocating weight lifted. Heard Jack roar at her to get the phone. "On the desk to the right of the fireplace. Call the Cube's special alert line; the number hasn't changed…leave it off the hook…then get out the window. Run."

She heard a grunt, a groan, the sound of someone hitting

the floor, then flesh on flesh contact. Hard. Brutal. Intended to maim, if not kill.

On her hands and knees, she scrabbled through the darkness. More grunts. More gasps. Furniture falling, ornaments smashing, and the sickening sound of fists driving into flesh and bone.

Her fingers brushed cold metal, the dark shape sinister. Jack's gun. She fisted it, continued her crawl, ignoring the sting of carpet burn to her knuckles.

Her fingers stubbed against the resistance of cool marble. The fireplace.

Relief warred with urgency. She squinted against the dark. Saw the shadowy outline of what looked like a desk. She scooted forward, throat so tight, air had difficulty passing through.

Gunshots.

Panic threatened to empty her stomach.

Oh God, Jack. Let him be all right. He was tough, trained for this. Expert in hand-to-hand combat. Deadly... So, was Smith. But neither was invincible against a bullet. Please not Jack, please not Jack...

...*Please not Jack*. The refrain tore her mind apart, an unrelenting echo that refused to silence and die.

She crawled faster, sprawled as her arms collapsed, pushed back up, scrambled forward, yanked on a trailing cord. The body of the phone made a dull thud as it hit the carpet. She patted the floor blindly, wildly, to locate the fallen instrument.

Found it, turned it upright.

She dragged her fingers across the surface of the unfamiliar keypad, roughly positioned the buttons in her mind and rapidly jabbed out the special alert number that would connect her to emergency operations at the Cube. She had no need to wait for the pick-up. Use of the number would immediately activate a trace, and a task force would be dispatched.

The door flew open, and light spilled in from the hall beyond. A looming hulk of a figure stood in silhouette, gun extended.

Too soon for help.

Lowry didn't hesitate. She had no idea if Jack was down. But the thuds, thumps, scuffling, and foul language of him and Smith fighting had ceased.

The silence terrified her.

Without thought, she brought up her arm, curled her finger round the trigger and fired. And fired again. Again and again.

The figure curled and slumped to the floor. She was dimly aware of someone screaming. She wanted to yell at them to shut the hell up. She needed to get the hideous sound out of her head.

More shots. Not from her.

The screaming wouldn't stop. *Dear God, it was her.*

She staggered to her feet, felt the sting of hot lead plow her shoulder, the force of the bullet's impact spinning her. She fell.

Her head connected with the marble fireplace.

It hurt to breathe. No, she couldn't breathe. She rolled onto her back to relieve the pressure on her chest. Found herself staring into the smoldering eyes of John Smith. They should have been wild, insane. Instead, they were empty.

He raised his hand, leveling the barrel of the pistol dead

center with the bridge of her nose. "Good-bye, bitch."

Her final thoughts were of Jack. She should have told him. Told him she loved him. That she'd never regretted doing so.

Silly thoughts. Wasted thoughts.

More gunfire. So much gunfire. She could taste cordite in the air.

She rolled onto her side, drew up her knees to her chest.

Someone was tugging at her, trying to stretch her out. She didn't have the strength to flap them away, so she curled tight into her own little ball and welcomed the darkness.

• • •

It was at her insistence that the medics reluctantly discharged her from the hospital after a fortnight. The bullet wound to her shoulder hadn't been life threatening, but the loss of blood had been. She'd needed transfusions. Jack's men hadn't hesitated.

Jack, she'd been told, had not been as lucky. He'd taken two bullets to the chest, one collapsing a lung. But even in that terribly injured state, when most men would not have been able to move, he'd found the strength to take Smith down, firing round after round into the man until convinced he was dead.

And when the second wave of rescuers had come to their aid, he'd held them at gunpoint, not letting them near her, until Marshall had arrived and personally vouched for each of the men.

He'd faced weeks of medical care, apparently swearing his way through his enforced rehabilitation, and was now back with the Service. She hadn't inquired too closely into what he was doing.

No one had understood her refusal to see him. They failed to understand her refusal to discuss him. And she didn't share with them that it just hurt too damned much to do so. Even now, weeks and weeks later, the pain was constant, a dull gnaw, deep within her, but she was learning to live with it. Sort of. Eventually her appetite would return.

She slipped her right shoulder free from the silk of her robe to examine the scar on her shoulder in the mirror and sighed a gale. The angry, puckered redness had finally paled. Now she had two visible scars as a mark of her past. How lucky could a girl get?

A knock sounded on her bedroom door. She hastily drew the silk back up over her shoulder. She'd built a damned fine façade against the world to prove she'd recovered, that she was in no way tormented by thoughts of Jack. She wasn't about to let anyone guess the truth. That she was falling apart on the inside.

"Come in."

"Morning, Lowry, found this on the doormat. It's addressed to you. Must have arrived sometime during the night."

She smiled at her father. Though still in pain, he was back where he belonged and happier for it. Back with the Service, like Jack. She seemed to be the only one still cut adrift.

She forced that thought from her mind. She'd shoot herself before she surrendered to self-pity. She still had her painting—or would have when she dredged up sufficient energy to consider picking up a brush—and the bridge between her father and her was getting stronger each day.

She frowned at the envelope in her hand. No stamp. No address, just her name. Typed.

She pulled a face, then slid the tip of her finger beneath the fold and jagged an uneven opening across the top. The leaf of paper inside was heavy. Expensive. The color of clotted cream.

Intrigued, she unfolded the document.

Got your cat — not sorry!

No signature, but Jack's handwriting. Strong. Bold. Unmistakable. Naturally, the arrogant bastard would assume she'd recognize his script and it irked that he was right.

Her vision narrowed. She'd sacrificed her heart for that damned man, and this was how he repaid her? By playing stupid games? "Where is he, Dad?"

"Harrick Hall. Want to commandeer my car? You know I'll cover for you if you're caught speeding."

"That cover extend to murder? Because that's exactly what I'm going to commit when I get my hands on him."

. . .

When she arrived at the Hall, tired and agitated, it was Richard who informed her that with the rewiring complete, Jack had holed-up in the west wing, and that's where she'd find him.

He snagged her wrist, his eyes dancing with amusement, as she moved past him. "You're not armed are you? Because you look kind of dangerous."

"Do I? Good. But no, I'm not carrying a gun. I'm angry

enough not to need one."

The quickest route to the west wing was to cut along the terrace. Not once did she let her eyes drift upwards. She had no wish to measure the height from which she could have fallen when scaling down the façade of the Hall.

It didn't take her long to find the bane of her bloody life. She stormed through the open French doors, marched the long length of the drawing room, her footsteps echoing around the emptiness of the sparsely furnished room that was still raw-plaster naked.

Hands on hips, her chest rising and falling with pent-up aggression, she parked herself in front of the television, deliberately blocking his view.

"I've come for my cat."

"Hoped you might."

Jack lay sprawled on the floor, his shoulders hitched low against the sofa. Discarded newspapers lay littered around him as if cast aside in impatience, and three of the family wolfhounds, looking decidedly hangdog, lounged beside him.

She was loath to admit it, but he looked criminally sexy. Barefoot. Faded jeans torn at one knee, and a very faded green T-shirt she vaguely remembered. He also looked pained and uncomfortable. Maybe his chest was bothering him.

"Why are you on the floor?"

"Because that damned cat of yours has staked a claim on the sofa and refuses to share. The dogs are terrified of him, and so am I."

She slow blinked at him. "He's not on there now."

"No, but we make so much as a move on those cushions,

he'll be back, and if he catches us, there will be hell to pay."

She notices the scratches on his arms and grimaced. "I'm surprised you haven't shot him."

"Oh believe me, I've thought about it. A lot. But being a reasonable man, I've decided if it keeps you happy, it would be better to let that vicious fur ball live here."

Reasonable? Hah, the man was insane—delectable, but insane. She licked her lips, saw that Jack appeared fascinated by her involuntary signal, and screwed her eyes tight shut. "He's not living with you, Jack. He's mine, and I want him back."

"You're welcome to him. But he's my hostage and will be living here at the Hall."

Her incredulity spiked. Her eyes flew open. "What is it you want, Jack? And what kind of a man steals a cat?"

"You. And a desperate one."

He might appear calm, nonchalant even, but she recognized that glint in his eye. The smoldering anger and frustration he was trying, and failing, to hide. Whatever the hell it was he wanted, he wasn't going to stop until he got it.

She dropped to her haunches, ducked her head to her knees—that's what people did who felt light headed, right?

"You okay?"

She shot him a filthy look. "Not really. I feel like I've crossed into some parallel universe where nothing is what it seems, and nothing makes sense."

"Know the feeling," he said dryly and then his tone turned flirtatious "I'm happy to play doctors and nurses if it'll make you feel better."

She shook her head. "I can't believe you just said something that asinine."

"Frankly, nor can I. But I'm prepared to make an idiot of myself to get some answers."

Faster than she could track it, his foot shot out and did something relatively painless to her knee that threw her off balance. He caught her before she hit the floor and deposited her beside him, one arm banding her tight.

He grinned at her abject indignation and shrugged his shoulders. "You know me; any way so long as it's my way. Now, start talking."

"I'm speechless."

"Yeah, welcome to my world. You fall in love with a woman and experience the equivalent of walking barefoot on razor blades to tell her so. You're told she feels the same way about you. You both get shot to pieces, but the bad guys die, and then there's supposed to be a happily ever after. But the woman refuses to take your calls. Refuses to even discuss you and spends her days making herself miserable pining for you—and don't deny it, because your father told me—does that sound crazy to you, or is it just me who's lost the plot?"

"You don't understand, Jack."

"Damn straight, I don't. What the hell has gotten into you? You're not traumatized by what happened. I know, because I got Richard to hack your medical records. So it's something else. Something about me that you can't face. So let's have it. And don't hold anything back, because that will just piss me off."

Her chest tightened. She flexed her shoulders to shrug off his arm. Half of her wanted to press so close she disappeared into him; the other half berated her for daring to even consider something so dangerous.

"Breathe, Lowry. You pass out on me, and my mother will evict me. She's already having second thoughts about me wanting to make the Hall my permanent home."

Christ, how to explain? Where to start? — and what did he mean about making the Hall his permanent home?

Jack maneuvered her so that her head was tucked beneath his chin, her cheek resting on his chest. "Not feeling particularly patient here. I am who I am, Lowry. That's not going to change. Think you can live with that?"

"No. Yes. No. I mean…" Damn it, what was he asking? She couldn't think straight with him wrapped around her. And she had a sneaky suspicion he knew it.

She struggled against him and felt oddly disappointed when he released her.

His slow grin kicked the thud of her heart into double time. Christ, he was up to something, and why was he reaching for her hand, his eyes never leaving hers?

Faster than a striking cobra, he slapped one half of a pair of handcuffs around her wrist, the other bracelet around his own.

"For God's sake, Ballentyne, what the hell are you doing?"

"Whatever it takes. The kissing you into submission comes next, just so you know."

"I don't even know what I'm supposed to be submitting to. I thought you wanted an explanation."

"I do. The cuffs are backup in case you run."

"That's ridiculous!"

"I agree. But then everything about this situation is ridiculous and I'm desperate, so start talking. Why won't you move in with me?"

Was he mad? "Well, for one you haven't asked, and second it would never work."

It didn't look much like he was listening. Not the way he was fixating on her hair, wrapping its new length around his forefinger and then releasing it, only to find a fresh lock with which to play.

"Jack."

"Hmm."

"Will you stop stroking me? I thought you wanted answers."

"Not really. After all, it's not like I'm going to let you walk away, whatever it is you have to say."

She pushed against his chest and leaned back. "The Service, Jack. It's your life…and I don't want it to be a part of mine. Too many bad memories, and I need to start afresh."

"Me too. That's why, having tied up some loose ends, I quit. For good this time. A desk job would have killed me or, more accurately, I would only have ended up shooting someone important. Too much tact and diplomacy required, and I don't have the patience to play politics."

"You can't quit, Jack. The Service is a part of who you are."

"Who I *was*. Setting up my own operation specializing in close protection makes more sense for a man intent on starting a family."

He was back to nuzzling her neck, delicious flames licked her skin. She curled the fingers of her free hand into his shirt and tried to hang on, while the walls tilted and spun around her.

She let his words percolate. "Jack, did you just propose?"

"Hell no. All that would get me is a flat-out refusal. I'm

asking you to move in. To give me a chance to prove I can make this work."

"Then hell no, right back at you." For an instant she could have sworn shock and yes, maybe fear, skirted his eyes. Not that he allowed her a closer look.

In an instant, she was under him, her lips trapped beneath his, his hands skimming. Teasing. His thigh eased between hers, pressing high. Christ, the man liked to play dirty.

Her blood fizzing, she deliberately wriggled her hips. Couldn't have him thinking she was without a few tricks of her own.

His groan vibrated against her flattened breasts. "Not stopping until you surrender. I'll kiss you all night and all over, if I have to, then I'll start again. A chance, Lowry, the last risk I'll ever ask you to take, I promise."

"Still no," she panted. "I don't *want* you to stop the kissing, so you won't be hearing any 'yes' from me."

She whimpered as he pulled away.

"Gotta find Richard. He's got the key, and I need these cuffs off. Bloody stupid idea. They get in the way."

She arched and curled her legs high and fast around his hips. "I like them." She liked the way his eyes suddenly burned more fiercely too. And the way his breathe quickened.

She refused to duck his intense stare, though there was little she could do about the slow-effusing flush that stained her cheeks.

"You really trust me that much?"

She nodded. "With my life. With my heart. Now prove you feel the same. Ask me to marry you—no conditions attached."

He hesitated, swallowed hard enough to bob his Adam's apple. "Okay. Will you be my"—there was no mistaking the choke—"wife?"

She nearly laughed. Jack Ballentyne loathed asking anything, hated asking period. But in their partnership, he'd do well to get used to it.

"No. Ask me again in a month's time, and probably several months' time after that. I like having the upper hand, Ballentyne, and knowing you love me too much to refuse me anything makes me feel deliciously naughty. Think you can cope with the insubordination?"

The last thing she heard, before all sound ceased to matter was a torn and heartfelt "Lowry-*bloody*-Fisk." Then, "Soon to be Lowry-*bloody*-Ballentyne."

Acknowledgments

To Tracy Montoya, Editor, for her endless patience, and tolerance of my 'voice'. Thank you. *Curtsies*

To Shehanne Moore, could my thanks ever be enough? Nope. Best company ever—keep waving the banners!

To the Naughties, and the Black Quills, for the friendship and entertainment you provide. Kudos. Thank you.

To the team at Entangled Publishing, for their contribution. Thank you, unsung heroes.

To the writers of the many books I have read, and will read in the future (yes, all of you). Thank you. For the colour. For the joy. For the journey.

About the Author

It took a swan dive from a roof to convince Incy (aged 5) she wasn't an avenging fairy and no, she most certainly couldn't fly. Bruised but undefeated she retreated deeper into her imaginary world populated with the brave and the poisonous.

When not fighting injustice and righting wrongs on 'Planet Incy' she works as a Marketing Director. (Unfortunately, her law degree languishes unused, the distinction between good and evil proving too worrisome in real life.)

Her five children are well versed in what scares her (most things) and delight in pushing her neurotic buttons — at their peril.

Also by Incy Black

HARD TO HOLD

Anna Key Marshall is pregnant. Granted, it's through a sperm donor instead of her ex-husband, but you can't have everything. When she becomes the target for murder, she'll do whatever it takes to protect her unborn child—even turning to her ex, the Black Ops specialist who broke her heart. Nick Marshall can't forgive the woman who betrayed him, but when she finds herself in trouble, he'll do what he does best—protect her at all costs. Fueled by a powerful love he can't leave behind, can he hold on to the woman he still loves?

Check out these other Ignite releases...

DOUBLE JEOPARDY
by Linda Wisdom

Medical Examiner Lauren Hunter has never known anyone like Assistant District Attorney Josh Brandon. Handsome, kind and tender, he's everything she has ever wanted in a man. Until he gets a new admirer who starts phoning Lauren with threats, then breaks into her home and rips her clothing. Someone is determined to come between Lauren and Josh. Someone whose rage is growing...

In the shadows of night, someone watches. And waits...for the perfect moment to strike. For if she can't have him alive, she'll see him dead.

Either way...he's hers.

WHATCHA GONNA DO WITH A COWBOY
by Jodi Linton

Too many cowboys and not enough time make for one helluva ride when it comes to Deputy Laney Briggs solving her next crime spree. When she stumbles across a cross dressing football coach and a deadly sexy Federal Marshal...she'll not only have to solve the case that opened a can worms in Pistol Rocks, but keep her bad boy Texas Ranger corralled in and out of the bedroom.

PERSONAL ASSISTANT
by Louisa Rose-Innes

Hannah Evans is on the run in a foreign country in the midst of a rebellion. Her only hope of survival depends on disgraced Special Forces operative, Tom Wilde. When he meets Hannah, Tom sees an opportunity to redeem himself. The information she holds is important enough to end the civil war—all he needs to do is get her out of the war-ridden country alive and back to Britain. With her life in his hands, can she trust him to get her to safety, or will he sacrifice her to save his own reputation?

CONVICTED
by Dee Tenorio

Retired Marine and new Sheriff's Deputy, Cade Evigan is on a mission to weed out a violent motorcycle crew from a small mountain town. Deep cover DEA Agent Katrina Killian is the last person he needs to fall for—especially when she appears to be one of the criminals he's out to take down. Unable to risk either of their lives with the truth, Katrina has to play both ends against the middle to keep Cade safe. But lies can only last so long and her time has just run out...

SECRETS AND SINS: CHAYOT
by Naima Simone

Months after Chayot Gray's darkest secret was exposed to the world, he's struggling to cope with the fallout. Shame and guilt threaten to consume him, and he longs for the anonymous, numb existence he's known for two decades. Then he interrupts the kidnapping of his neighbor, Aslyn. The pain-filled shadows darkening her eyes call to him, and her loveliness stirs a desire he didn't know existed. Now Chay must conquer his inner-demons in order to save her from a madman determined to finish the job he started...

HER SPECIAL FORCES
by Sophie Roslyn

Retired Marine Viper helo pilot Kacey O'Donnell is called out of retirement for a special assignment: to assist in extracting the kidnapped daughter of a U.S. Senator. With a young girl's life at stake, Kacey puts personal feelings aside and pulls Former SEAL hero Nathan Weatherly and his team together for one last assignment. But she finds it next to impossible to work with her former lover again—especially when she knows he wants so much more, and she has a dark secret to hide.

Secrets and Sins: Raphael
by Naima Simone

When Greer Addison's fiancé is found dead, she becomes the main suspect of a crime she can't remember. After their one night together, Raphael is stunned and suspicious when Greer shows up on his doorstep claiming she's carrying his baby. Worse, she's the target of a stalker bent on making her pay for a murder has no memory of. As Raphael begins to trust Greer, and fall in love with her, they must race against the clock to uncover a killer. Because Greer's memory is returning...

This Year's Black
by Avery Flynn

When someone embezzles millions under Devin Harris's watch, he isn't going to let the private investigator working the case go it alone—even if she is the woman who blew him away in bed and then blew him off. Allegra "Ryder" Falcon is a fighter, but just when it seems like it couldn't get any hotter between her and Devin, the case they're working takes them to a tropical paradise where the danger increases. From the catwalk to the pineapple fields, they have to work together to track down the missing millions before the thief finds—and kills—them.

Between the Sheets
by Genie Davis and Linda Marr

Erotic romance writer Jenna Brooks finds herself drawn into

her own stories, literally. When the seductive, mysterious Riley Stone rescues her from an attempted hit and run, she's plunged into a reckless, wild relationship unlike anything she's ever experienced—except on paper. A drug kingpin, a billion dollar development scheme, and a hostage situation have Jenna and Riley running for their lives. As Riley struggles to keep Jenna safe, the romance they've woven could force them to pay the ultimate price: admitting they've fallen in love—for real.

ALIVE AT 5
by Linda Bond

When Samantha's mentor dies while skydiving, she suspects he was murdered. Her investigative instincts lead her to irresistibly gorgeous Zack Hunter. An undercover police officer, Zack is investigating his uncle's diving death with the same adventure vacation company. He doesn't want Samantha's help because he's terrified of being responsible for a partner again. Still, Samantha's persistence is quite a turn-on, and he finds it harder and harder to stay away from her. But when the killer turns his attention to Zack, Samantha could be the only one who can save him.

LIE BY NIGHT
by Cathy Marlowe

Cole Stewart's mission to protect close friends from a criminal mastermind takes an unexpected turn when Emma Bailey runs head first into his investigation. He once spent one night falling in love with her, but now she's not only a danger to his heart, but her brother is a key suspect. In their race to keep the people they love safe, Cole and Emma betray each other's trust time and again, not realizing that trust—and their growing love for each other—is the only thing that can save them all.

Angeli
by Jody Wallace

Gregori's last mission is to save Earth from the demons threatening to take control. He doesn't care if he survives as long as he averts the impending apocalypse. But meeting Adelita, a human refugee, gives him a renewed reason to fight. And live. After Gregori saves Adelita from a demon attack, she vows to help him recover his faith and edge by any means necessary. But can she keep her own faith when she learns the truth about who and what Gregori really is?

CPSIA information can be obtained at www.ICGtesting.com
Printed in the USA
LVOW10s1959110815

449711LV00006B/189/P

9 781507 844786